The Santa
Klaus Murder

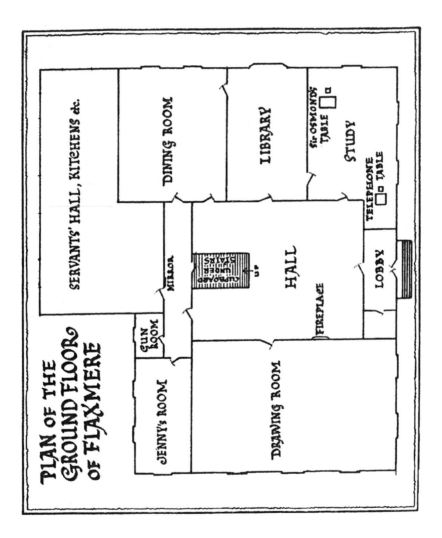

PLAN of THE
GROUND FLOOR
of FLAXMERE

SERVANTS' HALL, KITCHENS &c.

DINING ROOM

LIBRARY

Sir OSMONDS
TABLE

STUDY

TELEPHONE
TABLE

MIRROR

CUPBOARD
UNDER
STAIRS

HALL

LOBBY

FIREPLACE

GUN
ROOM

JENNY'S ROOM

DRAWING ROOM

The Santa Klaus Murder

Mavis Doriel Hay

Poisoned Pen Press

First Edition 2015 First US Trade Paperback Edition

10 9 8 7 6 5 4 3 2 1

Library of Congress Catalog Card Number: 201495

ISBN: 978146420   Trade Paperback

Poisoned Pen Press
6962 E. First Ave., Ste. 103
Scottsdale, AZ 85251
www.poisonedpenpress.com
info@poisonedpenpress.com

Printed in the United States of America

CONTENTS

People in the Story

Sir Osmond Melbury, of Flaxmere, in the county of Haulmshire.

George Melbury, his son.

Patricia, George's wife.

Their children: Enid—9.

                           Kit—8.

                           Clare—5.

Hilda Wynford, Sir Osmond's eldest daughter, a widow.

Carol, her daughter.

Edith (Dittie)—Lady Evershot, Sir Osmond's second daughter.

Sir David Evershot, her husband.

Eleanor Stickland, Sir Osmond's third daughter.

Gordon Stickland, her husband.

Their children: Osmond—6.

                           Anne—4.

Jennifer, Sir Osmond's youngest daughter.

Miss Mildred Melbury, Sir Osmond's sister.

Oliver Witcombe, a guest at Flaxmere.

Philip Cheriton, another guest.

Miss Grace Portisham, secretary and housekeeper to Sir Osmond.

Henry Bingham, Sir Osmond's chauffeur.

Parkins, Sir Osmond's manservant.
John Ashmore, former chauffeur at Flaxmere.
Colonel Halstock, Chief Constable of Haulmshire.
Detective-Inspector Rousdon.
Mr. Crewkerne, Sir Osmond's solicitor.
Kenneth Stour, an actor.

Chapter One

The Family at Flaxmere

by Philip Cheriton

I have known the Melbury family since the time when Jennifer, the youngest daughter, and I climbed trees and built wigwams together in the Flaxmere garden. I know enough about them, therefore, to set down as much of the history of the family as is necessary to an understanding of the general situation at that Christmas-time, 1935, when the Flaxmere crime was committed. At that date I had been engaged to Jennifer for three months, but her father, Sir Osmond Melbury, withheld his blessing, so the engagement wasn't publicly announced. Luckily for us, he did not forbid me to darken his doors, or anything of that sort. About nineteen years earlier he had tried the stern Victorian father business upon his eldest daughter, Hilda, when she fell in love with a young artist. Hilda had eloped—with her mother's connivance, it was said. So this time he tried a new method.

He evidently believed that I was a poor creature and that Jennifer would soon "see through me," especially if I were shown up unfavourably by contrast with a more eligible suitor. So he merely refused to take our engagement seriously; scoffed at us as too young to know our own minds; insisted that in any case we must wait; that Jennifer must stay at home to cherish her old father in the few years remaining to him; she couldn't possibly dream of leaving home; and so forth. Meanwhile he encouraged Oliver Witcombe to hang about the house and make himself pleasant to Jennifer.

I had been at school with Oliver and had always regarded him as a decent sort of fellow, though his film-star appearance put me off. One felt that there must be something wrong with a man who had such a perfect profile and such unnaturally natural waves in his crisp fair hair. Of course, Sir Osmond's behaviour—always, as it were, pushing Oliver forward and making him show off and treating him as if he were a clever and very well-trained dog—created rather a strained situation. I think Oliver and I both tried to forget this, but I, at any rate, felt horribly awkward when I met him at Flaxmere. That was typical of Sir Osmond; he had a genius for awkwardness. I would back him to arouse envy, hatred, and uncharitableness in any perfectly harmonious party of people in less than twenty-four hours.

Jennifer was the only one of his children still living with him at Flaxmere. This solid and rather grandiose mansion had been built by Sir Osmond's great-great-grandfather who had pulled down an Elizabethan house because he found it old-fashioned and cramped. It strikes me as one of the less fortunate products of the eighteenth century, but Sir Osmond considers it a fine old Georgian edifice.

Sir Osmond's father lost too much money on the turf and there was talk of selling the property, when young Osmond scandalised the family by going into business. When he made a nice little fortune out of biscuits the family discovered that business—the manufacturing side, of course—was really quite respectable nowadays; the best people go in for it; no one should be ashamed of putting his talents to their best use, and so forth. But Osmond Melbury, retiring, on his father's early death, from the atmosphere of biscuits to take his place in the county, had no idea of sharing out the profits of his bourgeois occupation amongst his gentlemanly brothers and uncles. He laid out some of his fortune in well-planned donations which secured, in time, the baronetcy he desired. He fitted the old house with electric light and sumptuous bathrooms, and he did it well. He also made it known to his children that they should be liberally endowed if they married suitably.

His plans did not seem to be working out very well when Hilda, at the age of nineteen, married the artist, Carl Wynford. I gather that Sir Osmond would have raised no objection to Hilda's engagement provided that she didn't marry Carl until it became quite certain that he was generally recognized as a great artist. Sir Osmond would even have given him commissions and helped him to get others. But Hilda was in love and in no mood to submit to this sort of bargain. Carl died about three years later, leaving Hilda with a baby daughter and a great many pictures. The art critics had already noticed Carl, and his death caused a bit of a boom in his pictures, which, at the end of the war, when people had money, helped Hilda a good deal. But she had worked pretty hard to educate her daughter, Carol, and her father had never helped her at all, except to invite her and the girl to stay at Flaxmere occasionally.

The queer part of all this is that Hilda, who was originally her father's favourite, has remained fond of him. At any rate, she seems to be, though it's nearly incredible. She must be nearly forty now and looks it, probably because of the hard times she's been through. She will say: "I can see father's point of view; the old simply cannot understand that the young

can't wait." She will never say more than that, and one feels
that she'd never fail in that sort of understanding herself,
however old she might be. I'm certain that she can't help
feeling pretty sore that her father wouldn't even fork out a
few hundreds, which he'd hardly miss, to give her daughter
Carol, who is now eighteen, the training she wants. The girl
is keen to be an architect and that costs more than Hilda
knows how to scrape together.

Four years after Hilda's marriage, in 1920, Lady Melbury
died. I was eleven then and I can just remember her as a
lovely, gracious woman, who looked older than the mothers of most of my friends and yet was much less fussy and
obstructive and easier to confide in. She left two-thirds of
her small personal fortune to Hilda and the rest to Jennifer,
as if she realized even then that Edith and Eleanor—the
other two daughters—would earn their father's reward for
obedient children, whilst Jennifer might well be glad of the
slight help that little portion could give her in escaping from
Sir Osmond's tyranny.

After Lady Melbury's death Sir Osmond's unmarried
sister went to live at Flaxmere and to preside over the social
functions which were so important because they were to
provide Edith—then aged seventeen—and later Eleanor,
with suitable husbands, and George, who was just twenty-
one, with a dutiful wife. Aunt Mildred did her work well.
Edith, generally known as Dittie, married Sir David Evershot
amid great, but decently restrained, family rejoicing. But
although they have now been married ten years there are no
children, a fact of which Sir Osmond strongly disapproves.
Dittie says they can't afford children; what she means, of
course, is that they might not be able to manage Kitzbühl
and Cannes and Scotland every year for a few years. Sir
Osmond has threatened to cut them out of his will if they
don't produce offspring; he has a theory that what he calls

"good stock"—that is to say, Melburies—ought to do their best to counterbalance the too numerous progeny of the less worthy. It is rumoured that there's some kind of lunacy in Sir David's family and that Edith is afraid it might come out in his children. I don't know the truth of that, but only for some pretty strong reason would she deliberately risk her share of Sir Osmond's fortune.

Eleanor, the third daughter, married Gordon Stickland, who is something fairly important in the City. Eleanor always had a flair for doing the right thing. When Gordon Stickland was drawn, by clever Aunt Mildred, to Flaxmere and turned out to be the completely desirable husband, in Sir Osmond's eyes, for one of his daughters, Eleanor was very charming to him, duly accepted his proposal, and produced quite a passable affection for him. She bore a son, immediately declared by everyone to be "a thorough Melbury," and christened him Osmond. There is also a daughter, Anne, who promises to be as beautiful as her grandmother. Eleanor knows all the right people, always wears the right clothes, is always seen at the right functions, and does it all much more economically than Edith.

George, the only son, married Patricia, a daughter of Lord Caundle, a girl with a good deal of money and rather glutinous charm, who kicks up an atmosphere of fuss about her like a cloud of dust, and whom Sir Osmond considers to be a thoroughly suitable daughter-in-law. They have three children, who are brought up to believe that they are the salt of the earth.

Aunt Mildred, having satisfactorily disposed of Sir Osmond's son and two daughters, was dismissed from Flaxmere in 1931, when Jennifer came of age. This was not Jennifer's doing, though I think Aunt Mildred always suspects that Jennifer had a hand in it. Aunt Mildred is certainly trying, with her sham humble attitude of "This is what I would advise, but I don't expect you to take any notice," but Jennifer was used to her and, moreover, was glad to have her there to companion Sir Osmond, who always expected some member of the family to be at hand to talk to him when he wasn't busy.

Probably the chief agent in the ousting of Aunt Mildred was Miss Portisham—the Portent, as Hilda and Jenny call her. Grace Portisham was the orphan daughter of someone at the place where Sir Osmond made his biscuits—a manager, I think—who came to Flaxmere as Sir Osmond's private secretary when she was a girl of twenty, four years before Aunt Mildred left. I don't think the secretarial work ever demanded very great talents; Miss Portisham was quick, neat and tactful and Sir Osmond was delighted. Then, during some absence of Aunt Mildred on a visit, Miss Portisham began to develop a perfect genius for looking after household affairs. She ran everything so perfectly that no one noticed that anyone *was* running things. Jennifer, who isn't at all a good housekeeper, was only too glad to leave everything to the secretary. Miss Portisham, having tasted power, and realizing how well she could exercise it, wanted to get the reins permanently in her own hands. So she unobtrusively planted and cultivated in Sir Osmond's mind the idea that it would be suitable for Jennifer when she reached the age of twenty-one, to preside over her father's house free from the guardianship of a maiden aunt.

None of the family took much notice of Grace Portisham during the first four years of her stay at Flaxmere. Jenny realized that it was a blessing to have her there; she was always willing to take responsibility, always understood Sir Osmond's wishes, and generally helped to make things run smoothly. But after Aunt Mildred left, in the summer of 1931, Miss Portisham began to make herself felt, though still gently and tactfully. During the next Christmas house-party

Edith and Eleanor and George noticed changes. The ten-year-old Daimler and the old coachman-turned-chauffeur had given place to a modern Sunbeam with a smart young Cockney at the wheel. Eleanor was the first to protest.

"I suppose you needed a new car, Father, but I don't like that young man; I don't like his attitude; it wouldn't surprise me to find that he's a Socialist. I very much doubt whether Jenny will know how to keep him in his place."

"And what's happened to Ashmore?" George inquired. "Gave me quite a nasty feelin', not seein' the old fellow at the station."

"He's been well-treated," Sir Osmond assured them. "Wouldn't have been safe to trust him with that car. Bingham is a far better driver and a trained mechanic as well. Miss Portisham's idea—the change. She's a smart girl."

From that time, Edith and George were accustomed to advertise their disapproval of Miss Portisham's choice by not letting Sir Osmond know beforehand the times of trains by which they were arriving at Bristol, and engaging old Ashmore—who had set up in the hiring business—to drive them to Flaxmere.

They found, too, that rooms had been done up in new colour schemes and there were various innovations in household organization. Edith expressed her disapproval of the changes and hinted at a lack of good taste. Always Sir Osmond pooh-poohed her criticism, boasted how economically everything had been done, and lauded Miss Portisham.

Edith and Eleanor and George became increasingly anxious about Grace Portisham. She was a schemer—and how far was she prepared to go? They would gladly have seized any opportunity to discredit her, but she was so discreet, so tactful, that she seemed invulnerable. Each Christmas they arrived in a greater state of anxiety, and soon after each New Year's Day they returned to their homes with their anxiety unallayed by the obvious facts that Miss Portisham greatly increased the comfort of life at Flaxmere and was never seen by anyone to presume above her station.

Sir Osmond, when he dismissed Aunt Mildred, also decided that Jennifer was not to marry but was to stay at Flaxmere as long as he lived. This might well be for twenty years; he was then sixty-six and seemed fit and tough. There was no earthly reason why Jennifer should throw away the best part of her life in order to decorate his household. With all her tolerance and good temper, she only got on with him by keeping her real opinions and interests to herself. She developed some sort of life of her own by working in the Women's Institutes, but these activities were hampered by Sir Osmond, who disapproved of what he considered the Bolshevist tendencies of the movement. He would have been happy for her to give the members a treat in the Flaxmere grounds every summer, with plenty of tea and buns and perhaps a conjuror. But he considered it unfitting for his daughter to drive thirty miles along country roads on a wet night to play games—games, indeed!—with "a batch of village women." The local school teachers ought to superintend that sort of nonsense, he declared; what are they paid for?

Aunt Mildred, of course, would have been only too happy to remain in the luxury of Flaxmere. Or, if Sir Osmond really wanted one of his daughters at home to act as hostess and be a companion to him, there was Hilda. She would have accepted the office gladly; thirteen years older than Jennifer, with love and aspirations and hard work behind her, she was ready to settle down to a peaceful middle age; she managed Sir Osmond well and she could have entertained his prosy old friends and their complacent wives with at least a superficial graciousness which Jennifer found it impossible to maintain at Sir Osmond's dinner parties.

But here you see Sir Osmond's cussedness again. He set his face against the obviously easy arrangement, which would have made everyone happy—even including himself, if he would allow himself to be happy. He had shown no objection to me or my family in the days when I had frequently stayed at Flaxmere in the school holidays. When I turned up again, after a gap of some six years, he only worked up his disapproval of me after Jennifer and I broke it to him that we wanted to get married quite soon. Oliver Witcombe, on the other hand, seemed willing to wait for an indefinite number of years, but I had a suspicion that if only I could be removed from the picture and himself installed as the accepted suitor, he meant to find some means of fixing a marriage date not too far ahead.

I have said that when Jennifer first told her father that she meant to marry me—in the summer of 1935—he was a very fit man for his age. He had always taken good care of himself. But in August he had some sort of heart attack, supposed to be a slight stroke, which aged him a good deal. His doctor, however, said that the old man might still last for many years, if he took life easily and was subject to no sudden shock or strain. He always seemed to thrive on the atmosphere of distrust and discomfort which he had such a knack of creating and although the Melbury family was riddled with feuds and jealousies, these were always conducted in a polite manner, with sarcasm and innuendo but never a healthy row. So, although Sir Osmond looked older and his memory began to get vague, Jennifer and I still thought of him as a man likely to live for many years.

At the end of August, as soon as Eleanor, Edith and George had news from Jennifer of their father's illness, they, and George's wife, all swooped down on Flaxmere like birds of prey. They hovered around, with flutterings and solicitous inquiries after his health, which thinly disguised their anxious peering and pecking after any shred of evidence as to the likeliness of his sudden death and the possibility that he was reconsidering his will.

"Very nice of you all to be so fond of me!" Sir Osmond sneered. "Now you can go back to your grouse and think no more of me until Christmas!"

That was all they got out of him. No one knew exactly how he would leave his money. He had been accustomed to say to his children when they were growing up: "If you show proper discretion in choosing husbands—or a wife, George—I'll see that you're properly dowered. If you don't, you can wait for my money till I've done with it myself."

From that, everyone supposed that Hilda would receive her share when her father died, but there was a good deal of speculation as to whether—after George had received enough to keep up Flaxmere—the rest would be divided equally among the girls, or whether the amounts which Edith and Eleanor had already received would be counted as part of their share. Edith, who had turned down a young man she was really fond of in order to please her father by marrying Sir David Evershot, had once been heard to remark that if, after all, she got less than Hilda when the old man died it would be grossly unfair. The others didn't express themselves so crudely, but probably held the same view.

George had less cause for anxiety than the others because Sir Osmond held strong views on the rights of the son and heir. But the increasing importance of Miss Grace Portisham disturbed even George and worried George's wife a good deal. They all considered that Jennifer's presence at home was some safeguard and after Sir Osmond's illness they felt this even more strongly.

"I do think father's right in wanting you to stay at Flax-mere," Eleanor told Jenny that August. "I wouldn't like to think of him left alone with Miss Portisham. You know one can't trust a woman of that class; she hasn't the same standards as we have. Oh, yes, of course she is clever and has acquired a superficial culture, but I don't think she's honest at bottom."

"Men of father's age, especially when their faculties are impaired by illness, sometimes do very foolish things," Edith had urged. "Look at Lord Litton Cheney's marriage, only the other day, to a woman who was nothing more than his daughters' governess! It's a dreadful thing for those girls!"

"Father's comment on that," Jennifer told them, "was that there's no fool like an old fool!"

"That proves nothing," said Edith. "I agree with Eleanor that you ought to be here. Father needs someone to look after him."

"And I'm no use for that, you know quite well," retorted Jennifer.

Edith ignored that and continued: "And it's no hardship for you. You've got every luxury; you've got your Women's Institutes that you're so devoted to; you can live your own life and have nothing to worry about."

"I *can't* live my own life; that's just the trouble!" Jennifer protested. "Father won't let me drive the Sunbeam alone at night, though I'm perfectly competent. He won't let me have a small car of my own and he always seems to arrange things so that Bingham isn't available when I want to go to a meeting."

"Those are details!" declared Edith, dismissing them airily. "You can't expect to have everything perfect and the fact remains that you ought to be here for the next few years."

As soon as Sir Osmond had recovered from his illness and the family had dispersed, Jennifer and I discussed the situation and decided to be married in the spring. When Hilda came to Flaxmere for Christmas we were going to tell her our plans and urge her to think out some way acceptable to Sir Osmond of installing herself in Jennifer's place. That wouldn't be easy, because Hilda was too proud to beg her father to give her a home. Of course the arrangement, if it could be brought about, would solve some of Hilda's problems, but she was so accustomed to the impossibility of getting any help from her father, that she would find it difficult to believe in a change of fortune.

I believe that Hilda, as well as Jennifer, was genuinely unconcerned about the question of how much Sir Osmond would leave and how he would allot it. She had given up any hope that money might come from him just when she most desperately needed it for Carol's training, and was not very interested in what might come later on. She was too fond of her father to allow herself even to think how his sudden death might help her daughter, and she accepted Jennifer's judgment that their father was likely to live for many years.

Jennifer and I realized that if we married in the spring we should be throwing away all chance of a dowry, but that couldn't be helped and we tried not to think of it though, goodness knows, we couldn't afford to turn up our noses at it.

Jennifer said: "It's no good thinking about it, because there simply isn't any money as far as you and I are concerned. For us it's non-existent. It may come along by the time we are middle-aged and probably we, like Hilda, shan't want it then."

My salary in the publishing firm would be considered by many people as a nice little income for a young married couple, but it wasn't going to provide an easy existence for Jennifer "in the state to which she had been accustomed." Her little inheritance from her mother, which she had saved carefully, would help and she had decided that economy would be amusing, and was ready to make a good job of our new life.

This was the state of affairs at Christmas, when all this crowd gathered at Flaxmere. It was the usual custom. Sir Osmond thought that a family gathering was the correct thing at Christmas and no one dared to object, though they generally had a pretty grim time. Aunt Mildred was always included in the party and was probably glad enough to enjoy the luxury of Flaxmere again for a short time. Oliver Witcombe was there, too, and even I was invited, partly because there was a preponderance of women in the party anyway and partly in pursuance of Sir Osmond's policy of comparing me unfavourably with Oliver. I guessed that the old man would be planning for one of the evenings some sort of diversion at which Oliver would be sure to shine and I would not; an easy matter, for Oliver is full of party tricks.

Hilda, with her daughter Carol, was coming as usual. I believe Sir Osmond liked to have her there, both from a genuine affection for her—though that's hard to believe in the light of his meanness to her—and also to throw it all in her teeth, as it were. "Just see what you've missed by going against my will!"

So there we all were; and, as we were so unpleasantly forced to realize later on, nearly all of us with good cause for wishing Sir Osmond dead and few with any cause to wish him long life.

Chapter Two

Saturday

by Hilda Wynford

Jennifer had asked me, as usual, to arrive before the rest of the family, so that we could have some private gossip. Carol and I caught an early train from London and were at Bristol soon after ten on Saturday morning. Old Ashmore was there to meet us, in the familiar high, square-looking car. Even his queer Bristol accent, with all the final l's vanishing into an indescribable sound, was home-like.

"Miss Jenny asked me to come for you, Ma'am. Sir Osmond is out drivin' this morn', I unnerstand."

We asked Ashmore how he was doing. It struck me that he looked haggard and ill, and I saw that his hands trembled as he opened the door for us, though he drove the car quite steadily, in his usual deliberate way.

"Not so bad, Ma'am, really, but of course there's a lo' of competition. I gets station work and there's some o' ladies has their drives reg'lar, but many peopah wants a more up-to-date lookin' car. They don' trust an o' bus like this for long distances, meanin' no offence, o' course, to Sir Osmond. It was a good car in its day."

"It still runs beautifully," Carol said. "I'm sure you look after it well."

"That I do, Missie!" the old coachman declared earnestly with a brief smile. "If anything went wrong wi' it, where shou' I be?" His face sagged again into tired lines.

I asked him if there were any chance of getting a new car soon.

"Not that I can see," he replied gloomily. "I paid a good price for this 'un, considerin' the age, an' a car like this is worth nothin' in the market now."

I was so surprised that I blurted out, "Why, I thought Sir Osmond gave you the car?"

Ashmore seemed embarrassed. "You see, Ma'am, it's like this-ere. Gennlemen like Sir Osmond, who've no concern with the motor trade an' don' buy a car every year or so, like some do, they don' hardly unnerstand the way these garages do business. If you've got an o' car to get rid of an' you're minded to buy a new one that costs a good sum, they allow you a top price for your o' car, just to encourage you like. Mebbe more'n you'd ever get if you so' it for cash. Weh, the garage named the sum they'd allow on this Daimler an' Sir Osmond, knowin' 'twas a good car an' had cost him a tidy lot, he said to me, 'Ashmore,' he says, 'you can have the Daimler for that; it's trade price an' a bargain for you.' Weh, Ma'am, it was in a way, me knowin' the car an' knowin' it'd bin weh handled. But it was a fair sight of money to pay an' I dunno when I see it back, with the wife so poorly an' aw."

"But, Ashmore, why didn't you tell Sir Osmond that the price was too high?" Carol exclaimed. "Of course it was! If grandfather had tried to sell the old car he'd never have got anything like what the garage offered. I know all about it.

Why, you might have got a more up-to-date car for less than you paid for this!"

"Weh, Missie, I couldn't bargain with Sir Osmond like. No doubt he meant weh. I don' want to complain. Don' quite know how I let it aw out! I wouldn't not for anything have it come to the ears of Sir Osmond what I've bin saying! I hope, Missie, that you—nor you, Ma'am, neither—won' speak to Sir Osmond about it. Mebbe things' uh mend."

I asked him about his wife and family and we talked no more about the car. But I gathered that he had had a lot of expense over his wife's illness and was really desperately anxious. Otherwise I am sure he would never have voiced any sort of complaint. He had worked at Flaxmere since he was a boy and taught all of us as children to ride our first ponies. Father is very much against pampering people and thinks they should work and save, as he did, and then stand on their own feet. He probably never realized that he was actually asking Ashmore a high price for the Daimler, but thought he was giving the man a chance to invest his savings profitably.

Carol was full of indignation, and when we arrived at the house she pushed half a crown into my hand, to add to the one I had ready for a tip to Ashmore. Jenny would have paid him for the drive, I knew. It was obvious from Ashmore's face that the five shillings was worth even more to him that it was to us. He muttered something about, "If on'y you was aw-ways here now, things'd be different." Which is the sort of remark an old retainer always makes to the married daughters of the house.

But I was worried about the man. I thought he looked as if he ought to go into a convalescent home for a month's rest and good feeding, and decided to discuss with Jenny whether anything could be done for him.

Jenny met us in the hall, gay and excited and prettier than ever. She told us that Father would be away all day, paying his usual round of Christmas calls with Aunt Mildred. That George and Patricia and the children would be coming by car that evening; Dittie and David, also motoring, were stopping on the way and would arrive on Sunday. Eleanor and Gordon and their children wouldn't arrive until Monday, owing to some complication about a new nurse, to replace one who had rushed off to the bedside of a sick mother. Two outsiders were to be included in the Christmas gathering. Jenny and I always agreed that the family was the better for dilution.

"Oliver Witcombe," Jennifer told me, curling her upper lip; "that too too perfect young man, is coming on Tuesday. Father likes him. And Philip will be here on Monday evening."

I hadn't known Philip Cheriton in the old days. I think his visits began just after I was married. But I had seen something of him in London in the last three or four years and I knew he had been at Flaxmere in the summer. Jenny had written a good deal about him, bringing him into her letters in a deliberately casual way which made me think he was important.

I asked whether Father liked Philip.

"He tolerates him," Jenny said. "I don't quite know why, for he definitely disapproves of him. But he thinks he'll do no harm. However, we'll talk about Philip later. How's Carol getting on?"

Carol was full of enthusiasm for her new job with a decorating firm, and had a lot to tell Jenny about it. She took it as second best, with the idea of getting some useful experience until we found it possible for her to start her proper training as an architect. Characteristically she had put her heart into the work and was doing it as if it were her life's career, besides which, she was thrilled at earning money for the first time.

At lunch time Carol announced: "Aunt Jenny!"—This was in mockery, for Jenny is only seven years older than Carol in years and younger in character, and they are more like sisters. "I know you and Mother want to nod your old heads together over James's rheumatism and young Emma's carryings-on and Peggy Jones's youngest, and so forth. I've got a frock I want to finish making. May I work in your room, Jenny?"

"Yes, of course; and you can use my new sewing machine."

"Marvellous!" mocked Carol. "Jenny with a sewing machine! Getting quite domesticated! What's the great idea? Well, it's rather nice that I shan't have to borrow the Portent's when I want one."

Jenny blushed and began to talk very hard about her Women's Institute work and how she had actually managed in the spring to attend a training "school" and had been appointed as an organiser.

"Superb!" Carol commented. "I'd love to see an Institute organized by you! They'd have lovely teas, and sing and dance like a beauty chorus, and would never have heard of minutes and probably forget to have a secretary!"

"Rot!" Jenny retorted, a little annoyed. "I've become frightfully businesslike, though Headquarters did recommend in appointing me that I should be used rather for the social side than for procedure! But the joke was that Lady Bredy, who was going too, persuaded Father to let me go. He thought it was a select party of the aristocracy. But when he heard later that Mrs. Plush—you know the Plushes, who have Linmead farm—was also there as a student, he got quite dramatic about it. He considered the whole thing unnecessary; my home training—I ask you!—should be enough to teach me how to manage these Institutes, as he puts it; and he simply hated the idea of Mrs. Plush and me sitting side by side to learn the elements of democratic government. Of course Mrs. Plush is a perfect pet and much more tactful with awkward presidents than I am."

Of course Carol sympathized and was amused and they were soon well away on a discussion of feudalism and democracy and points of view. They love talking about points of view, but they are both far too young to understand the point of view of anyone over forty. They're pathetically young and that's partly what makes them both so charming. Being so nearly forty myself I believe I really can get some inkling of how both the twenties, and the fifties and over, feel—though possibly that's just imagination and I'm really as self-centred as the rest.

The conversation shows how Jenny's ideas and Father's would always, inevitably, clash and I wished I could persuade him to let her get away from home. There were no violent rows and Jenny's plans were never completely frustrated; if she kept her mind fixed for long enough on what she wanted she got at least part of it in the end. But there was constant friction and unrest.

After lunch Jennifer and I settled into the sofa in front of the library fire and she explained all her plans about marrying Philip Cheriton. When I had just been wishing that Jenny could get away from home, it seemed absurd to feel aghast at this scheme. And yet it terrified me. Perhaps it was because I compared what Jenny was facing with what I had myself faced nearly twenty years ago. Jenny is older than I was then, but I believe she's much less fitted for the sort of struggle I had. I was always harder; more like Father. But if Jenny really had the strength of mind to carry this through, she wouldn't be living at Flaxmere now. She'd have found some means of getting away and making for herself the career she often talks of. I don't mean to be critical. I'm just trying to explain her character, and the strong-minded, determined people aren't always the nicest. Little, gay fair-haired Jenny still seemed very like the child who had sudden fits of naughtiness and defiance which generally ended in tears; who never defied authority for long at a time.

Jenny doesn't really know what she's letting herself in for, I thought. She'll hate living in a suburb or a semi-suburban country town; she'll hate all the petty details of managing her house and economizing. She may make a mess of it; and she'll hate failure worse than anything.

"Aren't you pleased, Hilda?" she asked me anxiously. "You've always said I ought to have a career."

"Yes; but is the career of the suburban young wife just the one you want?"

"You *would* put it that way!" she protested. "We think we can manage a house as far out of town as Guildford, or somewhere like that. It'll be practically country and it'll be a small house that won't take much managing, with a competent maid. Philip doesn't want me to be just a parasite; he hates parasitic wives. I shall have my own affairs—Institutes, perhaps. I might even write; I've got a marvellous idea for a novel and Philip believes I could do it."

"You think I'm middle-aged and that I've forgotten what you feel like, but it isn't that, Jennifer. It's because I remember so well that I'm afraid."

"But, hang it all, Hilda; I'm not marrying a pauper. Millions of people marry on less. We shan't have children at first. We can't afford it. Not in the way Dittie can't afford them, but really."

"It's always relative of course."

"Yes; I know. But Hilda, you've got to help me. And of course you mustn't breathe a word to Dittie or Eleanor or George. They think I ought to stay here and shield Father from the Portent. But that's all nonsense. I couldn't do anything if there *was* anything to be done. All I should be likely to do would be to throw him into her sympathetic arms. But I don't think they've really any cause for worry. He may intend to leave her some money, but there's enough to go round. Heaven knows, she's earning it! But to return to the point, you must come and live at Flaxmere after I've gone."

"But how can I? Of course I'd come if Father asked me. At least—would I? There's Carol, you see. Carol is you over again. You know, Jenny, you haven't exactly helped to put her in the right frame of mind to get on with Father."

"What I have said hasn't made any difference at all. Carol knows quite well that Father has treated you horribly meanly."

I had realized before this that Jenny and Carol did inevitably look at things from the same point of view, and to both of them Father's line of policy looked like meanness. I don't see it that way. I deliberately refused his way of life and chose my own. It was fair that I should follow that way, however it turned out, under my own steam, as Carol would say. I'm not sorry for anything. Father has been consistent and I like people to be consistent. I *have* followed my own way and have shown that I had the strength of character to do it. Father respects that and so we have always been good friends, though, of course, he was angry with me at the time.

"The point is," I explained to Jenny, "that even if Father should ask me to come back to Flaxmere and even if I should agree, how would Carol get on here?"

"She'll be away," said Jenny cheerfully; "getting her architectural training. For the sake of that she'd put up with some holidays spent with her grandfather. She'd get on better than I do really, for she's much more conversational and she'd amuse Father's old pals with her witty remarks. I'm quite tongue-tied with them. Anyway, I'll tell Carol the plan and see what she says."

I knew what she'd say. She'd see it all as Jenny did, with the difficult peaks of the prospect conveniently shrouded in mist. The adventure would appeal to her. She and Jenny would join forces—the forces of youth—in a trice.

"I'm not so sure," I said. "I don't know that Carol would be able to get her training."

"Anyway, she has her job."

"But she doesn't earn enough to live on—by herself."

"Well, how much does this architectural business cost? After all, you'd be living here with no expense. Wouldn't that leave enough for Carol's training when you consider that she'd also live here free of cost in the holidays?"

"But we can't assume all this!" I cried desperately. "It's fantastic. If Father didn't ask me to come, your house of cards topples to the ground."

"That's what you've got to manage—to get him to ask you. You know he'd love to have you here and you'd like to be here. You've proved your point, that you can stand on your own feet and live your own life. Even Father admits that to himself, I'm sure. Hilda, I do want you to help me. Of course Philip and I have quite definitely made up our minds and we shall get married anyway, but I should like to know you were backing me up."

"I must think it over," I told her. "My dear child, I want you to be happy. Can't we persuade Father to give Philip his blessing? That would be so much simpler and, after all, he can't object to him so much if he has him here to stay."

"I've suggested to Philip that he should write and publish a book that is at one and the same time an indisputable work of genius, a dignified production in the Victorian style and a best seller. That's the only way I can see of getting Father to accept him as a son-in-law. You know quite well that no one can *persuade* Father to anything. Except, perhaps, Miss Portisham, and no one knows how she does it. Of course I'm not expecting you to *persuade* Father to ask you to come and live here. You must wangle it in some clever way, so that it just happens."

I have recorded all this conversation, in the words which I remember very well, because it clearly shows Jenny's frame of mind just before Christmas Day. She wasn't in the least influenced by what I said and she was full of plans for her own escape from Flaxmere in the spring. She had no thought of her father's money, because she and Philip had decided that they could do quite well without it.

Chapter Three

Monday

by Jennifer Melbury

On Monday morning at nine o'clock most of us gathered in the dining-room for the family meal, which Father considered the correct thing. He liked to be "the head of the family in the old ancestral home." He was always playing a part of some kind and I believe that's why he has been so successful in material ways. He studied his role at each stage of his life and assumed the appropriate air. But he never bothered to study how to be the father of *this* family; I suppose he thinks *we* ought all to act our parts as members of the family of his imagination.

Eleanor and Gordon hadn't yet arrived at Flaxmere. Aunt Mildred had come several days before, but she doesn't feel at her best in the morning and therefore breakfasts in bed. Dittie, who goes in for being a bit languid, often does the same, but on this occasion she appeared in the dining-room with the rest of us, probably because she had only arrived the evening before and wanted to test the atmosphere and make her plans for the day accordingly.

After breakfast Hilda and Carol, Dittie and her husband David, Patricia and her children, and I were idling about in the hall, looking at papers, reading letters and making hurried notes of the names of people who'd sent early Christmas cards and whom we'd left off our lists. George, the only one of the family who dares to come down deliberately late for breakfast, was still in the dining-room, comfortably surrounded by toast and butter and marmalade and quite undisturbed by the fact that Father sternly presided at the head of the table.

Suddenly Patricia began to create a fuss in the hall; she'd forgotten, or thought she'd forgotten, to dispatch a present to an important rich uncle and decided that she must arrange a shopping expedition to Bristol, which is about twenty miles from us. But first we must all be asked whether it would be too dreadful if she had sent the old man a present after all and now sent him a second one. So, knowing that Patricia would certainly go shopping, whatever we said, we all gave our advice. Carol asked if she could go too. George and Patricia had come in their own car, so that would be available. Patricia was delighted to have Carol and I insisted that Patricia's only hope of salvation with this uncle was to go and buy this present and send it off at once, because I knew Carol had some shopping of her own to do in Bristol and there would be little hope of her getting the use of the Sunbeam.

"Hadn't we better wait till this afternoon?" Carol suggested insanely. "Aunt Eleanor will be here by lunch time and she may want to do some shopping too."

"It would be very difficult to manage *three* people's shopping in one car!" Patricia protested. "I mean, everyone has their own ideas about shops and we should all want to go in different directions and it's *so* confusing and there'd be all sorts of complications about waiting for everyone in different places. Besides, there'll be *such* a mob in the afternoon. It'll be bad enough this morning."

"Besides," Dittie reminded them, "Eleanor never forgets; she's like the elephant. *All* her presents will have been done up neatly in holly paper and all her cards addressed, and no one forgotten, long ago. You'd better be off as soon as you can, and be back punctually for lunch." Dittie had already announced that she and David were driving over to Manton to lunch with the FitzPaines, so she was rather pleased to remind Patricia that it was her duty to return punctually.

Then Patricia began to fuss again. "I'm really not sure whether it's better to risk sending the man *two* presents or none at all, and perhaps write later, if he didn't acknowledge it, and say I *hoped* it hadn't been lost in the post. You never can tell at Christmas time. It *is* difficult."

"Oh, Aunt Pat!" Carol protested. "We've gone over all that already. It's far, far better to risk sending him two; at the worst he'll think you're a little forgetful, but no one minds anyone being forgetful in *that* way. Now do get a move on!"

"All this hurrying business is no good at all while George is still hanging over the marmalade," Patricia pointed out.

"*I'll* go and stir him up!" cried Carol, bolting off.

She was back in a few minutes. "Aunt Pat! Marvellous! George says I may drive the Austin! I've got a driving license, because it so often comes in handy for driving other people's cars. He doesn't mind a bit and I'm awfully safe."

Carol is one of those fortunate people who inspire confidence and she often gets cars lent her.

"Well, of course, poor George does hate shopping—" began Patricia doubtfully.

"Now *rush* and do your hatting and furring, Aunt Pat, and we'll start in two minutes," Carol urged.

It is typical of the way Carol gets away with everything that she can call Patricia "Aunt Pat"—which is ridiculous, because George's wife is so obviously a thorough "Patricia"—and still be approved of. Other people get frightfully squashed if they use that name.

Just when Patricia was half-way upstairs, Parkins came in with the parcel post, which had just arrived. Enid, Kit and Clare, Patricia's three children, and also Carol, swooped on it. Patricia stopped, unable to decide whether to go on up or come down again. Father emerged from the dining-room. I could see at once that he was dramatising himself as the benevolent grandfather.

"Now, children!" he boomed. "No parcels for you! Don't you know that yours don't come by the postman? They come by the reindeer sleigh."

The children still scrambled and squealed. Enid, who is nearly ten, and Kit, who is eight, obviously disbelieved their grandfather's statement. Enid looked up to announce: "The postman's brought one for me, anyway! I saw it! Oh, Kit, you are clumsy; you've covered it up!" She caught her grandfather's look of disapproval and stopped grabbing at the parcels to say, "I expect he met the sleigh in the drive and brought this one along so that I'd get it quickly."

Enid is a great deal too clever to be a really nice child.

"Now, children! Don't forget your manners! Let me see these things. There's something I particularly want," said Father, still playing his benevolent role with rather an effort. He looked around and caught sight of Patricia, who had now decided to descend.

"Patricia! I really think the children should be better disciplined."

"Well, really; at Christmas time; children *ought* to be excited—" Patricia began and then, with relief, caught sight of her Nanny who had come to collect the children for a walk.

Father was rummaging in the pile of parcels without success, grumbling to himself loudly, so that no one could ignore the fact that he was in distress.

"Must be a good-sized box! Can't have come! Confound those people! Thoroughly unreliable! What business is coming to, I don't know! Plenty of notice and they can't even carry out a simple order punctually! Well, I might have known! Quite useless to arrange anything that depends on modern shopkeepers doing their job with reasonable efficiency! All my arrangements ruined! Doesn't matter to *them*, of course."

The benevolent grandfather had given place to the embittered man who has vainly tried to be a philanthropist but is foiled by the inefficiency of everyone else.

Patricia, who has the mistaken idea that it's a good thing to sympathize with Father in this mood, sniffed, "Christmas posts are so unreliable! These temporary postmen are often most dishonest; they'll steal whole bags of stuff to avoid the trouble of delivering it! The working class has no sense of responsibility nowadays."

I kept my mouth shut, for the sake of peace, though I longed to argue with her.

Dittie, aroused from the *Times* by all this fuss, remarked with her usual tactlessness, "It's no good talking as if someone had waylaid your parcel out of spite! It's not here, and that's that! Considering how awful some people's handwriting is, it's a marvel that so many things do arrive! Clare Mapperleigh has twins, I see." She sank back into the *Times*.

Hilda came to the rescue. "If it's something you particularly want, Father, is there anything we can do about it?" she inquired. "Send a telegram, perhaps?"

"I don't care!" Father declared, obviously untruthfully. "I wasn't thinking of myself! It's others who will be disappointed. I wash my hands of the whole affair."

This meant that he had worked himself into the belief that the non-arrival of his parcel was really due to the wickedness of his enemies, but he wasn't going to let them get the better of him.

"Perhaps it would be better to telephone," Hilda continued calmly.

"Quite right, Hilda!" Father agreed. "They don't charge you for the number of words on the telephone! Ha! Not that I'm a man of many words myself, but they shall know what I think of them. Miss Portisham shall put a trunk call through."

He fussed away into his study, where the Portent was dutifully awaiting his orders. Hilda and I had already received instructions from him to secure any Christmas parcels which arrived for the children, and we now began to collect these and took them into the study to stow them in a cupboard.

Miss Portisham was saying: "I think a trunk call, Sir Osmond, would be safer. Even the telegraph wires may be a little uncertain at this season. I will put the call through and I shall be *very* firm. The box must be despatched by passenger train, and Bingham shall meet the train and bring the box straight here."

"Yes, yes!" Father agreed. "I rather think you'd better go with Bingham yourself, to make sure there's no mistake."

"Oh, certainly, Sir Osmond! I am quite *sure* it will be all right. We may even get *two*, the other one coming by a later post."

"Make it quite clear that I'm only paying for one. They had plenty of notice and they know quite well that it's Christmas time! They should allow for postal delay."

"Oh, certainly, Sir Osmond. Shall I order the car for you now? I think you have some more calls to do? We shall hardly need it for the station until the 2.26."

"Yes, yes. But what about Eleanor and her husband and the children? They're coming before lunch."

"I rather think, Sir Osmond, that Mr. and Mrs. Stickland have arranged for Ashmore to meet them, doubtless thinking that you would be needing the car at such a time."

"Hm! Very well! See to that, then I'll look through these letters before I go."

Our parcels were packed away and we returned to the hall, to be greeted by George, who had just finished his breakfast, with, "What's all this to-do about a parcel which hasn't come for Father?"

I thought they'd better hear about it, but I warned them not to say I'd told them, because Father was probably planning a dramatic announcement.

I explained his idea that Santa Klaus should distribute the presents to the children from the Christmas tree on the evening of Christmas Day. He had decided on this last week, and sent for a Santa Klaus outfit from Dawson's. It was supposed to arrive on Saturday, but when it didn't turn up he was persuaded by the Portent to wait until Monday morning. Now, of course, he was thoroughly annoyed at this hitch in his plan, but doubtless the thing would turn up later, and the Portent would also secure a second one, and Father would be rather pleased that Dawson's had the trouble of sending two and would only be paid for one.

"And who's to have the honour of putting on the beard and the cotton wool?" George inquired. "You don't mean to say I'm cast for the part? Or does the old man do it himself?"

I told them I thought it was to be Oliver, though first of all Father had suggested that Philip should do it. Then I think it occurred to him that Philip, who is good at amateur theatricals, might make a great success of it and walk away with the honours, so he fixed on Oliver, who is such a stick and can't act for nuts. It wasn't to be one of the family, because Father thought the children would then identify him at once.

"You'd better coach the children a bit, Patricia," George advised his wife. "It would be just like Kit to spoil the game by blurting out that he can see Mr. Witcombe's trousers!"

"If it was to be done at all, it ought to have been done years ago, when the children were babies," said Dittie. "Children of eight and nine nowadays know that it's all rubbish, and I don't think they ought to be brought up in this atmosphere of shams."

"The kiddies will enjoy it all right," George assured her easily. "If they're told they've got to pretend, they'll pretend, won't they, Patricia?"

"I only hope so," she replied. "But Kit *is* so naughty. Of course, I like these old-fashioned customs, but governesses and schools are so *very* up-to-date and the children do seem to get such a grown-up point of view and know all about aeroplanes and which car you ought to buy; one can't keep pace with them. But I only hope it won't interfere with their bedtime."

Carol came bounding downstairs, ready to go out. She looked charming. I think that's partly why Patricia likes taking her about and patronising her a bit. Carol looks so distinguished; tall and with movements which I can only describe as well-sprung. She has Hilda's fine features and marvellous hair, really golden.

"Aunt Pat!" Carol called reproachfully. "I thought I saw you going upstairs to get ready, and here you are, not dressed at all! The car will be here in a moment. Bingham's bringing it round."

"There was some fuss about a parcel," Patricia explained meekly. "I came down again to see what it was about. I won't be a moment."

We got the two of them off, and Dittie and David started for Manton in their own Daimler. Father went in the Sunbeam on his round of visits, taking Hilda with him. He always paid a number of calls just before Christmas. I think his friends must have found it a bit of a curse, just when they were getting frantic about their holly and their turkeys and their dinner parties, but our great grandfather was quite famous for his Christmas rides on horseback, when he visited the families all round about and distributed largesse in the villages. Father omitted the largesse, but thought the rest of the custom was praiseworthy and ought to be kept up.

I had noticed George hovering around and wasn't surprised when he seized upon me, as soon as the others had all cleared off.

"Now, you haven't anything to do," he declared. "The Portent is seeing to the missing parcel and the holly and the mistletoe and the flowers for the table and father's correspondence and all the rest of it! I want a talk with you."

He settled himself into his favourite arm-chair in the library and assumed his most ponderous manner.

"Now tell me frankly, Jenny, what you think about Father!"

I couldn't help laughing at that. It was so impossible and so George-like.

"Joking apart; I mean his health and—well, the state of his mind. Strikes me the old man's aged a lot since his illness."

I assured George that I thought father's illness had very little effect on his general health. He certainly looked rather older; walked a little less certainly, though you couldn't say he tottered; and was more apt to forget things. Perhaps he got tired more quickly, but one couldn't be sure of that, because the illness had certainly alarmed him and he took more care of himself than ever. He was now apt to fuss about himself a good deal if he felt tired and was making a habit of resting in an easy chair, with his feet on a stool, in the afternoon.

"Well, it may be all right," said George moodily. "You know, Jennifer, I really think it's the right thing for you to be here with him. I gathered from Hilda that you were a bit restless."

I told George that I was fed to the teeth at being told by the rest of the family that it was my duty to stay at home. I told him, as I had told Eleanor and Edith in the summer, that I was quite sure I did nobody any good by remaining at home, and that I didn't want to argue about it any more. Of course, none of them knew of Philip's and my plans, but they seem to have got an inkling that something was in the air.

"All right, Jenny; I don't want to bother you," George said. I think he was afraid I would burst into tears, and this insistence on my staying at home was getting on my nerves so much that I almost felt like it. It made me frightened lest our private plans should somehow fall through. All this opposition, though it wasn't directed actually against my plans, of course, just made everything seem so difficult. I have made lots of plans in the past for getting away from home and making a career for myself and they have never come off, so I *am* afraid of failure. But with Philip, who's a very determined person, to help me, surely this plan ought to turn out successfully.

There was obviously something else that George wanted to say, but didn't quite know how to put into words.

"Old Crewkerne hasn't been here, I suppose?" he inquired at last. Crewkerne is Father's lawyer.

"Not that I know of. He easily might come without me knowing," I pointed out. "The Portent does all Father's business for him and he never discusses business with me at all. It's quite hopeless to think I can give you any inside information about Father's will or anything of that sort."

"The girls are worried," said George.

"And they've urged you to ask me to find out something! It's not the least use. Hilda's the only one who *might* be able to get anything out of Father, and she wouldn't. The only other thing I can suggest is that you sound Miss Portisham."

"Hang it all! I can't do that!" George protested. "So—so—well, really! Hardly decent!"

"Look here, George; you can't have it both ways! You're all frightfully anxious about Father's will; you know it's no use asking him, or you're afraid to ask him. Well, then, either you must just hope for the best, or else go and see Mr. Crewkerne. If it's not decent to fish for information in the only waters in which it's likely to be found, then you'll have to adopt direct methods or resign yourselves to not knowing."

"You don't understand these things, Jenny. I can't ask Crewkerne. If father's absolutely in his right mind—and I see no real grounds for supposing that he's not—then Crewkerne wouldn't tell me anything. In fact, I couldn't ask him. It's all very well for you to be so off-hand; you don't understand the value of money!"

Little he knew about that! Philip had been rubbing it in for a long time because he was afraid that I was going to find it hard to manage on the little we should have. We weren't worrying about it any longer because we had decided that was no use and we were ready to take the plunge. I couldn't explain all this to George, so I just pointed out that he needn't worry for himself. Father was so keen about the family going on and Flaxmere being kept up properly, he was sure to provide for George.

"All very well for you, with no responsibilities, to talk about not worrying," George grumbled. "The old man's more touchy than ever about money, and things aren't too easy with three kids. Kit's prep school fees are bad enough, but when it comes to Eton, Heaven knows how we shall manage."

George is now managing director of the family biscuits, and I have always gathered that he draws an enormous salary in return for lounging into an office now and then and slapping people on the back and signing cheques.

He went on. "It's the horses. Don't know what's come to horses nowadays! Don't run true to form!"

I told him he was a fool to lose money on the Turf, because we have all heard Father talk in his most moralising way of how his own Father did the same and nearly wrecked the whole family. Father would never make good what George had lost by that method.

"Besides, it's not only that," George went on. "It's the possibility of scandal. How would you like it if you found he'd left practically everything to that woman? I don't mean only the loss of your whack, but the gossip and all that?"

I reminded George again of how keen Father was about Flaxmere being kept in the family. "Besides," I said, "he must have a tremendous lot of money. I don't see why you all get into such a fuss about the possibility of him leaving a good fat legacy to Miss Portisham. 'To my faithful secretary, in gratitude for ten years' devoted service.' That sort of thing. Lots of people do it. There's enough to go round."

"Of course," George explained, "none of us would raise any objection to a suitable legacy. It's something much more—well, sensational—that we're afraid of."

"But really, George," I protested. "I don't believe Father considers her at all as a *woman*. She's a very useful machine. You've no idea what a treasure she is, looking after everything and getting things done and keeping Father in a good temper!"

"That's just it! She's got him completely in her toils."

"Rubbish!" I insisted. "It's not as if he had any difficulty in keeping her here. I believe she really likes being here; she loves running the house and managing. I often think she must be frightfully lonely, but that's only my idea. She doesn't seem to mope."

"Lonely?" asked George, horrified.

"Yes; she has no friends. She's rather better class than the servants and she sees very little of anyone else. I really don't know what she does in her free time. She sits in her room a good deal, I think; and she sometimes goes for walks alone. I took her to the W.I., thinking that might interest her, but she's too towny; she doesn't get on with the village people and is awfully afraid of losing her dignity. But it's a ghastly life for her. After all, she's under thirty!"

George guffawed. Of course, he always laughs at the W.I. "By Jove! I'm almost sorry for Miss Portisham! Taking her to a mothers' meeting to brighten her life! I must say, I'd never thought of it like this. It only makes the situation more dangerous, to my mind. But I suppose the woman can go into Bristol if she likes? Movies and theatres and shops and all that sort of thing."

"But she's all alone, if she does go. Of course, there's Bingham. You remember it was Miss Portisham who produced him; he comes from her part of the world. At first I thought she was walking out with him, or whatever the equivalent is in Miss Portisham's station of life. But I don't think they've been about together much lately."

"By Jove! If we could marry her off to Bingham, that'd solve the problem. They could live in the coachman's cottage and she could trot round every day and run the household! But you think that's off? Looks bad."

George really was obsessed with this idea of the danger of Miss Portisham. I thought I might divert his mind by returning to a point I had already mentioned.

"Father isn't *interested* in Miss Portisham," I urged. "Not a bit. All their conversation is frightfully formal. 'Have this done, Miss Portisham.' 'Yes, Sir Osmond.' Portisham has picked up good manners and all that sort of thing, but she doesn't *talk;* not like a human being."

"You don't know how they talk when you're not there," George pointed out.

I was sure it was just the same, whether I was there or not. If you go into a room where people are having an intimate conversation and they have to change the tone of it suddenly because you are there, you can always feel something in the atmosphere. A suspense; and a sort of tingling; as if their personalities had not got back properly into their shells of convention. I tried to explain this to George, but he wasn't really convinced.

"You don't understand these things, Jenny," he told me in his most fatherly manner. "Girls never do. Some men, especially elderly men, never marry a woman because what you call her personality interests them. They don't want her to make clever conversation. Miss Portisham is a good-looking girl; you must admit that. *You* just think of her as an efficient secretary, but any man can see that she's got a good figure and a good skin and nice hair. She's not my type, but, mind you, she'd be attractive to some men. You can't tell me that a girl of her age, with her figure, never thinks of getting married, not to mention marrying a rich man. And you say yourself that she sees no one."

Of course I'd heard this sort of talk before; it always disgusts me rather and I can't believe that Father would think of Miss Portisham like that. I told George so.

"Then there's this affair with Bingham. Apart from anything else, Father wouldn't want to lose his invaluable secretary. If he noticed anything between her and Bingham, he might be pretty keen to stop it."

"But you've just said yourself that they could live here and Mrs. Bingham could still run Flaxmere," I pointed out.

"Father mightn't see it that way. He might think she'd want to leave and he'd begin by telling her that she ought to do better for herself than that, and then he'd think of a sure way of keeping her here. I tell you, I don't like the situation."

"I'm sick of talking about it," I told him. "I can't do anything; I don't think that anything need be done, and I won't do anything. If you're really worried, the best thing you can do is to work it so that Father asks Hilda to come and live here. She is a companion to him, which I'm not; she could run the house very well, which I can't; she'd be the best possible antidote."

"By Jove!" said George. "That might be a solution!"

At least I had given George something new to think about. I warned him to be careful in anything he might say to Hilda. If she thought he was hatching a plot to coerce Father, she'd shy right off.

As far as I was concerned, I felt sorrier than ever for Miss Portisham. But the important thing about this conversation is that it shows how worried and *uncertain* George was about Father's will. He wouldn't want anything to happen to Father just then because he was afraid the will might produce "sensational revelations," but he did see a ray of hope in the idea of Hilda coming to Flaxmere, and he would be only too anxious to get that arranged and trust to her influence with Father to make the world safe for Melburys.

Chapter Four

Tuesday

by Mildred Melbury (Aunt Mildred)

Those days of waiting for Christmas, after the family has collected at Flaxmere, are always difficult. The children are excited and noisy and everyone is on edge, being afraid that things won't go smoothly and that Christmas Day will not be quite the festival of good will which we have a right to expect. Of course, none of us anticipated the shocking tragedy which was to occur, but I always do feel that families which have once broken up are best kept separate. There can be occasional visits, of course, but to attempt to bring everyone together again in the same happy family atmosphere they enjoyed as children is to my mind a mistake. And of course the "in-laws" complicate matters; not that Patricia and David and Gordon are not all very nice people, but they are not part of our own family, properly speaking, and cannot be expected to fit in perfectly. That, however, is only my own opinion; no criticism is intended, and of course my poor brother arranged things in his own house as he saw fit, though there is no knowing how far he may have been influenced by those who were scheming for their own ends.

As far as I am concerned, I am always glad to come back to Flaxmere. I am trying to describe the events of Tuesday— Christmas Eve—as they seemed to me at the time, so I will endeavour to write as if the terrible happening that took place on Christmas Day had never occurred. But I must emphasize that although there was a certain uneasiness in the party, as I have tried to explain, there was nothing, nothing whatever, to make me suspect for a moment that such a dastardly blow against my poor brother was even then being planned. For planned beforehand it certainly must have been.

Eleanor, with her husband, Gordon Stickland, and her two children, Osmond and little Anne, were the last of the party to arrive. That is to say they were the last of the *family* party, for Philip Cheriton came on Monday afternoon, and Mr. Witcombe on Tuesday morning. Eleanor and her family came from London by train on Monday, in time for lunch. If I had a favourite among the children—which at least I tried never to show when I took the place of their poor mother after her death in 1920—I think it was Eleanor. Hilda was married by then; in fact, she was already a widow; so I never knew her so well. Perhaps Dittie has more character, but she was not an easy girl to advise. Eleanor was always more easy to control; indeed she seemed to wait for advice and guidance before taking any definite step. Eleanor was the beauty of the family, very like her dear mother, with the same dark eyes and soft dark hair.

Everyone noticed, even on Monday, that Eleanor seemed worried. They noticed it because it is unlike her. She has always been the quietest of the girls, after Hilda; taking things as they are and never making mountains out of molehills. But now we all saw that Eleanor was *distrait* and sometimes didn't notice when people spoke to her. I don't consider that there is any need to make a great mystery of this or to look for any secret and sinister cause. Eleanor had been through a lot of anxiety, with her nurse—such an excellent woman—leaving her so suddenly and at such an awkward season and the difficulty of finding a new one to bring to Flaxmere. And of course it came out later that the new nurse held very unorthodox religious views and doubtless Eleanor knew it already, but too late to make a change, and only hoped that there might be no unpleasant results. But naturally such a devoted mother as Eleanor would be anxious about her children's moral welfare under those circumstances, and to add to her difficulty the new nurse was a very striking-looking girl. Rather a flashy type, I consider, with red hair; even the best of men and most devoted of husbands and fathers cannot avoid noticing a girl of that sort when she flaunts her charms under his very nose. Nurse Bryan flaunted naturally; she would probably have flaunted whilst walking in her sleep. And the knowledge that the girl had no Christian principles to restrain her, probably increased Eleanor's anxiety.

I must emphasize the fact that I have not witnessed anything unfitting between Gordon Stickland and Nurse Bryan. Gordon is a gentleman and, moreover, he is still in love with Eleanor. But he is the kind of man whom women can never resist, and he seems to regard a light-hearted flirtation with any pretty and lively woman as an everyday recreation. Eleanor understands him perfectly and, being sure of his affection, does not worry about his indiscretions. But her poor father, my brother Osmond, was a stern man and always ready to be critical of those who had married into his family. He would be the first to notice some foolish banter or frivolous glance passing between Gordon and Nurse Bryan, and then it would not be surprising if he caused a good deal of unpleasantness by rebuking Gordon before all the others. It was the danger of this possibility that was weighing on Eleanor's mind; of that I feel certain. One could not help noticing how she watched her husband and, in the midst of conversation with others, she would withdraw her attention, become oblivious to what they were saying, because she heard Gordon's voice and was all ears to know whom he was talking to and in what vein.

There was a conversation between them, which was overheard by others besides myself and has given rise to a good deal of speculation. What was heard—and I feel sure that no one could have heard any more than I did and that what has been added is merely the usual moss which rolling gossip always accumulates—what was actually heard, I repeat, merely bears out my view. None of the others, of course, is likely to give much weight to my opinion, but nevertheless I think I am better able than most of them to judge Eleanor's character.

This conversation took place in Osmond's study on Tuesday afternoon. It must have been in the early afternoon, because after tea the room was closed to us so that the Christmas tree and its lighting arrangements could be fixed up. It was overheard because the door opening into the library had been left ajar. My brother was at that time out in the park with his grandchildren, as I happened to know, and Miss Portisham was probably attending to household matters. It seemed to me that Gordon had first of all entered the study, perhaps to look for some book—my brother always kept all the books of reference there—or to telephone. Eleanor followed him for we, who were sitting in the library, suddenly heard her voice say, "Oh, Gordon!"—rather reproachfully.

Patricia and I, who were sitting by the fire in the library, knitting and chatting, certainly heard that much, but we didn't catch Gordon's reply. We heard Eleanor say again, "Oh, Gordon; it's not suitable," and more that was too low for us to distinguish. Gordon replied rather loudly, "Nonsense, Eleanor!" Hilda, who was also sitting in the library, writing letters, looked up suddenly, said, "There's a draught from the study door, I think," and went across and shut it. That is all that anyone can actually have heard, and it is quite easily explained by one who knows and thoroughly understands the people and the circumstances.

One disadvantage of these family reunions is that the presence of so many people in the house makes it very difficult to get hold of anyone for a heart-to-heart talk. As I had so much responsibility for the marriages of Eleanor and Dittie and George, I am naturally anxious to have a quiet chat with each of them and hear about the children and give them the opportunity to unburden their hearts of any private worries.

Patricia has no real worries, I believe. She always makes a great to-do about small things, but that is her nature. As usual, I heard how extravagant George is and how he will go on betting and always loses, and how much the children's education is costing, but that is just what I expect to hear from Patricia. I should guess that she herself is rather an expense to George, but then he would never have endured one of those careful wives who keep an eye on the family budget and are always telling their husbands that they can't afford this or that.

Dittie was the one I was really worried about and particularly wanted to have a quiet talk with. When Dittie married Sir David Evershot ten years ago it seemed a most desirable match in every respect. I was immensely relieved to see her so satisfactorily settled. A year or so earlier she had been definitely attracted by a young man, Kenneth Stour, who at that time stayed a good deal with the Tollards, whose place is only ten miles from Flaxmere. I did everything in my power to persuade Dittie that marriage with Kenneth

Stour would be a disaster. To begin with, he is an actor, and though one must admit that the man has a sort of flashy charm, he is, I feel sure, far too irresponsible ever to make any lasting success even of such a career as he has. I felt that he could not be depended upon in any way. His family is not well off, though they have a nice enough little place in Suffolk. They are really quite obscure people, and I have heard from friends of mine who live near them that they are most peculiar and entertain all sorts of foreigners and artists, and are entirely out of the ordinary social and sporting life of the county. They are not our sort of people at all, and Dittie could never have been happy for a year in the sort of life which Kenneth offered her. My brother did not approve of Kenneth and would never have countenanced the match.

It was easy to see why Kenneth was so persistent in his attentions to Dittie. She was a handsome girl and, more-over, her father's position would have been of great help to him in his career, providing the good social background which he lacked. Her money was doubtless a further attraction; I think he had little himself, and actors are always great spenders. It was more difficult to understand what Dittie saw in Kenneth, but he was one of those casual, incompetent, frivolous young men whom girls so often fall for. Dittie finally said no to him and sent him away, but although she did so of her own free will, having been persuaded that he would never make a good husband, she has never forgiven me, I fear, for the line I took. But I had my conscience to consider, as well as my duty to my brother, and—I repeat— I never for one moment thought that such a match could be a happy one.

It was not until Dittie had been married for a couple of years to Sir David Evershot that we first heard those disturbing rumours about his family history. I did my best to prevent them from reaching my poor brother's ears, for that could have done no good and he would certainly have blamed me for not being informed before the marriage. So far as I know, Osmond never heard the stories, for I feel sure he would have spoken to me had he done so.

To tell the truth, I had been prevented by financial stringency from moving much in society for many years before I took up my residence at Flaxmere, and therefore was not *au fait* with current society gossip. In any case I might not have heard anything, for the Evershot family is not of the kind that gets itself widely talked about, and their home is on the other side of England.

The rumour—I still do not know the truth of it—is that there was a strain of lunacy in David's grandmother's family, which showed itself in one of his uncles, who was sent abroad with a trusted attendant and lived and died under an assumed name in some remote corner of Europe, so that those people who had known him as a boy forgot about him and no one else ever connected him with the Evershot family. Sir David had a brother who was reported missing in the war and who is said to be still living, a hopeless lunatic in a private asylum.

These rumours were so vague that no one would trouble about them were it not for David's temper. We never saw the signs of this when he was courting Dittie; in fact, I feel sure that the tendency has developed since then, and I fear that Dittie's own lack of poise cannot be the best antidote to such tendencies. It was at Christmas time five or six years ago that Patricia's little Enid, then about three, toddled up to her Uncle David when he was writing in the library, pulled at his sleeve, and asked him to play bears with her. I suppose she shook his arm and spoilt his writing; he snapped at her crossly: "Get away, Enid!" and the child burst into tears and ran to her mother.

Patricia reproached David—quite moderately, I thought, considering how he had frightened the child. No one noticed anything more for a few minutes. Suddenly we realized that David was on his feet, striding up and down the room. His face horrified me; his eyes were blazing and his jaw was working as if he were gnashing his teeth, only he didn't quite gnash them. Then he burst out into what I can only describe as raving. I cannot remember all that he said, but there was something like, "So I'm not fit to touch a child! And the child knows it!" I was too shocked to take in all he said. Suddenly Dittie rushed in, looking very frightened, and she managed to get him away. He didn't appear again that day and Dittie made apologies about him having a frightful headache which was driving him frantic, but from what I know of David he is not the man to suffer in silence and he certainly had not mentioned any headache.

Similar scenes have occurred on a few occasions since then. Of course we all try to avoid annoying him, but it is difficult to know what will upset him; it is generally the slightest thing. There is no denying that the children are frightened of him.

Naturally Dittie's affairs give me some anxiety, and each Christmas I am on the watch to see how things are going. David must be difficult to live with, and Dittie is not of the character to put up with that easily. My poor brother did not make things easier for Dittie by his reproachful way of referring to the fact that she and David had no children, which personally I believe to have been deliberate on Dittie's part, owing to her fear that this hereditary insanity would show itself in them.

On Christmas Eve I managed to get hold of Dittie alone for a moment. I had heard that Kenneth Stour—who has been abroad, I understand—was in England again, and I feared she might renew her undesirable connection with him and wished to warn her against such imprudence. The man is still unmarried and Dittie still feels for him—or imagines that she feels—an affection that she would certainly no longer cherish if she had married him. I thought it unwise that she should get herself talked about in this way, especially since it would displease her father gravely if it came to his ears, and of course we were all a little anxious about his will, concerning which he would never give any information.

Dittie was very angry at what I said. She declared bitterly that she would be a different person now if she had been allowed to marry Kenneth—which may indeed be true, but not for the better. She said she could manage her own affairs and that Kenneth was the only person who sympathized with her and understood her. This alarmed me, because it is a sign of danger when a married woman says this about a man other than her husband. I pointed out that it is so much easier to sympathize with someone you do not have to live with.

She told me—less bitterly but very unhappily, I thought—that I couldn't understand. "The whole thing's a mess. I can only see one way out of it, and that's impossible—at present. Father would never understand. And then—I'm a coward."

Those words of Dittie's I remember very well. The meaning is plain to me. Osmond had been worrying her again about why she had no children, and she was afraid to tell him the reason why she refused to have any.

I urged her to discuss her troubles with me and accept my advice, but she only said, with that regrettable coarseness which I have noticed before, "Father shouldn't have counted his grandchildren before they were hatched."

The conversation did not decrease my anxiety, but I could do no more. Dittie is very self-willed.

The Christmas party was not made pleasanter by the inclusion in it of Osmond's secretary, Miss Portisham. By treating her as one of ourselves he gave the girl ideas above her station and deceived himself into thinking her better than she is. Some unpleasant things have been said about my poor brother's feelings for this girl, but I will not countenance this kind of gossip, though none of us could help being anxious about how much she would eventually wring out of my poor brother by her scheming and her affected pleasantness. I hope there is no need for me to point out that once this girl had achieved her avaricious purpose, it would be to her interest that my poor brother's life should not be prolonged.

Chapter Five

Christmas Day

by Grace Portisham

It was poor Sir Osmond's especial wish that I should take part in the family's Christmas Day festivities at Flaxmere, and naturally, being placed as I am and not wishing to hob-nob with the servants' hall nor to sit by myself at such a festive season, I was only too glad to conform to his wishes. Miss Jennifer is always kind, though perhaps she doesn't quite understand my tastes, but she certainly tries to make me feel at home. She has often remarked that it must be dull for me here, which is quite true, but there are many compensations, such as the advantage of living in refined surroundings in a gentleman's household.

Poor Sir Osmond was always kindness itself, and it seems dreadful to write now of that Christmas Day, which I little thought at the time would have such a shocking end. We were all so anxious that it should go well, and just when it seemed to have passed off happily this terrible thing occurred. It is difficult after such a shock and when my situation, which had seemed so settled and secure, has been thrown into uncertainty, to write down quite straightforwardly the events of Christmas Day, but that is what I will try to do.

As well as being anxious about how Sir Osmond's plans would go off—for this is a difficult family, I think, and things do not always run quite smoothly—I was also a little worried that the family might not like me taking part in everything like one of them. Miss Jennifer's eldest sister, Mrs. Wynford, is a very considerate lady, and her daughter, Miss Carol, always behaves quite respectfully to me; more respectfully, I might say, than she sometimes does to her aunts. But those are the manners of young people nowadays. I find Sir Osmond's other daughters rather stiff, but I dare say they feel a bit jealous of my position here, considering it used to be their own home, though I always do my best to have things the way they would like.

It was a funny thing that Harry Bingham had asked me, a week or so earlier, if I could manage for us both to have the day off after he had brought the family back from morning church, and he'd take me to Bristol, he said, and we'd have a real Christmas dinner at one of the hotels and some dancing.

He thought we might even be lent the car. Well, I did turn this over in my mind, but nothing was settled, me thinking I'd better wait and see how the arrangements for Christmas Day were turning out before I asked Sir Osmond about this plan of Harry's. It was a bit of a temptation to have some Christmas jollification on my own, and yet I wasn't sure if I really wanted to go with Harry Bingham. He was a bit put out because I didn't jump at the idea and agree at once. He went off in one of his moods, which I've noticed more often lately and which will do him no good in his career.

Well, as it turned out, when Sir Osmond got this notion of his for a Santa Klaus I didn't like the idea of not being at hand at the time. I was afraid something might go wrong and then Sir Osmond would be very put out. When he asked me to join the family party, I guessed that he'd be glad to have me there to help if need be, and I decided that I'd say nothing about Harry Bingham's plan. I thought maybe we could have our outing on New Year's Day instead, or some other time.

I felt that Harry had already made up his mind that I wouldn't go with him, but all the same I wasn't looking forward to telling him that was so. However, it happened all right. On the Saturday before Christmas Harry suggested to me himself that we should put off our party. Sir Osmond had spoken to him about fitting up the Christmas-tree lights, and Cook, it seems, had said something to him about hoping he'd be there for Christmas dinner. Of course he always had his meals in the servants' hall and seemed to enjoy their company all right, though he is really a cut above them.

"I've an idea," he said, "that Sir Osmond might not be best pleased if I turned up my nose, in a manner of speaking, at what he's providing for us. I dare say it'd make a difference to things. And then there's this Christmas-tree that I may have to see to, so maybe we can have our party some other time."

He seemed to have quite got over his disappointment and to be rather pleased with the way things had turned out. He talked about the Father Christmas arrangements, which he'd heard about from Sir Osmond when he was out driving, as if he was quite looking forward to it.

"*Santa Klaus*, we're to call the old buffer," he said, in a joking sort of way. I knew Sir Osmond was particular about us saying Santa Klaus; said we gave it up in the War, because it was German, but we oughtn't to mind that now and *Father Christmas* was just silly. The other meant Saint Nicholas, and that's who the old man with the reindeer sleigh really was. Harry had got it all pat.

Of course this Santa Klaus idea nearly didn't come off at all, with the costume not turning up on Saturday nor on Monday morning. I was very upset when it didn't arrive on Monday, having advised Sir Osmond to wait till then. He had set his heart on having this affair, and I knew he'd be very put out if the plan was spoilt. I made up my mind that if they didn't send the costume by train on Monday I'd buy some stuff in Bristol and run something up myself, though the beard would be a bit of a puzzle. I thought I might get one in Bristol. However, there was no need, for the costume came sure enough by the afternoon train. I went in with Harry and collected it and brought it back. The people said when I telephoned that they'd sent if off by post on Friday morning, but I dare say, with the Christmas rush, they didn't post it at all. Anyway, the one first ordered never turned up, so it was a good thing we'd got another sent down by train.

Christmas morning went off better than I'd expected. It was a nice fine day, though not exactly Christmassy, being quite warm for the time of year. It was Sir Osmond's wish that all should go to church and make a good family show at this season, and the family party being nearly as many as all the rest of the congregation put together, they certainly did liven up the village church.

There was some talk about whether the two youngest children, Mrs. Stickland's Anne and Mrs. George Melbury's Clare, should be left behind, but Sir Osmond said it was time they learnt to behave in church and both the nurses should go too. But it turned out that Mrs. Stickland's new nurse was some sort of a free-thinker and had no wish to go. In fact, she was quite nasty about it, saying she was engaged to look after children and that she would do, she said, but not outrage her convictions. Sir Osmond was considerably put out and so was Mrs. Stickland, she being such a one for having all correct and doubtless would never have engaged such a woman, but was not able to pick and choose, her own nurse being called away so inconveniently. My own opinion is that Nurse should have kept her views, if views they can be called, to herself, instead of upsetting the family in such a way.

However, it was all settled. I sat beside Harry in the Sunbeam car, with Sir Osmond, Miss Mildred Melbury and Mrs. Stickland's two children in the back. Harry made some sarcastic remark about him wondering I condescended to sit by him, me being now one of the family. Sometimes I can't make out what's in Harry's mind. Mr. George Melbury drove his Austin car and took his wife and his youngest daughter and their nurse and also Lady Evershot. The others all walked through the park. Lady Evershot said she had a headache and so she'd take the two youngest children out before the sermon and walk home with them and put them in charge of the nurse who was a free-thinker. Though I wonder that the Hon. Mrs. George Melbury liked her little girl to be put under the influence of such a woman, after what had been revealed.

Besides the family there were two gentlemen in the party at Flaxmere; Mr. Philip Cheriton, who is very much in favour with Miss Jennifer, though I can't say the same for Sir Osmond, and Mr. Oliver Witcombe, who is a very gentlemanly young man and extremely good-looking. Mr. Witcombe was to be Santa Klaus and dress up in the costume which had caused so much trouble. I don't think he liked the idea very much, but it was Sir Osmond's wish. Considering all the trouble Sir Osmond had been put to over this Santa Klaus business, and how he'd spent a long time planning it out, I didn't think the family seemed very grateful to him. The Hon. Mrs. George Melbury had a lot to say about her children being so highly strung that they couldn't stand a lot of excitement and little Clare's bedtime must not on any account be upset. Lady Evershot, who has no little ones of her own, is never behindhand in giving her opinion about other people's, and she seemed to have some idea that Santa Klaus was old-fashioned and the children would see through him. Well, I must say I like a bit of old-fashioned fun at this festive season myself.

Mrs. Stickland fell in better than the others with her father's ideas, but Mr. Stickland had some jokes with the children about looking for smuts on Santa Klaus' nose, because he came down the chimney, and wanted to take the stag's antlers that Sir Osmond shot in Scotland from the study wall and fix them on his head with the bearskin rug over him—what he called local colour. Sir Osmond was a bit put out over that. "I won't have you playing the fool, Gordon," he said. "This is not one of your modern pantomimes. Let the children use their imagination."

"Only Oliver is licensed to play the fool on this occasion," Mr. Cheriton said. "And he enjoys it less than anyone." Which was rather hard on Mr. Witcombe, I thought.

The Christmas-tree was stood in the library, and Bingham had fixed it up with little coloured lights, all electric. After lunch Mr. Witcombe went off to put on the red robe and the beard, and so on, and Mr. Cheriton went to help him. Sir Osmond had us all say good-bye to Mr. Witcombe, because he wanted the children to think that he had really gone away and Santa Klaus was a new person, so to speak. So we all said we were sorry he couldn't stay, and Lady Evershot said she hoped the journey wouldn't be too difficult. Then little Kit called out, "Mr. Witcombe hasn't packed! I looked just before lunch and he hasn't had a chance since! He can't go without his tooth-brush."

Mrs. Stickland quieted him by saying that we hoped Mr. Witcombe would be able to come back that night. Then Kit wanted to know what sort of car had come to fetch Mr. Witcombe and could he go and look at it, so he had to be quieted again. We were in the drawing-room, children and all. The children were all a bit restive because, except for their stockings in the morning, they hadn't had any Christmas presents yet, Sir Osmond having put all their parcels on the tree or piled up round it. Kit was the worst, of course. He's rather an obstreperous child. His elder sister, Enid, likes to please her grandfather, and she knew there was something up, and kept saying, "When's our surprise coming, Grandfather?"

At last Mr. Cheriton came back to us and said: "He's safely off!" That was the signal and meant that Santa Klaus was all ready in the library.

Sir Osmond said, "I think I heard a noise like reindeer." He had been quite put out that there wasn't any snow, because he had meant to say he heard the sound of the sleigh-runners. "All sorts of queer things happen at Christmas-time, you know, children. Anne, run into the library and see if anyone's there waiting for us."

Little Anne looked rather frightened at this. She is only four. "It'll be someone very nice," Mrs. Stickland said.

"Reindeer wouldn't go into the library!" little Kit piped up. "Shall I go and look in the drive?"

"Perhaps it was Mr. Witcombe come back for his tooth-brush!" said young Osmond.

"Nonsense!" said Sir Osmond, a bit sharply. Of course, children can be very trying. "Run along to the library, Anne!"

But Anne began to cry and ran to her mother. Luckily Clare, Mrs. George Melbury's youngest, who is a much bolder child, called out, "I'll go and see!" She ran across to the library door, which was open, and peeped in, and there was the big tree all lit up and Santa Klaus. She squeaked out: "Oh, oh, oh! It's the Christmas-tree!" and all the other children raced across after her, and we followed.

Everything went off all right. Santa Klaus gave out the presents, and the servants all came in to have a look, and certainly it was a lovely sight. There was a handsome gift from Sir Osmond for each of the grown-ups, and there were dozens of presents for the children, because all theirs had been saved until then. When everything had been opened and admired, the children began to play with their toys in the hall, because there was more room there. Kit began laying out some railway lines, and Enid hung around him, fussing over a big doll which Sir Osmond had given her, though it was easy to see that she very much wanted to play with Kit's new train. Some of the grown-ups were playing with the children in the hall, or looking on, whilst others had gone into the drawing-room to listen to the wireless.

When nearly everyone had left the library, which was all littered with wrappings and string, Sir Osmond told Bingham he could switch off the lights on the tree and then go. Bingham had been helping Kit with his train, showing him how it worked. Sir Osmond had been particular that he should stay near at hand until the lights were turned off, in case anything went wrong. Sir Osmond was rightly very careful about any electric apparatus in the house, seeing that so many fine old places had been destroyed by fire all through the electric wires.

Sir Osmond then told me he was going to the study; he was tired and wanted a little rest before tea. Also it was his custom to begin to write his letters of thanks on Christmas Day. He did all those himself, of course, and was very systematic about them, doing so many each day.

Now that morning Sir Osmond had received a letter which had come by hand and was marked "Personal." He had looked at it for a long time, though I could see it had only three or four lines of typewriting and no signature, and he never told me what was in it. But he said to me to remind him if necessary—because his memory was not what it used to be—that he had an appointment between three-thirty and four-thirty that afternoon. I thought this rather funny, Christmas Day not being usual for a business appointment, and I suppose I showed it, for Sir Osmond said it was only a personal matter, but he wanted to be in the study ready. From that I took it that he was expecting some private telephone call.

So on that afternoon of Christmas Day, when he said he was going into the study, I at once thought he had the engagement in mind, but to make sure I just said that I supposed it was not necessary to remind him of the call he was expecting, and he said that was all right. Those were the last words I ever spoke to Sir Osmond, and his last words to me, as he went into the study, were: "Thank you, Grace. It's a pleasure to me to know there is someone I can always rely on."

Sir Osmond then called to Mr. Witcombe, who was still waiting in the library, as Santa Klaus, to follow him into the study, to have his instructions, I suppose, about giving out the presents in the servants' hall. It had been arranged that he was to do this in his Santa Klaus dress and Sir Osmond was very particular that it should be done just so, with a special remark of a jocular nature to each one of them. We all knew that Mr. Witcombe didn't relish this part of the business, because of course the servants all knew who he was and he probably felt a bit silly.

When Sir Osmond went into the study with Mr. Witcombe, there was only Bingham there in the library, seeing to the lights, and me, and I don't suppose anyone else knew exactly where Sir Osmond was or when he went into the study. I began tidying up the papers and string, but Harry, who was still busy with his electrical business, came and swept everything up into a corner and told me not to bother with the mess now, when I ought to be enjoying the party. So I went and joined the others in the hall and went round to look at the children's presents.

Santa Klaus, that is to say Mr. Witcombe, came out of the study not long afterwards and crossed the hall and went out by the door at the back, under the left-hand branch of the staircase; soon he came back again into the hall, from the dining-room, I think—on the right-hand side—holding a lot of crackers in his arms. He went up to Kit, who was kneeling on the floor over his train, and held out a cracker for him to pull. The cracker went off with a big bang, which attracted the attention of the other children, who came running up, and Santa Klaus divided his armful amongst them and they ran around pulling them with us who were in the hall and making a tremendous noise. Santa Klaus went into the library, I suppose to pick up the presents for the servants' hall.

It was some time later when we saw Santa Klaus come into the hall again, through the door from the back passage. He came to the bottom of the big staircase and waved his empty sack to show that he'd given away all the presents, and called out something to the children about saying good-bye soon, until next Christmas. Then he went into the library. We weren't quite sure what was to happen next and I think everyone was waiting to see. I knew the original idea was for him to report to Sir Osmond, who would come into the hall and gather us all together to see Santa Klaus off from the front door. He had evidently gone into the study through the library, which happened to be the nearest door to him. Now that there had been this private letter to Sir Osmond about the appointment I didn't know whether the plan might be altered or what we were supposed to do, so I kept a look-out to be ready.

Then I heard a rattling of the handle of the study door, like someone trying to get out and not being able to turn it. I ran up to the door and tried it, but it was locked and the key wasn't on the outside. I called out that the key must be inside, as was to be expected, but in a moment Santa Klaus appeared from the library, shutting the door carefully behind him. He looked round quickly and came up to Mrs. Wynford, who was standing near me, as we had been talking together. We saw that he had a sort of ghastly look, though with the false eyebrows and beard and his cheeks rouged, it was difficult to see what he really looked like until he came quite close. There seemed to be two expressions; this ghastly one looking through the jolly Santa Klaus one.

He said very quietly to Mrs. Wynford: "Get the children away somewhere. There's been an accident. Do you know where George is?"

She gave a sort of gasp and put her hand to her mouth and looked towards the study and at him again, and didn't seem able to say a word.

He just nodded and said: "Yes: Sir Osmond. I think he's shot himself." He held her by the arm as he said it, as if to warn her not to scream and to hold her in case she fainted. But she seemed to get control of herself.

She said: "I must go to him—a doctor—Grace had better telephone."

Mr. Witcombe said quickly, before I could run to the study, where the telephone was, "Hilda! I'm afraid it's no good; you can't do anything. Don't go into the study; wait for George. Miss Portisham, will you see that someone looks after the children."

I knew from his manner as well as from what he said that it was very serious and I felt dreadfully frightened, but I knew we mustn't have a scene and get all the children screaming. But he looked so awful in the Santa Klaus dress and make-up and his staring eyes that I wanted to laugh, even when I felt frightened and trembling and almost crying at the same time. I managed to tell him that I thought Mr. George Melbury was in the drawing-room; I'd noticed him go in there a little earlier. Mrs. Wynford stood, looking about her, very pale, but she seemed able to look after herself. Then I caught sight of Nurse Poole and was going to ask her to see to the children, when it occurred to me that there might be some feeling if I gave orders to her. But I saw Mrs. Stickland, and thankful that it was her, who is always so quiet, and not the Hon. Mrs. George Melbury, I went and told her what Mr. Witcombe had said.

I don't know exactly what happened after that, but everything was awfully quiet. Even the children were quiet, for a wonder, and Mrs. Stickland and the nurses got them all away without much fuss. I was still thinking that I ought to telephone, so I went into the library, remembering that the study door was locked, and as I went in I saw Mrs. Wynford at the study door, which was closed. Mr. Witcombe, still dressed up, which seemed so dreadful, but I think he had forgotten about it, came hurrying up just as Mrs. Wynford opened the door and he followed her into the study, and I went in behind him.

We were surprised—at least, I was—to see Lady Evershot standing in the study with her back to the window that looks out at the side of the house. She was standing a little to one side and behind the chair in which Sir Osmond usually sat at his table in the corner, when he was writing, and I could just see that Sir Osmond was in the chair, not sitting up but dropped over one arm of the chair, with his head below the table. Lady Evershot looked very white and I could see her hands were trembling.

Mrs. Wynford ran forward, round Sir Osmond's table, taking no notice of her sister; she stood there, looking down at her father, drawing in her breath and seeming to go all stiff, with her hands spread out.

Mr. George Melbury came in quickly and said, "Wait, Hilda!" He went up to her and put his hand on her arm, as if to hold her back, while Mr. Witcombe said: "You can't do anything." She pulled herself away and took a step nearer to her father. Mr. Witcombe said again, "It's no good, Mrs. Wynford. We ought not to touch anything." Then he turned to me and asked me to ring up the doctor.

I went across to the little table in the other corner, where the telephone stood, and sat down and everything seemed to swim and my hands trembled so that I could hardly dial the number, though I knew it well enough. As I was waiting for the number I heard Mrs. Wynford say in a queer, high voice, "Where are Jenny and Carol?"

I think Mr. Witcombe took her and Lady Evershot out of the room, and Mr. George came over to me and when he heard by what I said that Doctor Tarrant was coming at once, he asked me if I knew the number of Colonel Halstock, who was a neighbour of Sir Osmond's and the Chief Constable of the county. I gave him the number and he sat down and began to dial it. I didn't know whether to go away, so I waited. I walked a little back from the telephone table to where I could see Sir Osmond better. He lay all sort of collapsed sideways in his chair, leaning over towards the wall, and I could see a dark hole in the side of his forehead and a trickle of blood, and a long pistol lay on the table in front of him. It made me feel quite awful. I was afraid to touch him; he looked so dead; but it seemed dreadful to leave him like that.

Then I heard voices in the library and in came Miss Jennifer, and went straight up to Sir Osmond's table and stood there and said in a low voice: "Oh!" Very long drawn out it was. And then she just said: "How frightful!"

She stood there a moment or so and then she walked up to the table and picked up the pistol. Mr. George was speaking through the telephone, with his back to her, but he had noticed her come in and now I suppose he heard the noise of her picking up the pistol and he said, very sharply, "You mustn't touch anything, Jennifer!" Then he went on speaking into the telephone.

I didn't like to do or say anything. Miss Jennifer seemed to take no notice of her brother, but she held the pistol for a moment and then put it down again very carefully and stood there looking at the table and everything on it. Then she turned and saw me.

"I don't know what I ought to do!" she said, but almost as if she were speaking to herself.

Mr. George had just finished telephoning and he got up and said, "Really Jenny, you mustn't touch anything in the room. It's no good staying here, you know."

He looked towards me, as if wanting me to do something. I was very frightened and as if rooted to the ground, especially because I thought Miss Jenny was really half off her head with the shock. She looked white as a ghost. I went up to her and persuaded her out of the study and into the library.

There sat Mrs. Wynford, still with that frozen look, as if she didn't know what was going on round her. Lady Evershot was standing with her back against the window, just in the same position she had stood in the study, and she was gripping the window ledge with her hands and looking as if she might faint. Then Sir David came in at the library door and looked all round the room rather wildly and saw his wife and went and stood near her, but she took no notice of him at all.

The others came in one by one. Mrs. Stickland was very quiet, but she was crying. Mr. Stickland followed her in and they went and sat down together. Mr. Witcombe, who seemed to have been finding them all and telling them, came in holding Sir Osmond's sister by the arm and half supporting her. She was sobbing and calling out, very loudly, it seemed:

"Look after the others! Where is George? He ought to be looking after his poor wife and sisters. Oh dear, oh dear! How can such a thing have happened? I always said these Christmas gatherings were not wise; but of course, no one would listen. Oh dear, oh dear!" She sat down and went on crying and calling out, "Oh dear! Oh dear!" over and over again.

Mr. George's wife followed them in and she was talking too, rather wildly, I thought, and saying, "At such a time, too! Oh, it's dreadful, dreadful! Do you think the children will be all right? We must *do* something. To-day of all days! Just when we were doing our best! It's frightful!"

No one took much notice of her, except that Mr. Witcombe, after he had put Miss Melbury into a chair, went up to her and tried to quiet her. He had taken off his Santa Klaus dress, and the beard and false eyebrows, but the rouge was still on his face. I suppose no one liked to tell him about it.

The door opened suddenly and Miss Carol sort of burst in and then stopped and said: "Oh! Where's mother? What's the matter?" There was a sort of shocked silence and then she saw her mother signing to her and went and sat beside her, talking to her in a low voice.

Then Mr. Cheriton came in and he also seemed as if he had rushed to the library in a hurry, which of course was only natural. He looked round anxiously till he saw Miss Jennifer, who looked towards him as though she were relieved that he had come, and he went up to her and began to talk to her.

Just then Mrs. Stickland came up to me and asked me to go and see that tea was served to the children and nurses in the day nursery and to give a message to nurse about putting them to bed. I was rather glad to have something to do and to get away. I couldn't get used to the idea that Sir Osmond was dead and I was very uncomfortable in the library, not knowing whether I should stay, because I might be needed over some business, but feeling that they didn't want me there. In fact, it seemed as if each one of them didn't want some of the others there. As each one came in, someone would look up at them as if somehow that made it all worse. It was like a group of people having a private conversation, which makes them feel awkward when someone walks in upon them suddenly. I suppose it was the awful shock and no one quite understanding what had really happened.

Chapter Six

Review of the Situation

by Col. Halstock, Chief Constable of Haulmshire

Certainly the most difficult and painful situation I have ever found myself involved in! My old friend, Sir Osmond Melbury, found shot in his study on Christmas Day. Evidence seems to point to someone in the household as the criminal, and the large party gathered there consists almost entirely of members of his family, whom I have known from their childhood.

Here and now (11.40 p.m. on Christmas Day—just returned from Flaxmere) I will record my personal impressions, as well as the bare facts.

Facts which seem to be generally agreed upon:

After Christmas-tree business Sir Osmond went to his study at about 3.30. Miss Portisham and Bingham, the chauffeur, last saw him in the library at this time. Mr. Witcombe, impersonating Santa Klaus, followed him into the study and was there instructed by him concerning distribution of presents in servants' hall. Sir Osmond said he would be in his study until tea time (4.30) and was expecting a telephone call. Mr. Witcombe was to report to him there when he had finished his Santa Klaus job. (Only Mr. Witcombe's evidence for this conversation.)

Rest of the party were for the next half-hour scattered about hall and drawing-room. Miss Portisham and Hilda Wynford say they were in the hall all the time and confirm each other's evidence on this point pretty well, declaring that they were talking to each other after the first five or ten minutes. No one seems sure of having seen any of the others during the whole of this half-hour.

George Melbury's wife, Patricia, was talking to Eleanor Stickland in the drawing-room and then went into the hall to quieten two of the children who were quarrelling. Eleanor followed her into the hall when she heard the crackers being pulled, as she thought her daughter would be frightened. Edith Evershot says she was in the drawing-room all the time. Miss Melbury went upstairs at some point to fetch her knitting. Jennifer says she was "all over the place," chiefly playing with the children in the hall. Carol Wynford says the same. So much for the women.

Of the men, George Melbury, David Evershot and Gordon Stickland say they were in the drawing-room most of the time. George went into the hall once to see what was going on, he says, because he was on the look-out for some summons to them all from his father "to see Santa Klaus off the premises." He returned to the drawing-room. Gordon Stickland says he sat in the drawing-room all the time, working out a crossword puzzle, and didn't particularly notice who else came and went. David Evershot says he looked into the hall when the cracker-pulling began, to see what was up, and then, because of the noise and smell, felt he must get some fresh air, so he went out of the front door and took a breather up and down the drive in front of the house, returning after about five minutes.

Philip Cheriton says he was moving about, chiefly talking to Jennifer and Carol, who both agree that they were talking to him "practically all the time," but they struck me as rather vague about this. In short, it seems impossible to be sure of anyone's exact movements during that half-hour.

No one admits seeing anyone enter the study after Oliver Witcombe left Sir Osmond there, until Witcombe returned and found him dead. Clearly he was shot after Witcombe left. *Evidence for this*: Miss Portisham, who remained in the library when Witcombe followed Sir Osmond into the study, testifies that the door was left open and she heard their voices in conversation until she went into the hall. Bingham, who was also in the library for some time, agrees that the door was left open. Witcombe knew they were there and can hardly have known when they left, so we can wipe out the possibility that he followed Sir Osmond into the study to murder him.

Witcombe left the study by the door leading into the hall. But the study can be entered from the library and there is a door between the library and dining-room—in fact a route by which you can get from the passage behind the hall to the study without entering the hall or, providing the library door is shut, being seen from it.

The next visitor to the study, as far as anyone admits, was Oliver Witcombe again, acting on Sir Osmond's instructions, he says, to report when he had distributed the presents in the servants' hall. He entered library from hall (seen by several) and so into study. About 4 p.m. Found Sir Osmond seated at his writing table, shot in side of head; dead. Pistol on table before him.

Witcombe says he felt Sir Osmond's heart but otherwise touched nothing. Attempted to open door into hall but found it locked. (Door certainly locked when I arrived and key not yet found.) Came round into hall through library, locking study door behind him, lest the children might run in. Spoke to Hilda Wynford and Miss Portisham, found George Melbury in drawing-room and spoke to him, and returned to library. As he entered he saw Miss Portisham there and Mrs. Wynford, the latter just opening the study door. He followed her in and they found Lady Evershot already there. George Melbury came into the study soon after them.

At George's request, Miss Portisham telephoned to Doctor Tarrant. (He says she sounded very upset; the gist of her message was that Sir Osmond had shot himself.) George himself telephoned to me. (By my own observation it was 4.12 when I reached the telephone. There was a little delay in getting hold of me, and the line was not clear; I couldn't make out at first what George was saying. George remained in the study until Doctor Tarrant arrived at 4.27. Jennifer Melbury came into the study while he was telephoning. He seems to have cleared them all out when he had finished telephoning to me and he remained there alone. I was there at 4.46. The police and police surgeon (notified by me) arrived soon after. The only people who seem to have been alone in the study with the corpse, after Witcombe gave the alarm, were, first Edith Evershot, and then George.

The gist of the doctors' report is that Sir Osmond was shot at close range—a foot or two, probably—in the *left* side of the head, almost certainly by the weapon found on the table in front of him. One bullet had been fired from it. The bullet which killed Sir Osmond, extracted from his head by the doctors, fits the weapon. Doctors consider it quite impossible that Sir Osmond could have shot himself. He was not left-handed (my own knowledge, as well as evidence of members of the family). The weapon was not held with barrel pressed against head—the almost inevitable position in cases of suicide, and one which would be clearly shown by scorching. The weapon had not been dropped on floor, though Sir Osmond's arms hung down over sides of chair, but had been replaced on table. As we found it, it lay across the table in front of him, with the butt nearest to the right hand side of the table as one stood facing the body. (But see notes *re* Jennifer.) Oliver Witcombe says he noticed the revolver when first he saw the body, but did not particularly notice its position.

The weapon is identified by George positively as a .22 target pistol belonging to Sir Osmond and usually kept in the gun room. Nobody remembers seeing it lately, either in the gun room, the study, or elsewhere. Ammunition could have been obtained from the gun room. Gun room was generally locked but key hung on hook, above children's reach, in passage near gun room door (at back of hall). This seems to have been common knowledge.

No signs of disorder in the study or of a violent quarrel, or of robbery as motive. George, Miss Portisham, and others, testify that nothing was displaced or missing, so far as a hasty survey could show.

Soon after Sir Osmond entered the study there was a good deal of cracker-pulling in the hall. A pistol-shot might easily have been unnoticed; doors and walls are thick. No one admits hearing a shot. There was probably also a good deal of general noise in the hall from children playing, toy train, etc. In fact no one admits hearing any noise at all from the study—raised voices, or anything of that sort.

Impressions of members of the house party.

Must face the obvious fact that nearly every member of the party probably had something to gain by Sir Osmond's death, although just how much is not clear until we see the will.

George Melbury showed natural state of distress and shock. Nothing unusual. Seems to have taken correct course of action, except for allowing other members of the family to go in and out of the study and behave rather oddly after the tragedy had been discovered.

Jennifer Melbury may stand to gain more than her sisters, because Sir Osmond's death removes the obstacle to her marriage with Philip Cheriton, and probably provides her with the income which will make this possible without hardship.

Says she happened to enter the library (after the tragedy was discovered), saw Oliver Witcombe and others there and learnt that her father was shot. Went at once into study. George was telephoning. (His call to me.)

In the midst of this telephone conversation I heard part of a remark addressed by George to her: ... "You mustn't ... Jennifer." When I asked George about this, he said he couldn't see Jennifer from where he was sitting, but heard a "sort of jarring noise," thought she had bumped against Sir Osmond's table, and therefore warned her not to touch anything. Jennifer, when questioned, was very distressed; said she hardly knew what she was doing; it was such a shock seeing her father like that. Thinks she did touch the pistol— "Just because it was a strange thing there; I couldn't connect it with anything at the moment." Doesn't remember exactly how it was lying, or if she changed its position.

Jennifer's evidence is undeniably vague and confused, but she is obviously suffering from shock.

Miss Portisham probably stands to gain nothing comparable with her loss of a good position. Appears very distressed; also very frightened (natural, I think, in her position, with some members of the family not very well disposed towards her). Her evidence is very clear. She followed George and Hilda into the study, having been asked to telephone to the doctor, and she left the study with Jennifer.

Hilda Wynford says that on hearing news from Witcombe, her first thought was to go to her father. Knew the study door into hall was locked, as she had been standing near it when Witcombe tried it from inside. So went through library into study. On opening study door, found her sister Edith there. Left, after a few minutes, with Witcombe.

Obviously very distressed; seems stunned; but clear in her statements.

Carol Wynford says that Parkins, the manservant, told her that "there had been an accident in the study" and then she realized that everyone else had gone into the library and she followed them. Doesn't know how it was that no one else had told her or that she didn't notice that anything was amiss, but there was a general atmosphere all the afternoon of "what's going to happen next" in connection with the Santa Klaus affair, which she says she was rather bored with. Blasé younger generation attitude! She struck me as knowing a little more than she was ready to give away.

Patricia Melbury, the fluffy type. Heard the news in the hall and "hardly knows who told her" and didn't seem to think I had any right to ask. Very upset and incoherent.

Edith Evershot says she was told that something had happened in the study and she went through the library into the study, unlocking the door (locked by Witcombe behind him). *N.B.* According to other evidence, she shut the door again behind her. Says that on seeing her father she was too shocked to do anything at all, and that Hilda and others came in almost at once.

Is in a highly nervous state and struck me as frightened of something.

Sir David Evershot—curious character; restless and jumpy; unhelpful. Snarled at me: "I tell you I know nothing; haven't been into the study at all to-day. I was outside on the drive—my usual confounded luck—just before it happened, but I don't know anything."

Eleanor Stickland, always a placid sort of woman and now in a state of subdued grief. Learnt news from Miss Portisham in hall; gave orders to nurse to keep children out of the way and helped shepherd them from the hall before she went into the library.

Gordon Stickland; suave, detached; answered questions clearly. Suggested possibility of entry to study from outside the house (but shutters were all closed and hooked on inside).

Miss Mildred Melbury probably stands to gain nothing by her brother's death. Almost hysterical and unable to give any clear evidence, but Witcombe states that he found her in drawing-room, that she broke down on hearing the news, and he took her into the library to join the others. She seems to take the curious view that she always said no good would come of these family gatherings at Christmas; but gave no clear idea of what misfortune she had expected, or why.

Oliver Witcombe seems to be the one member of the party who has nothing whatever to gain by Sir Osmond's death and something to lose. I should say he never had much chance with Jennifer and now has not an earthly. But he never struck me as a very ardent suitor—though that may be merely modern manners. I think he is not very popular with the rest of the family.

No doubt he had opportunity, more than most of the others, so far as can be seen. His Santa Klaus rig-out would make it easy to conceal the pistol. He hardly had opportunity to get it when he went to dress up, as Philip Cheriton went with him, and it is highly unlikely that those two would plot anything together. But after Witcombe left Sir Osmond in the study his movements are not clear. Some discrepancy between his own statement and those of others. (*Clear this up.*) Apparently he went out through hall and by door into passage at back, but came back again through dining-room with crackers. (He could easily have gone into gun room on the way and got pistol.) He left hall again by door into library—presumably to go through dining-room to back premises—but it would have been a simple move to go from library into study, where he knew Sir Osmond was, shoot him, lock door into hall to prevent premature discovery of crime, return through library and dining-room to servants' hall.

Philip Cheriton obviously stands to gain a good deal—the way clear to marry Jennifer, and Jennifer's money which she presumably inherits from her father.

He answered my questions fairly clearly, but seemed worried. A bit vague about how he spent the fatal half-hour; was "here and there," talking to Jennifer and Carol. He seems to have been deputed by Sir Osmond to help Witcombe, so probably knew the plan of his movements exactly and may have known that Sir Osmond would be in the study.

Possibly Jennifer and Carol suspect something and are trying to shield Cheriton by saying they were talking to him all the time. He may have slipped out at the back of the hall unobtrusively as soon as Witcombe was out of the way; taken pistol from gun room, gone by passage, through dining-room and library into study, and back into hall the same way. Possible that he may even have wangled Witcombe's movements, so as to make suspicion fall on him.

That accounts for all the house party. Servants all seem straight and none of them has any motive, so far as I can see at present, for getting rid of a master who may have been stern but was not unjust. Most of them have been at Flaxmere for some years.

Henry Bingham, the chauffeur, was in attendance on the Christmas-tree until the lights were switched off; says he left the library whilst Witcombe was still talking to Sir Osmond in the study. *Look into Bingham's subsequent movements*—when did he reach the servants' hall? Could have gone back to the library?

Witcombe is sure Bingham was in the servants' hall when he distributed the presents and also maintains that none of the others could have been absent because Sir Osmond expressly stated that there was a parcel for each and Witcombe found a recipient for every parcel. There are also the two nurses, the Sticklands' nurse recently engaged by them, but they were occupied with the children and in every way unlikely suspects.

In spite of my hypothetical case against Philip Cheriton, which is nothing but a demonstration of the possibility that he *could* do it, the facts really point to Oliver Witcombe as our man. But as well as his lack of motive, there seems to be a lack of reason in his movements if they were really part of a plan for murder. Detective-Inspector Rousdon was all for arresting him last night and obviously thought me an old fool to leave him at large. But he is under close observation. A point which carries a good deal of weight with me, though it's too vague to explain to Rousdon, is that the family don't seem to suspect him. They must know a good deal more about this than they have yet admitted; they do suspect someone. If Witcombe had any motive some of them would surely know of it and they would connect it at once with the obvious facts against him. Moreover, they would be less likely to shield him than one of themselves, or even Philip Cheriton, whom some of them certainly like and who is a much older friend of the family than Witcombe. I believe I do know all they can tell me about Witcombe, but probably not about anyone else.

I feel sure that the important facts, which will clear up the case, lie within the knowledge of at least one member of the family and must be extracted, though it's a damned unpleasant job.

Chapter Seven

The Open Window

by Col. Halstock

Arriving at Flaxmere early on the morning of Boxing Day, thanking heaven that no newspapers were published on that day and we could pursue our investigations in privacy, I found Rousdon in a state of annoyance.

"Remember those shutters in the study, sir?" he inquired unnecessarily. "We found them all hooked shut on the inside last night, but when one of the men left on duty here opened them this morning, one of the windows was wide open at the bottom!"

The murder was beginning to look like an outside job, after all, and of course he was riled, having been so sure about Witcombe last night.

I made light of it. "Careless maid?" I suggested. But it seemed a bit queer, for I had looked at the shutters myself the night before and was sure they were all closed and hooked. I asked Rousdon which window was open.

"The one looking out at the side of the house, almost behind Sir Osmond's chair," he told me. "I've just sent for the girl who was responsible for closing the windows and shutters last night—name of Betty Willett."

Constable Mere ushered the girl in with a benevolent air; I think he'd been trying to reassure her outside the door, but she looked thoroughly scared. She told us in a whisper, that she had been in service at Flaxmere for three years.

Yes—still in a whisper, with her eyes starting out of her head—she closed the shutters in the study last night.

"You needn't be scared!" Rousdon exhorted her. "We're not blaming you! When did you attend to these shutters?"

"Before the Christmas tree was lit, sir. That was Sir Osmond's orders, given me by Miss Portisham. I was to close the shutters of the lib'ery d'reckly after lunch, to show off the lights, you see, sir; an' I was to close the shutters of the study at the same time, because Sir Osmond didn't want to be disturbed when I went round later to draw the curtains in the other rooms—they haven't all got shutters; on'y the study an' lib'ery an' dinin'-room. An' that's what I did, sir."

We questioned her closely about closing the windows. She always closed any windows that were open, she declared; "those are orders." She remembered that one of the study windows at the front of the house was open a bit at the top and she shut it. She was quite sure the other windows were all shut and was quite shocked at the idea that any of them might have been open at the bottom. "Sir Osmond never had the study windows open at the bottom in the winter," she maintained. She was also quite certain that she had hooked all the shutters; Sir Osmond was very particular about that, she said.

I asked if she drew the curtains. She said, no, Sir Osmond never had the curtains drawn over the shutters in the study. This was in accordance with what we had observed. We dismissed the girl and went into the study to look at the window.

The shutters were now all folded back. Sir Osmond's study always impressed me as rather a forbidding room and now, fireless, in the thin light of a wet winter morning, the shiny leather chairs, the office furniture and the brown cord carpet looked positively bleak. The window behind Sir Osmond's table, which looked out on to a wide paved path with a naked flower border beyond, was open about two feet at the bottom. Cold, damp air flowed in. I fetched my gloves and closed the shutters and stood near the chair in which the body had been found. I could feel a draught round my neck; he could never have sat there for a moment without noticing it. Clearly the window was opened after he was killed.

Rousdon and I examined the shutters and the catch; it didn't seem possible to fasten the hook from outside, though of course it would have been easy to draw the shutters together and then push down the window.

I sent Rousdon round to the path outside the window, not letting him climb out over the sill, and made him experiment on the hooked shutters with the blade of a pen-knife, after we had examined them for any marks of previous work of the same kind, which we failed to find.

After a good deal of scratching and scraping he got the hook open. Then I tried to balance the hook so that when the shutters were pulled to from outside, it would fall into its eye. It didn't work very well.

I was trying my best to demonstrate that the murder might have been done by someone who escaped through the window. It would give us the problem of catching an unknown, vanished, criminal, instead of merely picking one out from a batch of suspects under our noses, but it would exculpate the family.

Rousdon, who submitted to the experiments impatiently, finally disposed of my idea—which I didn't really believe in but wanted to make possible.

"These windows are heavy and noisy," he pointed out. "If anyone pushed up the bottom sash, Sir Osmond couldn't help hearing; he wouldn't have stayed quietly in his chair with his back to the window, in the position in which he was shot."

Still, the window might have been opened and the catch of the shutters unfastened before Sir Osmond entered the study; the murderer could have waited—no; it wouldn't do. Whoever came in was expected or at least didn't alarm Sir Osmond. He had been sitting in his chair at the table, expecting no danger.

"Besides," said Rousdon; "why should anyone going out of that window fiddle about with the catch in the hope of making it fall into the eye, which was chancy, and then not push down the sash, which was easy and obvious?"

He noticed me scrutinizing the path and flowerbed beyond.

"Been over everything, sir," he assured me. "Window ledge, wall and all, and the window frame for any sign of forcing the catch, though I admit it wouldn't be too difficult to push that back from outside with a pen-knife and leave no scratch. Finger-print man has been all over it and taken photographs. There *are* prints; quite a lot; the maid's, of course; and perhaps others. As for the path, you could walk up and down on those paving-stones all night and not leave a mark, after this rain."

I called Rousdon indoors and sent for Parkins, who for years had combined the duties of butler and valet to Sir Osmond. I knew him and trusted him. He was a pale man with a big nose and thick wrinkles down his cheeks, and this morning he looked worried and paler than ever.

I asked him first if he was perfectly certain that every member of the staff was in the servants' hall when Mr. Witcombe entered to distribute the presents.

"I'll swear to that, sir," Parkins declared eagerly. "In accordance with Sir Osmond's orders I had assembled the staff in the library to see the tree lighted up, and we then returned to the servants' hall; all except Bingham, that is. He was to stay on duty by the tree. But he was back with us before Mr. Witcombe arrived, entering in a hurry and saying, jocular like, 'So I haven't missed the bus?' meanin', sir, that he was in time to receive his gift, having been kept, doubtless, seein' to the lights."

I made particular note of this for it cleared Bingham completely. He wouldn't have risked going to the study by any route whilst Witcombe was still wandering about the hall and library with his crackers, and if he got to the servants' hall before Witcombe arrived, he couldn't have had a chance to do the shooting. I was frowning—a trick I have when concentrating—in the effort to picture their movements exactly, and apparently Parkins thought I didn't believe him.

"It's quite all right about Bingham, sir; I assure you, sir," he insisted. "He always got on very well with Sir Osmond—if you'll pardon the liberty, sir. And he couldn't have done it; he came in and Mr. Witcombe followed close on his heels, sir, as the saying is."

"All right," I assured him. "You've cleared that up. Now what about that girl, Elizabeth Willett; is she a bit careless? Is it likely that she left a shutter unhooked in the study, or a window open, and wouldn't remember? Girls are sometimes unreliable." I thought the girl had spoken the exact truth, but I wanted to make sure.

"That they are, sir," Parkins agreed with feeling. "But Betty is a good girl and very careful in her work. Most methodical she is, sir, and if she said she closed a window I'd take her word for it without going to look at it myself, which is more than I'd do with some."

I thanked the man and dismissed him, but he hesitated and then jerked out, "Excuse me, sir, but maybe you didn't notice, seeing it's a small thing and gentlemen are not always so partic'lar about noticing things like that when they know there's someone else will attend to them, which of course it's my duty to notice and attend to in the usual course—" He suddenly dried up.

I prompted him; "Yes, Parkins. What is it?"

"Well, sir!" His words now came in a rush, as if he had suddenly got rid of some obstruction in his throat. "When I saw my poor master's clothes I couldn't help but notice his coat and all the fluff on it; or rather, sir, not exactly fluff, but little white hairs, sir, as if off some cheap fur. It was all I could do to keep from going at once for the clothes-brush, sir, and I couldn't help thinking it odd, being sure that I had brushed the coat most particularly, so that there wasn't a speck on it, before Sir Osmond put it on yesterday morning."

I asked quickly if he had touched the coat.

"No, sir; I kept my hands off it and you can see for yourself, sir. All along the top of the pockets."

"When did you notice this?"

"Last night, sir. You remember, sir, you sent me for a sheet to cover the body? And when I brought it into the study, sir, and looked at my poor master, I noticed it at once."

"Why didn't you tell us at the time?" growled Rousdon.

"It's difficult to explain, sir," said Parkins, answering Rousdon's question but addressing himself to me. "I noticed it as it might be Sir Osmond was going out and I was giving him a final look-over and brush-down, quite automatic as it were, and then I received instructions from you, sir, about seeing that all was clear for carrying the body through the hall, and I put the other out of my mind. But it came back to me, quite sudden-like, this morning, sir, and I thought I ought to draw your attention to it. I hope I was right, sir?" He looked quite pathetically anxious.

I assured him that he had done the right thing and I asked him if he knew what Sir Osmond habitually carried in his pockets.

"Oh yes, indeed, sir. Sir Osmond was very methodical and I know just what articles he usually placed in the pocket of each suit. Hundreds of times I've laid those things out, sir."

We took him into the study, where the clothing from Sir Osmond's body was stacked in a neat heap. Rousdon couldn't restrain his triumphant satisfaction. He picked up the coat and examined it carefully. On the dark blue cloth were certainly a great many tiny white hairs, chiefly along the edges of the pockets and on the fold of the right-hand lapel. Parkins watched eagerly with his pale, prominent eyes.

"You see what I mean, sir?"

I directed his attention to a table on which lay several little collections of objects, labelled to show which pockets they had been taken from. I asked the man to notice carefully whether anything which Sir Osmond would normally have carried was missing, or in the wrong pocket, or if there were anything unusual there.

Parkins surveyed the notebook, fountain-pen, ivory-handled pen-knife, gold watch, note-case, coins and other items, moving his lips as if he were reciting a prayer. Finally he turned to me and reported, "All correct, sir, as it seems. All in the right pockets, too, according to the labels."

He couldn't give us any idea of the amount of money Sir Osmond was carrying but thought Miss Portisham would know. I dismissed him with orders to send Miss Portisham to the library and an injunction not to talk to anyone about the white hairs.

"What the deuce did Mr. Witcombe find, or expect to find, in Sir Osmond's pockets?" grunted Rousdon as Parkins shut the door behind him. The fellow was positively gloating. I left him to question Miss Portisham about the money Sir Osmond had, though I didn't suppose she would be able to tell us anything really helpful, and went out to take a look round outside the study window.

As I left the library I met Miss Portisham. She looked rather "dressed up" in a black silk frock but I had an idea that she had put on her best because it was the only black one she had. It showed up her dark auburn hair, which looked very smooth and shining. I said good morning to her and she threw me a sudden, appealing and rather scared look from her blue eyes. She was certainly an attractive young woman; a bit plump, perhaps, but with a neat little figure. I don't wonder she caused the family some anxiety, though I felt positive there was no serious cause for it. I thought to myself that this was a nasty jar for her, with all the family looking at her askance, no doubt, and a good job gone. But she looked plucky.

After an unfruitful survey of the paved path and flower border outside the study window, I spoke to Constable Stapley who was on duty there, and returned to the front door. As I did so a sports car hummed up the drive and stopped. A tall man of about thirty-five crept out from under the hood. That hawk nose and square chin were familiar. I hurried forward.

"Morning, sir!" called out Kenneth Stour. "I'm staying with the Tollards, you know, and we heard the news this morning. Shocking business. I thought I'd better come round—might be of use? And I'd like to see Dittie."

The shiny car, the really good leather coat, the whole air of the man suggested a prosperity that I had never associated with Kenneth, but I hadn't seen him for years and I knew he was making some name on the London stage now. His breezy manner was just the same as ever. I wasn't too pleased to see any visitor at this moment and asked him rather abruptly how he had heard the news when there were no papers.

"News just leaks, y'know," he replied. "Probably the Flaxmere milkman has a cousin who's walking out with the boy who delivers the bread to the Tollards!"

I pointed out that no one delivers bread on Bank Holiday and no one walks out before ten o'clock in the morning, but I know how news does seep out and float abroad, apparently on the air. Another point struck me. "So you know Dittie is here?" I asked him.

"Bound to be; whole family always comes for Christmas. But why this cross-examination?"

I don't know why I should have felt so suspicious of him, but it struck me as odd, his driving up at that moment. I took him inside the front door and advised him to ring the bell and ask Parkins if Dittie would see him. I hadn't seen any of the family that morning.

"I don't think I'll ring the bell just yet," he announced coolly. "That is, if you can spare me a moment, Colonel."

I didn't feel inclined for a friendly chat with anyone. I'd just been making mental notes of half a dozen points I wanted to inquire into. I suppose I growled at him. I told him I was up to my eyes in a difficult business.

"I rather thought it might be difficult," he remarked. "Look here, sir; I really want to speak to you. I think I might possibly be able to help."

I told him that if he had anything relevant to tell me, he'd better tell it quickly; the hall was empty; I went over to the fireplace and stood before the blazing logs. I was leaving the drawing-room free for the use of the family and I didn't want him to entrench himself in the library.

"I'm a student of human nature, Colonel Halstock, and a bit of a criminologist," he began grandly. "Oh yes, you think that all rot, but at least you know that I've got brains and if I give you my word that I won't do any fool detective work on my own and that I'll obey orders, will you let me help you in any way I can?"

I asked him how he knew that I wanted help.

"Oh, I know you've got your trained men and finger-print experts and all that. But sometimes a private individual can pick up information. I worked with you once before, you remember, and you were good enough to say—"

"You were younger then, and less cocksure," I told him, and asked what he was after, anyway. Did he *know* anything? If so, he'd better tell me and have done with it.

"I don't know anything in the police sense. You'd be the last man to encourage anyone to communicate unfounded suspicions," he had the cheek to say. "But I know the family— some of them—pretty well."

I told him that so did I, and that was my trouble. I didn't admit, however, that I'd been half inclined to call in Scotland Yard straight away last night. I did say that I hoped we might have the whole case straightened out in half an hour.

"And if you haven't," he said, not in the least discouraged, "you'll tell me how things stand and give me a chance. Colonel Halstock, you know how I felt about Dittie, ten years ago. My feelings haven't changed. This is a rotten thing for them all and in some ways it's worst of all for her, because she has no one who can really help her. David—well, you know David! I don't want publicity. I merely want to be of use. That's hard for you to believe, of an actor. But perhaps you can believe it of Kenneth Stour whom you've known for thirty-five years."

It's impossible to describe Kenneth Stour's charm; that sounds an effeminate word, but there's nothing of the sissy-boy about him. Opposition simply doesn't affect him; he behaves as if he couldn't see or feel it. By persisting in the assumption that you're agreeing with everything he suggests, he hypnotises you into doing so. That's the only way I can explain why I trusted him as I did in this case, although I met him with a feeling of suspicion which I didn't shake off for a long time.

I made no promise to him at the moment, but told him to go and see Dittie, if she were willing, and warned him that I would not be responsible for giving him the run of the place. I wasn't sure how pleased the family would be to see him at Flaxmere at this time.

He smiled at me as if I were an approving first-night audience, and then a slight noise drew our attention towards the wide staircase at the far end of the hall and, glancing round, I saw Dittie stepping down deliberately from stair to stair. She was looking down at her feet all the time, and biting her under-lip, as if she were negotiating some unfamiliar or difficult descent. She was concentrated on what she was doing—or perhaps on her thoughts—and quite unaware of us until Kenneth strode out towards the foot of the staircase.

Hearing his steps, she raised her eyes and saw us. She stopped, with a half-uttered, half-choked cry of his name and swayed backwards. Her right hand, already on the rail, gripped it and steadied her. Her left hand groped wildly for the other rail and found it. I could see the fingers, whitened by her grip, moving uneasily.

We all stood there a moment without speaking; Dittie's eyes wavered from Kenneth to me; I saw terror in them; they turned back to Kenneth. Then he ran up the stairs and put his hand on her arm.

I heard him saying, "Dittie—my dear—," with such tenderness in his voice that I had an uneasy feeling of eavesdropping and slunk into the library. But of course, the man is an actor.

Chapter Eight

Who Left Flaxmere?

by Col. Halstock

Constable Stapley came panting after me into the library, with mud sticking to his boots, holding out a large white handkerchief carefully folded over something in his palm.

"Key, sir!" he announced.

He had found it in the flower-bed, where I told him to look, about five yards from the house, directly in front of the open study window. It fitted the lock of the study door into the hall.

"He just opened the window to throw out the key," Rousdon asserted. "All that shutter business is just a blind!"

Constable Stapley, who was a smart young man and knew how to appreciate the jokes of his superiors, uttered a loud guffaw. Rousdon, who hadn't intended the pun, glared at him and he retired abashed.

Rousdon picked up the red Santa Klaus costume, trimmed with white rabbit fur, from a chair.

"He threw the things off in the drawing-room last night; Mr. Melbury—Sir George, I suppose we must call him now—said, you remember, that Witcombe went in there to tell them Sir Osmond was shot and didn't seem to realize he was still dressed up. It's the same fur, right enough, that is sticking to Sir Osmond's coat!"

I examined the fur. "Regular moulting, it is," said Rousdon scornfully. "Comes off on everything you touch, and that's lucky for us! Shall we have him in?"

But I hoped to clear up a few points before we roused a sensation in the household, so I told Rousdon that his victim would keep.

"He'll keep all right. Cool as you like! Ate a hearty breakfast in the dining-room this morning. Rest had theirs in bed."

He had got a pretty detailed account from Miss Portisham of what money Sir Osmond had. In the note-case found on the body there was a five pound note and three pounds more in notes and some silver. She had cashed a cheque for him on Monday afternoon and knew pretty well what he had spent; it all agreed with the amount found on him and some more notes in a locked drawer in the study which she pointed out. Any possibility of robbery as a motive seemed definitely ruled out.

Further examination of Sir David Evershot was the next item on my agenda and, being sent for, he strode jerkily into the library and sank into a deep arm-chair. He gave me the impression of being ill at ease and making an effort to conceal it. I knew he was touchy and difficult and I didn't want to get him worked up. Everyone had been on edge last night and I hoped he might be more amenable this morning. I told him we had now found out a bit more and thought he might be able to confirm some of our facts.

"Most unlikely!" he snarled. "I had no idea Sir Osmond was about to be murdered, so I didn't take particular note of what was going on."

"I think you said that you went out of the front door while the crackers were being pulled in the hall?"

"That's so. Beastly stench they made!"

"Do you remember whether you shut the lobby door behind you?"

"I haven't the least idea, and I don't suppose it will help you if I invent an answer."

I continued my questions just as if he was behaving with ordinary politeness.

"And the front door?"

"Probably. But, mind you, I'm not going to swear any oath on that!"

"You walked up and down on the gravel drive in front of the house for about five minutes?"

"If you say so, you're probably right. I'm not going to contradict the Chief Constable."

"Did you see anyone about?"

"Didn't look. D'you think I was spying on Santa Klaus and his damfool reindeer?"

"Do you happen to remember whether you heard any particular sounds from the house?"

"What sort of sounds?" Sir David seemed suddenly suspicious.

"We hardly know what sort of sounds you *may* have heard. Possibly voices raised in anger; possibly a shot?"

"Shot! Nobody would hear a shot with those damned crackers banging right and left."

"But you couldn't hear crackers from the drive?"

"You think I'm lying! I tell you I heard one."

"Just one?" Rousdon pressed him.

"Confound your questions! I wasn't in a mood to count the crackers, I tell you."

"Anything else? Any other sound to suggest what the people in the house were doing?"

"I didn't care what the people in the house were doing. And I'll tell you this. If someone chose to shoot Sir Osmond last night, it's not my affair. It's just my blasted luck to be in the house at the time, but I don't mean to be mixed up in the business any more than I can help! I believe someone shut a window while I was outside, if that's any damn use to you! A maid upstairs, probably, going the round of the bedrooms. And that's all I can tell you."

"You *heard* a window being shut—or perhaps being opened?" I pressed him. "Are you sure it was upstairs?"

"Call it opened if you like; if you think anyone in this house would ever open a window when it was getting dark. Sir Osmond had a Victorian fear of the night air. I don't know what window it was; I didn't care and didn't look to see. I won't answer any more fool questions! What's the good of badgering me when I tell you I know nothing? It's the wrong method, I tell you, trying to get information where it doesn't exist. Why you fix on me, and question me and question me again, hounding me till I don't even know what I did do or hear—"

He was working himself into a fury. He heaved his lean body out of the chair and strode up and down the room heavily, running his fingers through his thin pale hair. I fell into step beside him and talked quietly to him.

"I know we're being troublesome, but we have to pick up every scrap of information we can," I said, and so forth. Thanked him for answering our questions and then ventured to ask whether he heard the window opened—or shut—before he heard the cracker. He had been calming down but that roused him again.

"Those hellish crackers were going off in my head, I tell you!" he shouted. "They were going off all the time! I want to forget them!"

I gave it up and let him go.

"The man's not normal!" Rousdon commented superfluously. "Now, if it looked like a crime committed in a sudden fury, I'd plump for him. But it doesn't. He heard the shot all right. He couldn't hear a cracker out there, and he knows it. And he heard the window opened. I'll make sure about the maids, but it's almost certain they weren't shutting windows then because they were all gathered in the servants' hall."

No one, so far as we had discovered, had noticed Sir David going out or coming in again. I began trying to reconstruct his movements on the drive. Assuming that he heard the shot fired in the study and recognized it for something more than a cracker, he would stand still, wait. Then he heard the window opened for the murderer to throw out the key, and he crept round the corner of the house. The murderer hadn't switched off the light and Sir David saw Sir Osmond slumped in his chair with a hole in his head. He climbed in through the window. Then——? Did he find some evidence which he destroyed in order to shield the murderer? Or did he merely realize that his own position there might be difficult to explain? In either case, he slunk out through the library and dining-room and so back into the hall, first closing and hooking the shutters—why? Just an instinctive action, perhaps.

This might explain Sir David's state of mind, which struck me as more agitated than I should have expected even in the irritable man I knew him to be, but it wasn't very helpful. Except that it pointed to some murderer whom Sir David would be anxious to shield—and that was surely not Witcombe.

I had one more job to do before I let Rousdon loose on that gentleman. I sent for Sir George and while waiting for him asked Rousdon if he had collected all the details of the Santa Klaus outfit. He had the fur-trimmed robe with its hood, the beard on wires and a pair of eyebrows which had to be attached with gum; there was also an empty sack, which had held the presents.

"Probably used that to carry the pistol in," Rousdon surmised. "No pockets in this garment. But the sleeves are wide; you might just hold the pistol ready in your hand and draw it back under the sleeve and no one'd notice. We've found no gloves, though he's pretty sure to have worn them, since he left the pistol lying on the table and he seems to be a careful chap. That pistol's covered with finger-prints, almost as if someone had handled it on purpose to wipe out anything that might have been there before, but I don't suppose that the prints of the hand that pulled the trigger were ever there at all. It would be easy enough to drop those gloves into the fire in the hail. We've sifted the ashes this morning, and there's nothing to show, but that's only what I'd expect."

George Melbury opened the door and looked at me inquiringly. "Mornin', Colonel! You wanted me? Anything discovered?"

"Nothing definite," I told him, watching him pretty closely. He looked distinctly disappointed, and I don't think he's capable of simulating it.

First I asked him if he knew what kept Sir Osmond in his study after the Christmas present distribution yesterday afternoon.

"He was waitin' for a telephone call," George declared. "Some private business. The old man didn't confide in anyone much about his private affairs, not even me. I think he'd made an arrangement with some friend, maybe a business acquaintance, to ring him up at that time. None of us thought much about him shutting himself up alone like that. He'd get sudden fits of being tired, y'know, and go off into his study at any time."

"Did that telephone call for which he was waiting ever come through?" I asked.

George looked puzzled. "That's rum! Never thought about it before, but now I do come to think of it, I don't know of any call coming through."

"Could it have come before your father was shot? Would anyone have heard it then?" I knew that all calls to Flaxmere must go direct to the study, because Sir Osmond had refused to have a telephone extension to any other part of the house.

"Depends on how the bell was fixed," George told me. "Y'see, it rings out in the hall or in the study, accordin' to how it's switched. The old man had that fixed because people used to ring up and get no answer if the study was empty and no one happened to be about within hearing. Miss Portisham would probably know all about it; she had to arrange for it to be switched the right way."

That seemed to be all the light he could throw on Sir Osmond's appointment. He had some inquiries of his own to make. Could he go ahead with arrangements for the funeral and had we yet got into touch with Crewkerne, Sir Osmond's solicitor? George knew we were trying to get hold of him. We agreed that he should arrange for the funeral to be held on Saturday.

"Don't want to make a big parade, under the circs.," he mumbled. "Must have a notice in the *Times* but I thought of putting *funeral very quiet*, or something of that sort. Don't want the countryside flockin' and askin' awkward questions. My aunt would like to put, *struck down by the hand of a foul assassin*, in the *Times* notice, but we can't have that sort of thing, of course. Now, there's another thing, Colonel; sorry to bother you and all that, but the ladies are all gettin' in a state about their mournin'; must have it for the funeral, y'know. Of course nothing can be done to-day, but they want to make a shoppin' expedition into Bristol to-morrow."

I saw Rousdon cock his head at that and scowl. He wasn't so dead sure of Witcombe that he was ready to give anyone else the chance of making an easy escape, or else he felt sure that Witcombe had accomplices and he did not want to let them out of his sight. Personally I felt that we had a great deal yet to discover and that everyone was safer under observation. So I had to tell George that the shopping expedition was banned. Surely they could get their blacks without going to Bristol themselves? They had permission to telephone to the shops and get things sent up.

"Of course," George pointed out gloomily, "that takes all the kick out of shopping! As a married man yourself you'll understand that. But I've no doubt they can get their things all right that way."

He seemed very downcast, doubtless at the prospect of having to break this news to his wife and sisters, and inclined to discuss his troubles, but I was impatient to get on to the main business for which I had summoned him.

I explained to him that there were numerous finger-prints in the study, which were probably left by various people in the house when about their lawful occupations. I wanted him to help me persuade everyone to have their finger-prints taken, so that we could identify and eliminate those which had nothing to do with the murder—those of Miss Portisham, who would naturally handle many things in the study, of the maid who closed the shutters, and so forth.

George looked thoughtful. "You're welcome to mine, of course. I'll do my best to get the others to follow suit, but—er—well, some of 'em may object. I mean they might think it a bit odd without really having any reason to be afraid of giving them; I mean to say, I hope you don't mean to put 'em under arrest and all that, on the spot, if they refuse?"

I pointed out that anyone had a right to refuse and I couldn't enforce the ordeal unless I brought a definite accusation against the recalcitrant. I have often found that the best way to persuade anyone to do something they suspect is to explain that they really need not do it.

I arranged that George should first assemble all the house party in the hall, and that we would take the domestic staff afterwards.

"It's those who're likely to kick up a fuss, I'm afraid, but perhaps our example—moral effect, y'know—"

He went off and before long Parkins came to report that all the family and guests were in the hall. I went out and took up a station on the stairs. They were standing in separate little groups, which told me a good deal. Kenneth Stour with Dittie near the back; there was anxiety still in Dittie's eyes. Not far from them Sir David stood alone, staring into the fire, taking no notice of anyone. Miss Portisham was also alone, on the opposite side of the hall, looking about her anxiously. Carol Wynford and Philip Cheriton were talking together near the foot of the stairs. I looked for Jennifer. At this moment, when everyone was a little apprehensive of what was before them, I had expected that she would be with Philip. But she stood at some distance from him, looking a bit forlorn, I thought, until Hilda Wynford joined her. Witcombe was moving here and there, with the air of a man who will not recognize that he is being ignored. Eleanor and her aunt and George's wife were a little gossiping group. Gordon Stickland and George were at the back of the hall, keeping a watchful eye on the rest.

I made my little speech, asking for their cooperation. They were surprised, annoyed, suspicious. Dittie clutched suddenly at Kenneth's sleeve. Aunt Mildred stopped knitting and glowered at me. A buzz of talk rose, which stopped when George raised his voice.

"I'm ready, to begin with, to give my finger-prints, and I propose that everyone else does the same. It's up to us to help the Chief Constable all we can to track the skunk who shot my father!"

"O.K. by me!" Witcombe declared. Several turned to look at him.

Miss Melbury raised her voice. "Really, it's monstrous! I never entered the study after luncheon yesterday! Treating us like common criminals!"

I was passing near her to speak to the man who was stationed with his apparatus at a table on the study side of the hall. There was a good deal I should have liked to say to her, but I refrained. Patricia—the new Lady Melbury—sympathized loudly enough for me to hear.

"It's definitely frightful, Aunt Mildred! *I* didn't go into the study either. Just officiousness! So like the police! No discrimination! I wonder they don't ask for the children's finger-prints!"

George came up and I heard him blustering gently at her.

"You don't know what you're talking about! Just like a woman! I'm submitting to this business; isn't that good enough for you?" And then to Miss Melbury: "Be a sport, Aunt Mildred! Seems a bit queer, what? But we're in a queer fix. Don't make things more difficult!"

Jennifer followed me up to the table. "You're welcome to *my* finger-prints, Colonel Halstock!" she seemed pleased at the idea.

The ceremony began and as George left the table he signed to me and I followed him across the hall.

"Sorry, Colonel, but Sir David has gone off in a huff. I know it looks bad, but if you knew him as well as we do, you'd not be surprised. Nerves, y'know; shell-shocked in the war. Thrown right off his balance by this business. *I* d'know what to do—"

I told him not to bother; that it probably wouldn't matter, and relief spread over George's broad face. As I left the hall,

Miss Melbury was proclaiming shrilly: "Really, I fail to understand why you all submit to this outrage! Perfectly useless. Now if someone would take my advice—" At that point she saw that I was making my escape and arrested me with an imperious, "Colonel Halstock!" I turned to her with all the civility I could assume.

"I understand, Colonel Halstock," Miss Melbury said icily, "that you even refuse to allow us to obtain decent mourning for my poor brother. That is really too much! Poor Osmond may go unavenged but he shall not go unmourned!"

"I think you have misunderstood the orders I was compelled by the situation to give," I pointed out. "You can telephone to the shops and have clothes sent up for you to choose from. I should imagine that, while you are still suffering from grief and shock, you might prefer to try on frocks in the privacy of your own room, rather than have to face the crowds and noise of the city." I thought that was rather neat. Eleanor passed near us and I called her to my aid, but she didn't back me up quite as I had hoped.

"It doesn't concern me at all," she announced; "because I have telephoned to my maid to pack my mourning clothes and send them at once. I always have them at hand because one never knows what may happen and one seems to have to go to funerals so often. It is so much more satisfactory to wear things which one has been able to choose and have made at leisure!"

"Really, Eleanor!" Aunt Mildred protested. "I don't approve of the *spirit* of that at all! To be prepared, for what none of us, none of *us*, I repeat, could possibly have expected! Of course we all know that one person in the house was able to make a fine parade of mourning *immediately*, and some of us can read between the lines and see that there is more in that than meets the eye." She shot a venomous glance at poor Miss Portisham's neat black-gowned figure.

"Well, poor father would have been pleased to see his dutiful secretary still doing the right thing," Eleanor remarked.

"I won't hear a word against my poor brother!" Miss Melbury protested unreasonably.

"I'm saying nothing against him," Eleanor retorted.

They had apparently forgotten me and I made a move towards the library door, reflecting that the situation was playing havoc with their nerves, for it was unusual for Eleanor to be snappy or for Miss Melbury to reprove her favourite niece. I turned at the door to see if Patricia was still withholding her fingers, but she was standing meekly behind a group of others near the table. My hesitation gave Kenneth Stour a chance to catch me before I could escape into the library.

"Of course I was miles away last night, Colonel, but as some of the others seem to wonder what I'm doing here, perhaps I'd better go in with the rest in this?" he suggested.

I told him he could if he liked, though it seemed rather off the point. In the library I found Rousdon talking to the police surgeon, Caundle, who had just arrived. I told Rousdon that Sir David and Miss Melbury shrank from the ordeal and he had better take the opportunity, while there was no one about upstairs, to go to their rooms and try to secure prints from some objects there.

Caundle, a desiccated little man with stubbly, sand-coloured hair, stood warming his back at the fire. I asked him whether he had any startling news for us.

"Not a thing, Colonel!" he told me. "No revelation! No sensation! Sir Osmond was killed by the bullet from the .22; he hadn't been drugged or poisoned, he was in pretty good health and had no gnawing pains in his vitals that might drive him to suicide. It positively couldn't be suicide, anyway. Here's the report in all the correct language. But what I do want to know is, who left the house just after the murder was discovered yesterday?"

That was a sensational revelation all right. I had been assured by George and the servants and everyone else that no one had left Flaxmere.

"When you sent for me yesterday afternoon," Caundle explained; "I came up here through the village and by the back drive—much quicker for me than going round by the main gate—and just before I turned into the drive a car came out of it, turned into the road and passed me. Now that's a bit odd?"

I inquired why the dickens he didn't tell me yesterday.

"It didn't strike me at the moment as odd, and when I got up here I had other things to think of. It jumped into my mind again later. It *is* odd."

Something jumped into *my* mind. I asked him whether it was by chance a big sports car, of shiny metal, which he saw.

He thought not. "It was getting dark, you know, and my headlights were on, which means I saw very little of anything that wasn't in their beams. But as far as I remember, it would be a darkcoloured fair-sized saloon, and not a very modern one, either. Not one of those stream-lined affairs, but a dignified, comfortable car. It came slowly out of the gate."

There didn't seem any sense in it. I couldn't picture our murderer driving slowly out of the back drive in a big old-fashioned saloon car, but who *would* have been doing so on Christmas afternoon? Caundle had told Rousdon, he said, and the detective was very peeved because he hadn't got the number of the car.

Sir Osmond's Sunbeam was four or five years old and George had an Austin which was definitely old-fashioned in outline now, but if either of them was in use, who drove it? It was incredible that anyone should come to Flaxmere with criminal intentions and keep a big car conspicuously waiting in the drive. Perhaps after all some neighbour had sent a belated Christmas gift and in the scurry and alarm after the murder everyone had forgotten the event. I went off to interview the domestic staff and prepare them for the finger-print ordeal.

Chapter Nine

Peregrinations of Santa Klaus

by Col. Halstock

By the time we had secured the finger-prints of everyone in the house, either by open approach or by strategy, it was getting on for midday. The spectacle of Parkins majestically submitting his fingers, with the remark, "It's not what I am accustomed to, of course, but I am ready to suffer in the cause of justice, as the saying is," produced meek submission in the rest of the staff. The experts were now busy sorting and identifying the prints.

Rousdon had meanwhile questioned Miss Portisham about the telephone bells. She had shown him the switch in the study, by which the bell could be made to ring there or in the hall. It was then switched on to ring in the hall, and so she had set it on the morning of Christmas Day, she said, because they were not likely to be occupying the study continually. She did not know whether Sir Osmond had altered it himself when he went into the study on Christmas afternoon, but it seemed that he hadn't, for Rousdon couldn't discover that anyone had switched it back again later.

In any case Miss Portisham thought that she would have heard the bell if a call had come through, because she was in the hall all the time and was sitting on a divan quite near the study door, talking to Hilda, most of the time. From the hall you could plainly hear the bell ringing in the study.

"Even above the noise of crackers?" Rousdon asked.

Miss Portisham thought so. Crackers, she explained, did not make a continuous noise; one would hear the telephone bell between the bangs.

Rousdon also questioned Mrs. Wynford, who had been sitting near the study door all the time and had heard no telephone bell and felt sure she would have heard it if it had rung, even in the study.

"I've been in touch with the local exchange, too," Rousdon told me. "They've no record of any call to Flaxmere on Christmas afternoon. That fixes this telephone appointment as a put-up job. It was an excuse to get Sir Osmond in the study. There never was a call and there never would have been a call. But I don't quite see why he didn't switch the bell to ring in his study. It seems, however, that you could also hear it in the study from the hall, and perhaps he forgot about it. It was Miss Portisham's business to attend to it as a rule."

Rousdon could by now hardly be restrained from bringing his victim down. I was anxious to postpone an arrest, because I didn't think we really had enough to go on and I felt that some of the information which the family must be holding might leak out if we kept them in uncertainty. But in any case Witcombe must be questioned and I was glad enough to leave the job to Rousdon.

Oliver Witcombe was always so conventionally correct in his appearance that he reminded me of an advertisement of one of the best tailors. From the little I knew of him he struck me as having about that much individuality. He was good-looking in an uninteresting kind of way, without any liveliness of expression. I watched him now from my seat in the background (at a table in the library bow window) as he sat down rather carefully in a chair opposite to Rousdon and leaned forward a little. It would have seemed appropriate if he had inquired, "And what can I do for you, sir?"

"I want to ask you, Mr. Witcombe," Rousdon began portentously, "to make a statement about your movements yesterday afternoon, from the moment when you followed Sir Osmond out of this room here into his study. And I must warn you that anything you say may be used in evidence."

Witcombe blinked at that, obviously a bit surprised. He threw a sideways look at Constable Mere who was sitting at the big library table, prepared to write.

"Yes, of course, I see that it's important; I was the last person to see Sir Osmond alive—"

"Do you really mean that?" snapped Rousdon.

Witcombe blinked again. "Oh, I see what you mean! Always excepting the murderer, of course."

There was a pause. Then Witcombe began his statement, speaking slowly and carefully. Except for a few unimportant additional details, he gave exactly the same account as he had given to me on Christmas evening. He did not mention his return to the hall with crackers after he had gone out towards the servants' quarters.

"When you returned to the study to report to Sir Osmond, and found him dead, as you say, did you notice anything unusual about the room?" Rousdon asked. This was my question which he had rather unwillingly agreed to put.

"There was the pistol on the table; I think I mentioned that." Witcombe closed his eyes and considered. "Of course!" he exclaimed suddenly. "The window!"

"What about the window?" Rousdon inquired coldly.

"It was open—the window behind Sir Osmond—wide open at the bottom!"

"How could you tell?"

"How could I tell? I could see it—it was straight in front of me when I faced Sir Osmond's table."

"But the shutters?" Rousdon asked.

"Oh, of course; I'd forgotten there are shutters. They must have been open."

"You're sure about that?" asked Rousdon sternly.

"Well, if I clearly saw an open window, there can't have been any shutters in front of it. You can see that for yourself, surely?"

"Did you close the shutters yourself?"

"No, certainly not. Having made sure that Sir Osmond was dead, my one thought was to let George and the others know."

"Having made sure that Sir Osmond was dead," Rousdon repeated slowly and heavily. Witcombe gazed at him in mild surprise. "How did you make sure?" Rousdon suddenly snapped out.

"I think I mentioned that before; I felt his heart; there was no movement at all. As a matter of fact, I felt pretty sure as soon as I saw that hole in his head."

"I suppose you were quite sure where the heart would be found?" inquired Rousdon sarcastically.

"Absolutely! I have taken a course of Red Cross classes. Are you implying that Sir Osmond wasn't dead when I found him?"

"Oh, no," said Rousdon with a nasty grin. "You made sure that he was dead all right. But you seem to have done a good deal of feeling about; if you weren't feeling for his heart, what were you looking for?"

"I haven't the least idea what you mean," Witcombe replied. He seemed quite unshaken by Rousdon's questions and had given away nothing of value. I didn't like Rousdon's method and I couldn't help feeling a certain satisfaction that it wasn't proving very successful.

"Then how," Rousdon asked, "do you account for the fact that Sir Osmond's coat was strewn about with white hairs from the trimming on your Santa Klaus dress?"

"Do I have to account for that?" Witcombe asked with mild surprise.

"You do!" Rousdon growled. "The hairs are all over Sir Osmond's coat and they came off the costume that you were wearing."

"Well, they did come out very easily. My own clothes were in a bit of a mess, I noticed this morning. And there are wide, floppy sleeves, you know, on the garment." Witcombe had all the appearance of a man trying his best to be helpful. "Tell you what! D'you mind being the body? Just slump in your chair the way Sir Osmond was when I found him, and I'll give a demonstration of how I felt his heart!"

Rousdon, looking mistrustful, as if he thought Witcombe might suddenly produce a pistol and press the trigger and say, "That's how I did it," leant awkwardly across one arm of his chair.

Witcombe stood up and surveyed him thoughtfully; then closed his eyes. "You're a bit stiff!" he observed critically. "Can't you slump more? And—yes; I think the arms hung outside the arms of the chair."

Rousdon slumped a bit more and moved his arms.

"Yes; I think that's about how he was. I came up between his table and the wall and bent down like this—" Witcombe bent over Rousdon, who followed his movements watchfully.

"Wait!" Rousdon shouted suddenly. "Didn't you put something down?"

Witcombe started back and considered again. "Oh, the sack? It was empty, of course. I can't remember; I was pretty well shaken, you know. I may have dropped it—"

"Never mind!" Rousdon growled. "Go on."

Witcombe undid the top button of Rousdon's coat and slid his right hand inside. "My first is a bull, I think!" he remarked complacently. "Here is the heart, beating quite nicely! Now, imagine that wide Santa Klaus sleeve; it would brush across the right side of the coat, as you see, leaving its little trail."

Witcombe stood back, well pleased with himself. His "model" sat up. "Yes; the lower part of the right side, but not just below the collar. And what about the left side?"

"What about it?" inquired Witcombe amiably.

"How do you account for it being covered with white hairs?"

"I really don't see how I can account for it," Witcombe admitted, as if slightly pained. "Except that I was upset, as I have pointed out, and therefore probably not so neat in my movements as I was just now, and I suppose I must have flicked the sleeve across the other side of the coat. Of course, I didn't notice that I'd left the hairs sticking there."

"I guessed that," said Rousdon with some satisfaction. "Now, another point. To return to that window. Was it open when you came back into the study?"

"Was it open—oh, of course; it was open before. Well now, that's funny, but I can't remember. I wasn't specially noticing. But probably one of the others can tell you; Mrs. Wynford went in at the same time, you know, and someone else—George, I think." He sat still, looking puzzled.

Rousdon leant forward towards him. "Mr. Witcombe, can you explain this: you went into Sir Osmond's study; you found him, as you say, lying there dead; you noticed a window open behind him. But you said nothing to us about that window. Didn't you think it of any importance?"

"I was too fussed to think about it. Look here, is there some catch in this?" Witcombe asked quickly. For the first time during the cross-questioning he was showing signs of uneasiness. "I certainly think I remember seeing a window open when I went into the study, but all I thought of then was to fetch George or someone. Tell you the truth, my first idea was that Sir Osmond had shot himself, so I didn't think of anyone having come in by the window. It never came into my mind again. After all, *I'm* not doing the detective work. It wasn't my job to remember every detail I'd seen and point it out to you, was it? If there was an open window, anyone could see it. I didn't shut it; I can swear to that."

"In fact," suggested Rousdon; "you thought it might be better if someone else did notice it and point it out?"

"You've no right to imagine what I thought; and you're wrong; I didn't think anything of the kind," he retorted angrily.

"All right," said Rousdon soothingly. "Now there's one more little detail. Just why did you go to Sir Osmond's study?"

"That's simple," Witcombe replied with some relief. "When I left him in the study before I went to do the Santa Klaus business in the servants' hall, he asked me to go back there and let him know when I had finished."

"Did Sir Osmond say why he was staying in the study?"

"I don't think so. But he wasn't a man to explain himself much. I thought he was a bit tired with the children's racket. It wasn't unusual for him to go and sit there by himself."

"Did he give you any instruction about the crackers?"

"He never mentioned crackers. Everyone's been talking about crackers, but I don't know where they come in and I certainly didn't have anything to do with them."

Rousdon hardly concealed his surprise, but he merely asked firmly, "So the cracker distribution in the hall was quite your own idea?"

"I've told you, I don't know anything about it. It certainly wasn't my idea. I don't even know who did it; I can't get anyone to tell me. You know, there's some mystery about those crackers; you might think that one of them was a bomb, from the way people talk about them—or rather, *don't* talk about them."

Rousdon stared at him incredulously. "You're not telling me that you yourself didn't hand out crackers to the children before you went out to give the servants their presents?"

"That's what I'm telling you. *I* give out crackers? It's absurd. I never saw a cracker."

"Do you know that two or three people saw you handing out those crackers in the hall?"

"They couldn't have seen me," Witcombe persisted. "If they say they did, it's a lie! It's a conspiracy! I don't know what the point of those crackers is, but I had nothing to do with them."

Rousdon was nonplussed. He looked at Witcombe as if unable to make up his mind whether the man were sane or not. He hadn't been flustered into this denial, so far as I could see. He had been disturbed by the questions about the window, but had calmed down again afterwards. I had before me a plan of the ground floor at Flaxmere and I called to Witcombe to come and show me, on this, his movements from the time he left Sir Osmond's study. He came over to my table in the window, took out a pencil and traced on the plan a path from the study door across the hall and out by the door at the back; then across the passage and through the door into the servants' quarters.

Rousdon stood over him and, when he got to that point, snatched the pencil, exclaiming, "You've left something out!"

Witcombe jumped and looked rather concerned. He watched very attentively whilst Rousdon traced a line along the passage into the dining-room and out of the other dining-room door into the hall again. Then he looked up at Witcombe, who shook his head. "No; that's not the way I came back. And anyway, what's that door?" He pointed to the one between the dining-room and library. "There's no door there, surely? The map's wrong." He looked up from the plan towards the corner of the library.

The door is a concealed one. It was not generally used and I didn't know of its existence until this investigation. On the dining-room side it is covered with the same paper as the walls and there are bookshelves attached to it on the library side, which swing back absurdly when you open the door. You could see that it was a door if you looked closely, as Witcombe did now.

"Yes, of course, I remember now. The servants came through that way to see the Christmas-tree. But I'd never noticed it before."

"Not very observant, are you?" sneered Rousdon.

"I think I'm pretty average, but there wasn't any reason why I should notice that. Anyway, I didn't use it. I came back into the hall the same way as I went out."

"Not the first time," put in Rousdon quietly.

"I don't know what you mean by the first time. I went out to the servants' hall and then I came back and returned to Sir Osmond's study."

"Do you mean to say that you didn't come back again after you went out, and before you went through to the servants' quarters?"

"I do mean to say that. I showed you on the plan how I went out and I came back the same way."

Rousdon, now quite hot and ruffled, gave it up and very ungraciously told Witcombe he could go. The latter turned to me.

"My original plans, Colonel Halstock, were to return home to-morrow. I suppose there is nothing against that?" he asked, rather anxiously, I thought.

"As things stand at the moment, I'm afraid there is," I told him. "You are a material witness and we may want you again. I can't allow any one of the party to leave this house until—well, until certain facts are cleared up."

"Yes; I see. Well, I shall be very grateful if you'll let me go as soon as possible. I'm thinking of the family, you know," he added. "After all, they don't want visitors around at the moment."

I asked him one more question before he left. Had he at any time taken off the Santa Klaus costume from the time he put it on until after Sir Osmond was found dead.

"Good heavens, no! Though I'd have been glad enough to get rid of it. But I was under orders to play the part until I left the house as Santa Klaus; then I was to go round to the back door and come in again as myself," he explained.

Rousdon exploded when Witcombe had gone. "It's lunatic! The man's a fool! How can he expect us to believe that? It's Mrs. Wynford's and Miss Portisham's word against his, and they were the clearest witnesses we had. They'll swear to it, I know."

I only asked him, "Exactly *what* will they swear to?" When he was cooler, I thought, he would reach the same idea as was now in my mind. But I had noticed two things that Rousdon hadn't been able to see. One was Witcombe's look of genuine surprise when he had noticed the door marked on the plan between the dining-room and library. The other was his worried, perhaps guilty, look when Rousdon said, "You've left something out!" and the way the muscles of his face relaxed again into an expression of relief when Rousdon's pencil took a line from the door at the back of the hall into the dining-room.

Rousdon stood by the fireplace, staring at me gloomily. Just then Kenneth Stour passed outside the window, strolling along the paved path with a pipe in his mouth.

"You still don't want that man arrested?" Rousdon inquired.

"Less than ever, unless he does anything that justifies it; watch him closely," I advised.

Kenneth passed again and looked in through the window as he did so, caught my eye and raised his eyebrows inquiringly.

"You might see whether you can trace that old-fashioned saloon car the doctor saw," I suggested to the Inspector. "And see whether your men have been able to get into touch with Sir Osmond's solicitor yet and when he's coming back from his Christmas holiday," I suggested.

I left him blasting all Bank Holidays, and went to find Kenneth and see what he had to tell.

The rain had cleared away and I found him strolling up and down on the gravel sweep between the front door and the paved path that ran under the study and library windows.

"You haven't reached your solution yet?" he asked. "Nor has anyone else. The family don't *know* who did it. They see that the known facts point to Witcombe, but they can't think of any reason why he should want to shoot Sir Osmond, so they let their suspicions range around. Now I believe that if we could get them to tell us all that happened on the few days before Christmas—since they arrived here—we should see the whole thing plain."

"Of course!" I agreed sarcastically. "The murderer would then tell us exactly how he did the job and why!"

"I'm making an exception of the murderer. I believe that the others hold the clue within their knowledge, but partly they don't realize that and partly they're reluctant to tell you anything because they don't know whom they're inculpating."

I didn't need him to come over to Flaxmere to tell me all this, as I pointed out.

Disregarding me he continued: "I've given Hilda and Jennifer and Philip Cheriton something to keep them quiet for the next twenty-four hours, or perhaps longer. I've asked each of them to write a confidential account of events leading up to the murder. Philip is to deal with the family situation in general, as it seemed to an outsider. Hilda is to describe Saturday and Sunday and Jennifer, Monday. They are to put down as much as they can remember of trivial incidents, conversations and so forth. Now I want you to ask Miss Melbury and Miss Portisham to do the same for Tuesday and Christmas Day. I don't know them well enough to ask them and I don't want to approach them as your emissary."

"I should think not indeed!" I was able to say.

Of course he met all my objections; his idea was that they would be partly off their guard when they sat down to write; they might reveal something of value which they thought too trivial to mention to me and which I couldn't extract from them by questions because I was too much in the dark, and so forth. He had chosen the people who might, he thought, write fairly connected narratives without much difficulty. Philip Cheriton as a literary man, Jennifer because she had literary aspirations, Miss Portisham because she was businesslike (and also because she was in close touch with Sir Osmond), Hilda because she had been a school teacher and because he considered her more capable of a detached point of view than any other member of the family. Dittie was too upset, he said, to be bothered. Eleanor and Patricia and George would be hopeless; they couldn't write three grammatical sentences on end, he was sure. Gordon Stickland wouldn't be reliable; he was too self-conscious; he'd write what he thought fit and would never forget that intention.

I was interested in Kenneth's reasons for his choice and asked him why Carol wasn't included. She was well-educated, she was self-possessed and I felt sure she was observant.

He looked a bit worried. "Ask her, too, if you like," he said. "I don't know her well. I don't think she could add anything to what Jennifer and Hilda can tell us."

"And why not Witcombe?" I asked.

"Strikes me as too obtuse. No imagination."

"But we don't want imaginings; we want facts," I pointed out.

"You need imagination to see the facts."

"And why on earth do you include Miss Melbury?" I asked him finally.

"I hear that Aunt Mildred is famous for her long letters; she writes frequently to all her acquaintances, giving them all the news and explaining everything. Her account will be full of gossip; it may be malicious gossip. Any reasons she gives for anyone's behaviour will certainly be wrong, but she overhears a good deal; she's a specialist in other people's affairs; she may give us something of value."

Of course, by criticizing Kenneth's choice of writers and discussing them with him I had implicitly accepted his scheme. That's his way. He makes some monstrous proposal and you are drawn into a discussion of it and before long you find that you are talking of it as a plan you have agreed to. Anyhow, I promised to ask Miss Portisham and Miss Melbury to write their stories and Kenneth went off to join the family at lunch.

I lingered a few minutes on the drive, from which a lawn—a patch of strong bright green in the bleached winter landscape—sloped down to the dull pewter surface of the swimming-pool. I was wondering if I had time before luncheon—which George had insisted I must take with the family—to stroll down to the pool and through the copse behind it. I noticed two figures by the edge of the pool, who moved slowly towards the path that climbs the slope and began to come up to the house—a glint of auburn hair, as well as the black frock which flicked out from under a dark coat hugged round her, identified the smaller one as Miss Portisham. Her jaunty, gaitered companion was Bingham, the chauffeur. I remembered having heard some talk of tender feelings between them and was glad to know that Miss Portisham had at least one friend in the hostile household. I abandoned my idea of a stroll because I saw an opportunity of waylaying Miss Portisham to make the request to which Kenneth had committed me.

Note.   *The accounts which were written by Philip Cheriton, Hilda Wynford, Jennifer Melbury, "Aunt Mildred," and Miss Portisham, have been used, with very little editing, to form the first five chapters of this narrative.*

Chapter Ten

The Clue of the Glove

by Col. Halstock

Miss Portisham entered the hall quite buoyantly and with a little smile on her lips. When I asked her to write for me an account of the events of Christmas Day, in the manner of a story rather than as a statement of evidence, I was relieved that she didn't seem to think the request at all unusual. I think she welcomed it as a job of some kind. I asked her not to mention it to the others. She agreed to this in a voice that implied that she wouldn't have dreamt of doing so. She turned away and then hesitated.

"Colonel Halstock—do you think I might have my typewriter—from the study? If it is not required, of course."

I went with her to fetch it. It was on the telephone table in the alcove, with its cover on, but on looking more closely at it we both saw that the cover was not properly fitted but loosely put on, slightly askew, and not latched.

"Oh, I see!" exclaimed Miss Portisham brightly. "Perhaps Inspector Rousdon, or one of his men, has had occasion to use it and they didn't know, of course, how to fit the cover.

It's a bit tricky if you don't happen to know this machine. A Remington; I think they're so good, don't you? You see, you have to press this knob in—so; then it clicks and the cover will fit on. But I wonder if I ought to take the machine, if Inspector Rousdon is using it?"

I thought that Mere might have been typing his notes of Witcombe's answers, but he could borrow the machine again if he really needed it, so I told her to take it.

"By the way," I asked her. "When did you use it last? I suppose you always put the cover on after you had done with it?"

"Oh yes. Sir Osmond was very particular. He didn't like to see the machine standing uncovered. Now, let me see; I did no typing on Christmas Day, of course. Yes, it would be on Tuesday morning, when Sir Osmond dictated a few letters."

I asked her whether Sir Osmond ever used the typewriter. She was sure that he didn't. She didn't think he understood it. He dictated most of his letters, even personal ones.

"But, of course," she added; "I have no objection to anyone using the machine, though it really is my own. And anyone could remove the cover quite easily and work the machine. I quite understand how they didn't manage to replace it correctly, and no harm is done. Thank you so much."

She had put the cover on and picked it up by the handle. Again she stood hesitating.

"Colonel Halstock; I am in some difficulty. Really, I don't quite know what my position is now. I am so anxious to do the right thing and what Sir Osmond would have wished, of course. Do you think that I ought to make my arrangements to leave Flaxmere as soon as possible? Really, I don't know what I ought to do!"

I promised her that I would speak to Sir George, but that at any rate we should need her here for some days. She trotted off, looking happier.

They had sent a luncheon tray into the library for Rous-don, who was eating heartily. I asked him about the type-writer. He was sure that Mere hadn't used it and he himself hadn't touched it. One of the men, he thought, might have taken off the lid when searching the study, though that was unlikely.

He had some news about Crewkerne, Sir Osmond's solici-tor, who had shut up his house and gone away for Christmas and whom the police had been trying to trace.

"He's getting back to Bristol this afternoon, cursing like hell. Says he can't come out to see you, because he's given his chauffeur a holiday for the rest of the week and he can't get in touch with him and doesn't drive himself and doesn't think he can hire a car on Bank Holiday and doesn't know about the buses. Full of difficulties, he was, so I told him we'd send to meet his train. But I think one of us must go. No one ought to be allowed out of this house except under supervision."

Envying Rousdon's peaceful repast, I went into the dining-room, late and reluctant. The others were all at the table. It was a buffet meal, so I helped myself and found a seat between George and Dittie. It wasn't a comfortable meal. Miss Melbury and Patricia, who were chatting confi-dentially at the far end of the table, eyed me coldly. During one of the many awkward gaps in the conversation, Miss Melbury's peevish voice reached me, declaring, "—not done a thing, which means of course, dear, that the unspeakable criminal who struck down your dear father is still in our midst, red-handed. I shall not be in the least surprised if there is another terrible crime before many days are out! Well, at least I have said what I can, but of course no one will consider my warning—"

George made a valiant but unfortunate effort to blot her out. Leaning forward, very red in the face, to Sir David who sat opposite, he blurted out: "Feel like takin' a little air this afternoon, David? We're to be allowed out on the drive, the Colonel tells me. We can't get at the bunnies, but how about a little target practice?"

"George, you're an ass!" said Gordon Stickland to his plate. The fall of that brick had silenced everyone again. Looking up, Gordon announced loudly, "Enid's been taking some photographs with her new camera and now she wants someone to help her develop them in the dark room. Who's an expert?"

Unfortunately the dark room—which had been rigged up many years earlier, for George, in the disused dairy—had been made to serve as a mortuary, which several of those at the table knew, though Gordon didn't. Whilst we were at lunch, Bingham and Parkins were conveying the body from that "dark room" to Sir Osmond's bedroom. Stickland was dismayed by the awful silence, broken only by Witcombe volunteering nervously.

"Well, I have done a bit in that line—" and letting the sentence fade out because everyone looked at him so ominously.

Carol muttered, "Hell! This is a ghastly day! Nothing's safe."

Dittie, curiously enough, seemed to be the only one with her wits about her, for it was she who began a conversation about Kenneth's theatrical tour in the States, into which everyone who was near enough plunged with relief.

They must be having a pretty awful time, I realized, especially as they were, most of them, not much given to intellectual occupations. They were forbidden to leave the house, except to walk up and down the drive within sight. They could find nothing to do except sit about and suspect one another.

I finished my lunch and got up as soon as I could. Passing Kenneth on the way out I murmured that I wanted a word with him. I hung about the hall for a few minutes and soon he appeared. I told him that if Miss Melbury's account of events was to be written he must ask her to do it. I didn't feel that she was prepared to comply with any request made by me.

"You're missing a grand opportunity!" Kenneth declared. "She'd think you had come to your senses at last and were really seeking help in the right quarter. Besides, she's a very poor opinion of me. She hasn't such a bad one of you, really, but she thinks you don't take enough notice of her. It would cramp her style to know that I should read what she was writing—" As the dining-room door opened he slipped quickly away and left me standing in the middle of the hall as several of the party came out. I buttonholed Aunt Mildred at once, being still under Kenneth's ridiculous influence and therefore convinced that it was important to persuade her to write an account of the events of Christmas Eve. She was, as Kenneth had foretold, delighted and pretended to see at once why that day was selected.

"Of course; I shall be delighted to give my poor little bit of help, Colonel Halstock. Not that I can tell you anything of importance, of course, but I think anyone will admit that I am observant and, of course, under the circumstances, all of us being so anxious, I noted everything most particularly. This is quite confidential, I suppose?"

I assured her that it was so and she trotted off. I didn't attempt to find out why they were all so anxious on Tuesday because I had already tried to probe to the foundations of a hint of this sort and found nothing but a quagmire of nervousness induced, apparently, by any gathering together of the Melbury family.

After she had gone I waited about for George in order to ask him about the car. When that was settled, I still stood by the fireplace for a few minutes, thinking out my plans. Bingham came into the hall from the door at the back, with a large rug over his arm. I thought he had come to fetch me and was surprised that he had got the car ready so quickly. Seeing me, he remarked:

"Car will be round in five or ten minutes, sir. Takes a bit of time to warm up. This 'ere—" (indicating the rug) "got damp through bein' put over the bonnet on Christmas Day, an' it's jest bin dried out."

He fumbled in one of his pockets and produced a glove, a man's hogskin glove of an ordinary type. "Picked this up, sir," he mumbled, "in the lib'ry, when I was a'clearin' up my electrical stuff this mornin'. Wasn't on'y the one. Thought mebbe you oughter know, sir."

The man seemed half-ashamed of his discovery. I pretended to be only faintly interested, but asked just where he had found it. He said it was in the far corner, amongst a lot of wrapping paper which had been piled up there. It was only by chance that he noticed the glove; it might quite easily have been carried away and burnt with the paper. But having found it, he looked, he said, for its fellow, which he failed to find.

I gathered that the man had been carrying this treasure about in his pocket all day and felt pretty mad with him, but I didn't want to frighten him because he struck me as the sort of man who will quickly resort to lies in self-defence if he thinks he is being blamed. I only inquired quite mildly why he didn't tell one of us at once. It seems that he made the find very early, before Rousdon or I was on the scene. There was no one about at the time, except a maid or two, and in any case he thought nothing of it at first except that someone had lost a glove. Later on it occurred to him that it was an odd place in which to lose a glove and there might be some significance in it.

"'Ope I've done right, sir?" he finished up anxiously.

I assured him that he'd certainly done right to hand over the glove and probably the delay wasn't important, and sent him off to get the car. I took the glove in to Rousdon and told him Bingham's story. His eyes gleamed, but after examining the glove very carefully he looked a bit disappointed.

"Yes; one gent's glove is very like another gent's glove," I told him. "Unless the owner has been so incredibly foolish as to keep the fellow, you'll have some difficulty."

"But he *is* a pretty fair-sized ass!" Rousdon declared. "What did he want to drop it there for? Though it's true he couldn't destroy it here or in the study—not in these gas fires. There's a good open blaze in the hall, but people may have been about there all the time. But if he could get all the rest of his outfit away, why drop one glove? Can't make up my mind whether there's sheer lunacy or something really devilish clever at the bottom of all this."

He jerked his mind away from this problem for a minute to tell me that the crackers which had been distributed by Santa Klaus were some of a quantity which had been ordered by Miss Portisham, together with other Christmas supplies, for a party which was to have been held next week. They had been stored in a cupboard in the dining-room, where anyone could find them. The general idea in the household was that they were not intended for use on Christmas Day.

I left him brooding over the glove and went off to Bristol to meet Crewkerne and learn the contents of Sir Osmond's will.

Chapter Eleven

Sir Osmond's Will

by Col. Halstock

I sat beside Bingham during the drive to Bristol, for now that I had time at my disposal I was willing to encourage him to talk, as he was ready to do at every opportunity. Even the gossip of the servants' hall may contain valuable specks of information. Bingham might well have picked up something less tangible but more useful to me than an unidentifiable glove.

His chief concern was for those "pore li'l kiddies. A norrible thing for them, 'avin' their grandad shot like that within a few yards of them, where they was playin' so innercent an' enjoyin' their crackers an' all. Sir Osmond too, 'e thought a lot of them kiddies an' 'e was that set up with the idear of that Santer Klaus; talked ter me abaht it, 'e did, because a-course I was ter fix up the tree an' all. Little did 'e think what it would lead to."

I asked Bingham if he would recognize Crewkerne, because I was myself only slightly acquainted with the lawyer and thought that he and I might not recognize each other in a station crowd.

"Yes, sir; I know 'im well enough. I reckon I can pick 'im out. I fetched 'im up from Bristol once to see Sir Osmond, though the las' time my poor master saw 'im 'e went into Bristol 'imself, to Mr. Crewkerne's orfice. The Thursday before Christmas, that would be. I reckerleck it pertic'ler because Sir Osmond, 'e sat at the back of the car all the way ter Bristol, makin' notes. An' I can't help thinkin'," Bingham declared piously, "that if Sir Osmond was makin' a will, which a-course I don' *know*, but it nater'ly comes to mind, speakin' of lawyers an' my poor master's death, then it's all ter the good that 'e got it done before 'e was bumped off like that, so as now it'll all be divided up in the way 'e would wish, whatsoever that may be. Makes you wonder, don't it, sir, whether 'e 'ad any premonition, as they say. Might've known of some secret enemy, don' you think, sir, with a grudge aginst 'im?"

I thought Bingham had been too often to the movies, but I asked him if he had any ideas about Sir Osmond's possible private enemies.

"Why, no, sir! Can't think 'oo'd want to shoot 'im through the 'ead like that. It's a fair mystery to me."

From under the bogus embattlements which so strangely adorn Temple Meads station at Bristol surged a Bank Holiday crowd, from which Bingham extricated a tall, gaunt, stooping figure whom he followed towards the car in which I was waiting. Mr. Crewkerne's black eyebrows were drawn together angrily, his long nose was red and the rest of his face yellow. He was not mellowed by Christmas feasting.

I had moved to the back of the car and he got in beside me, after giving Bingham some directions.

"I've asked Bingham to drive us straight to my office," he said. "Fortunately, I've got all the keys and I can lay my hands on that will in a moment—I take it that it's in order to get a sight of it that you've given me this deplorable journey on this unspeakable day? Shocking affair, very."

He then proceeded to describe the iniquity of railway officials, the rowdiness of football crowds, and the regrettable state of affairs in the country generally.

At the door of his office he announced, "Come in, do! Most inviting, I assure you. Yule log on the hearth and bunches of mistletoe over the door! Ha! Ha!"

I suggested that probably a few moments would be enough to show me the main points of the will and then we could drive him to his house at Clifton.

"Ah! I can promise you a fine welcome there!" he growled. "Maids all sent home for a holiday; house shut; silver at the bank! Oh, you'll find a festive household!"

The obvious solution was that we should both drive out to my house and I could send him home later. He had already sent a telegram to his housekeeper, who was spending the holiday with relatives in Bristol, and he thought she would have the house ready for him by dinner-time. He was considerably soothed by my suggestion and he unlocked the outer door and skipped upstairs quite briskly to fetch Sir Osmond's will.

We discussed it in low voices on the drive out to my place, Twaybrooks. Sir Osmond had, as Bingham had said, visited Crewkerne on the Thursday before Christmas and had discussed with him some alterations to his will. The existing will had been taken out and Sir Osmond had gone through it, making notes on it of the alterations he was considering. He had a little slip of paper on which he had evidently been planning these beforehand, and he took it away with him. Crewkerne made notes while Sir Osmond talked, and he had these and also Sir Osmond's figures on the will itself. He hadn't drafted the new will yet. Sir Osmond had said that he didn't want to see it until about a week after Christmas. Crewkerne gathered that his client hadn't quite made up his mind and that his final decision might depend on the opinions he formed of various members of his family during their Christmas visit.

"He wasn't a man to talk much about how he intended to dispose of his fortune, from what I knew of him," Crewkerne stated. "But something may have been said, and in my opinion you'll find two sets of motives in this nice little document. There are several people who would lose a good deal under the proposed new will, and it would be to their interests to prevent that will from being executed. There is another group who stand to gain substantially under the new will and if they were to hear some garbled account of what the old man had been doing they might suppose that the alterations were already made, or that these notes were valid, and that now was their time to strike."

The lawyer licked his lips. "It's a very pretty little problem, Colonel Halstock. Very pretty indeed."

He showed no interest at all in the crime itself, not asking how it had been committed or even whether we had made an arrest.

"The ordinary layman, Colonel Halstock," he continued, "is singularly ill-informed, culpably ill-informed, I may say, about a matter so important in the lives of us all, the making of a will. I would not be in the least surprised to learn that anyone who knows of these alterations to the will—if anyone does know of them—has assumed that they would be upheld as the late Sir Osmond's duly executed testament."

I asked him whether they would have any force at all; whether those who benefited under the alterations would have grounds for trying to upset the original provisions of the will.

"No grounds at all!" Crewkerne declared, leaning back in the seat, pursing his lips and tapping the tips of his fingers together. "Those notes carry no weight; not the least gramme! Quite apart from the evidence I could give that they do not represent any definite decision by Sir Osmond, I had determined not to draft the new will until I heard again from my client, because I fully anticipated that he would change his mind."

At Twaybrooks I took Crewkerne into my study and ordered some tea. Then he untied the pink tape and unrolled the document. I had realized on the drive that Crewkerne felt it would be improper to discuss on the highway anything more than generalizations. So I had merely speculated as to whether Witcombe's name would appear in the notes. A quick survey of the will convinced me that he was not mentioned.

Flaxmere and all other real estate was left to George, with the exception of the Dower House, which went to Miss Melbury. A grim jest, that. The Dower House was in the village almost at the drive gates, and Sir Osmond would not have his sister at such close quarters whilst he was living, but he had dumped her neatly on George. Miss Melbury also received a legacy of £500, which would not please her much, I thought. There were small legacies to all employed at Flaxmere, in the house and grounds, who had been there more than three years, Parkins and Bingham receiving the most, £500 each. A few gifts to charities amounted to less than £10,000. Carol Wynford received £1,000 and Grace Portisham £1,000. A substantial legacy, that, for a private secretary, but yet nothing for the family to get on their hind legs about, I felt. The residue of the estate was to be divided into six parts, of which two went to George and one each to Hilda, Eleanor, Edith and Jennifer.

There was nothing sensational in the will; it was much what one might have expected and I thought the family would be relieved. Crewkerne scanned my face as I sat considering it.

"Quite a sound allocation, yes? Ah—but now look at the notes or, if you can't read them—his writing was very small at times—look at my own notes of them." He passed a sheet of paper across to me and I turned to it in relief from Sir Osmond's tiny scribbled figures on the margin of the will, connected by lines like scraps of spider's web with the relevant parts of the document.

In the revised version the legacies to charities, to employees and to Miss Melbury remained unaltered. The names of Carol and of Miss Portisham were removed from this list. The residue was now to be divided into eight parts, of which George received two parts, as before; Hilda, Eleanor and also Carol one part each; Jennifer, if she were single at the time of her father's death, two parts; whilst Edith shared the remaining part equally with Grace Portisham. If Jennifer had married, she was to receive one-eighth and the remaining eighth was to be divided between Hilda, Carol, Eleanor and Edith.

I have set forth the two different divisions of the property, as it concerned the chief legatees.

	RECEIVED UNDER THE WILL:	UNDER THE REVISION:
George	one-third	one-quarter
Hilda	one-sixth	one-eighth
Carol	£1,000	one-eighth
Eleanor	one-sixth	one-eighth
Edith	one-sixth	one-sixteenth
Jennifer	one-sixth	if single, one-quarter
		if married, one-eighth
G. Portisham	£1,000	one-sixteenth

When I had taken in the gist of Sir Osmond's after-thoughts, my first idea was of thankfulness that he had not executed a valid will on these lines. It would be bad enough when the family learnt what he had contemplated! I suspected that a double share was willed to Jennifer under the condition that she was still single because her father felt convinced that she would not be single much longer. It was to be dangled before her as a punishment, because she had not obeyed his wishes.

"And now," I asked Crewkerne, who was regarding me sardonically, "what does all this mean? Roughly what does the estate amount to?"

"He'll cut up pretty well; pretty well. He was a careful man. But neither I nor anyone else can say for certain at this juncture what he is worth. I'll say this, in confidence, mind you; I shall be surprised if the estate, quite apart from Flaxmere and the other property, amounts to much less than two hundred thousand."

I made some quick calculations. "So the girls may get about thirty-three thousand each. And under the revised allocation they would have had about twenty-five thousand, excepting Edith. Those who would chiefly have benefited under the revision are: Carol, who would get some £25,000 instead of a mere thousand; Grace Portisham, who would get £12,500—a tremendous fortune for her; enough to make her comfortable for life; and Jennifer, if she were single, when she would get about £50,000 instead of £33,000." I considered that and didn't like the look of it very much.

"You've estimated it at maximum figures," Crewkerne pointed out. "There are the miscellaneous legacies to be deducted from the total before you divide it into lots, and then there are the death duties."

"Never mind," I told him. "My figures give the propor-tions, and if the estate is anything like what you suggest, the sums won't be so far off what I've put down. Now let's consider the losers under the revised version. First of all Edith would get a miserable £12,500 instead of £33,000. That's the most important. George and Eleanor would each lose a bit, Eleanor about £8,000, in fact, and George twice that; but they still get a good whack. Jennifer would lose a bit if married, but we need hardly consider that; she must be classed under the winners. Hilda's loss of £8,000 would be more than offset by her daughter's gain of £24,000."

"This'll give the Melburys something to think about for a bit!" Crewkerne chuckled.

"You're quite sure that the properly executed will can't possibly be upset in favour of these notes?" I asked him again.

"Not a hope! Those notes don't constitute a will at all; they're signed, it's true, but not witnessed. That's not to say that there aren't people fools enough to try to get the will upset, or men in my profession irresponsible enough to help them. And then there's the possibility of a sort of blackmail. A person who stood to benefit substantially under the proposed new will, in a way which might be distasteful to the family, could threaten to bring an action, not with any real hope of winning it, but with the idea of frightening the family into buying her off to avoid sensational publicity. You know the sort of thing I mean: newspaper headlines: *Wealthy Man's Family contest Claims of Pretty Typist.* Very unsavoury."

I couldn't picture Grace Portisham embarking on that sort of trick, but, of course, she might have a needy and avid family in the background who would force her into it.

I had been so absorbed in working out the implications of the will and the notes, that I had forgotten the tea and I began to apologize to Crewkerne, when I saw that he had quietly poured out a cup for himself. In fact, I suspected from the lightness of the teapot that he had manged to drink one and pour out a second whilst I was occupied with making notes and calculations.

I now had all the information I wanted from the will and I handed it back to Crewkerne, asking him whether he would have to read out the notes when he read the will.

"No; they do not properly belong to the will. But any of them has a right to look at the will, and you can count on them rushing at it. People always do! They seem to think I must have made mistakes in the figures or that they'll find a sentence or two I haven't noticed." He chuckled dryly.

I heard the telephone bell ring and a few moments later the bell of the extension in my study told me it was my call. I had had a message telephoned to Flaxmere as soon as I reached home to tell Rousdon where he could find me.

When I picked up the receiver I was deafened by a loud buzzing, through which filtered faintly some confused chatter from the exchange. The instrument had been working abominably on Christmas Day and the news of Sir Osmond's death had made me forget to report the trouble. It was still just as bad. At last I caught Rousdon's voice repeating peevishly, "*Are* you there? Hal*lo!* Hal*lo!*"

When I answered, he announced distinctly, "Remember what you said about gents' gloves? Well, the owner *has* been so incredibly foolish! And still more so. I've got him here safe!"

There was a good deal more indistinct talk overwhelmed by a loud buzzing from the telephone. I could make out nothing except that Rousdon was taking Witcombe to the police station and there was no need for me to go over to Flaxmere to see either of them. I told Rousdon to send me some information by Kenneth Stour who, I gathered, was still in the house and who would pass by our gates on his way back to the Tollards. I said he could trust Kenneth, which he answered by a snort.

I arranged for Bingham to drive Crewkerne back to Bristol and ordered the chauffeur to return straight back to Flaxmere after that. I didn't see what harm he could do; he couldn't have foreseen that he would be left alone and he had been watched while he was getting the car out—a precaution of which I was now glad, for I believed there was something hidden at Flaxmere which I hoped to find before long.

As I was seeing Crewkerne off, my wife came into the hall. I told her that I was expecting Kenneth Stour and wanted to see him alone in the study.

"Kenneth Stour—that's the young man who used to come here a lot, years ago, isn't it? Yes, of course I remember him; charming smile! Quite a famous actor now, isn't he? And—yes—I saw him for a moment at the Tollards, just before Christmas; it was on Monday and Dittie Evershot was there too."

"Dittie? Are you sure?" I questioned.

"Of course I am! I've known Dittie since before she was married to that frightful man. I thought she'd aged terribly; she's got such a hard look now and she can't be much over thirty. Poor Dittie! You know, she's much nicer than you'd ever think if you didn't know her well. She's always been very shut up inside herself. There was talk of an affair between her and Kenneth Stour once; she probably ought to have married him, but, like most of that family, she was too fond of money and he had none then."

I began to wish I could discuss the Melbury case with my wife. I only asked her whether Sir David was at the Tollards, on Monday.

"No, I'm sure he wasn't. But I didn't stay long; I only called to take some presents for the children. Dittie wasn't staying there, you know; she had driven over from Flaxmere, I think. Ask young Stour to lunch or to dine or something; I *do* like the way he smiles at one, as if one were the only person in the world! I expect he does it to everyone, but I enjoy it just the same."

I thought all this over. I had asked Kenneth when he turned up so unexpectedly at Flaxmere how he knew that Dittie was there and he had avoided the obvious reply that he had seen her on Monday. I had let him come poking about in this case because I knew him and because—as my wife would have said—he has a way with him. But I began to feel uneasy.

I rang up Max Tollard, whom I knew well, to ask him if he could provide Kenneth with a good alibi for Christmas Day. I made light of the matter, suggesting that as Kenneth was running in and out of Flaxmere it was only right to inquire about his movements as we had done about those of everyone in the house. Tollard was quite sure that Kenneth had been with them all the afternoon and evening. His wife and daughters and several guests could swear to that, he said. "He's very discreet," Tollard added. "We can't get a thing out of him and I suppose I mustn't ask you, but this is a ghastly affair for the Melburys, and I shall be thankful when I hear that you've cleared it up."

Chapter Twelve

Fight with Fire-Irons

by Col. Halstock

IT was nearly dinner-time when Kenneth arrived at Tway-brooks, primed with a pretty complete account of the events of the afternoon at Flaxmere. Rousdon, elated by what had happened, had been quite expansive; Kenneth had collected further details from George and Carol and Witcombe himself and added some embroidery of his own. This was his story:

Although Witcombe emerged pretty well from his inter-view with Rousdon in the morning, he had been worried. ("Of course he didn't do it," Kenneth commented; "and he doesn't know who did.") So he had nosed around during the afternoon, trying to pick up a clue of some sort (and perhaps looking for a chance to plant one) which would point the pursuit towards someone else. But Rousdon had set Mere to watch Witcombe and Kenneth himself was also keeping an eye on him. The household had been given permission to take the air on the gravel sweep in front of the house and the paved path under the windows on the study side, and here

Witcombe prowled for a time. But there was Mere stolidly contemplating the view of the pool and there was Kenneth on the drive, polishing his windscreen or inspecting the early snowdrops. So at last Witcombe gave it up and returned to the hall with a harassed air.

Mere skipped round by the back door and the back stairs and so reached the main staircase and took up a station on one of the branches that lead off at right angles from the first flight. Here he could peer down through the banisters into the hall. Witcombe didn't notice him there and probably assumed that the constable's vigilance had only been to prevent any funny business out of doors. Actually Mere was not only observing Witcombe in the hall but also guarding the stairs, whilst Constable Stapley searched Witcombe's bedroom.

Jenny, Miss Melbury, Miss Portisham and Philip were all busily engaged in their own rooms on what Kenneth calls their "homework" and most of the others were in the drawing-room, as Witcombe knew. He drew an armchair up to the fire in the hall and picked up a copy of the *Tatler*. After turning over the pages for a bit, he propped it up against the arm of his chair and then seemed to fumble in his breast-pocket. Mere couldn't see exactly what happened behind the *Tatler*, which was doubtless intended as a screen against the eyes of anyone who might happen to enter the hall.

Mere's impression was that Witcombe drew out a pocket-book or wallet, extracted something and then replaced the wallet in his pocket. He gave a hasty glance round the hall. Mere was on tiptoe with expectation and after that he ventured a stair or two lower. Witcombe picked up a poker and stirred the fire, which had been newly made up and was dull, until a flame shot up. At once Mere came bounding down the stairs. Witcombe heard him, lost his head, and snatched at the thing he had taken from his wallet, which turned out to be a sheet of notepaper. He fumbled it, because the *Tatler* had fallen on to it, but he did manage to crumple the paper and hurl it, with part of a leaf of the *Tatler*, into the fire, not very accurately. By that time Mere was upon him, seized the tongs and raked frantically at the paper. A whole lot of the fire fell out on to the hearth, and some of it scattered on to the floor.

Witcombe still held the poker and he swiped with it at Mere, a tall hefty man, who parried with the tongs and yelled for help. The two of them grappled and rolled on the floor. George came rushing out of the drawing-room, followed by others; Patricia stood at the door and screamed; Rousdon dashed out of the library and Stapley from upstairs. Kenneth himself heard the shout from the drive and ran in, in time to see Witcombe on the floor in the grip of George and Rousdon whilst Mere, who had extricated himself, rolled over rather ludicrously towards the fireplace and began routing with the tongs among the litter of coals and cinders.

The thick shiny paper of the *Tatler*, which didn't burn easily, had protected the other piece of paper; it had caught at one edge and smouldered, but part of it was rescued. This fragment of a note in Sir Osmond's handwriting—identified by George and others—had been sealed up in an envelope by Rousdon and was now handed to me by Kenneth.

A note from Rousdon enclosed with the charred piece of paper ran: *I assume this refers to the will. Can the last name be Witcombe's?*

Witcombe cooled down on the floor, in the grip of George and Rousdon, and when he was allowed to get up he went off quite meekly into the library, only protesting that "that great lout rushed at me like a mad elephant and attacked me with the tongs."

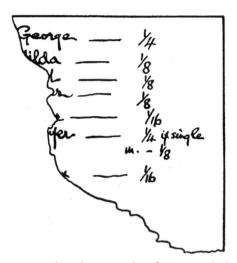

Stapley returned to his search of Witcombe's room and before long he came down triumphantly with the fellow to the glove which Bingham had picked up in the library. He had found this prize in a drawer of the dressing-table, pushed to the back and under some handkerchiefs, but not very effectively hidden.

The two gloves were shown to Witcombe and he was asked if they were his. Quite calmly he agreed that they looked like a pair he had with him at Flaxmere; in fact, he pointed out his initials, O.W., neatly marked inside them. He wanted to know where they had been found and what they had to do with the case? Rousdon asked if he could account for the fact that one had been found hidden in the library.

"Now, look here," Witcombe declared. "I can't account for anything more. You really mustn't expect me to solve all your little problems, especially this one of why someone has been monkeying with my gloves." (Witcombe himself had later repeated this speech to Kenneth). "If you're still harping on that cracker business, send for Miss Wynford. She can tell you that when I left Sir Osmond and went out of the hall I didn't go back, because I stood talking to her in the passage for some minutes."

Carol was sent for and arrived to find Witcombe facing Rousdon, a bit pale but quite composed. They were eyeing each other warily, she said, as if each was looking for a chance to grapple.

Rousdon asked him sternly what he had to say to Carol.

Witcombe looked a bit embarrassed. "Carol," he said, "do you mind telling Inspector Rousdon what I did when I went through the door from the hall into the back passage on Christmas afternoon, in the Santa Klaus rig-out?"

Carol got rather hot (her own confession) and said indignantly, "I don't see how *I* can tell what you did!"

Witcombe said, "It's serious, Carol. Inspector Rousdon"— he glanced at Rousdon's stony face—"thinks of accusing me of murdering your grandfather; of going back through the dining-room to murder him immediately after I went out into the passage and met you there."

"Oh! Well, of course—" Carol turned to Rousdon; "I know Mr. Witcombe didn't go back to the study because I met him, as he says, in the back passage and I talked to him there for some minutes."

"You say you met him as he left the hall; please show me on this plan just where you met him," Rousdon requested.

Carol pointed to the passage into which the door at the back of the hall leads; to a spot, in fact, very near the gun-room door.

"And how did you come to be there, Miss Wynford?" Rousdon asked her freezingly.

"Oh, I'd been to Jennifer's room to fetch something— a cigarette case, which I'd left there."

It was, of course, just outside the door of Jennifer's own little room that Carol claimed to have met Witcombe.

"And how do you know that when you met Mr. Witcombe he hadn't already come out of the hall once, returned with the crackers and come out a second time?" (According to accounts of course, Witcombe had *not* gone out by that door on the second occasion, after the cracker business, but Rousdon was setting a trap—or two traps, as I guessed. Witcombe did not fall into it by exclaiming, "But I didn't go out that way the second time!" as Rousdon doubtless hoped he would).

"I'm sure that was the first time Mr. Witcombe came out," Carol insisted.

"How can you be sure?"

Carol considered her answer. "Why, of course, the crackers hadn't begun when he came out of the hall. I'm sure of that, because I heard the first one, very loud, a few minutes later, and it made me jump. You remember that, don't you?" she appealed to Witcombe.

"Yes, of course," he agreed. "You know, I haven't got frightfully good hearing and I didn't notice the cracker, but I did notice Miss Wynford jump. I remember it now quite well."

"You mean to tell me," Rousdon asked her very deliberately, "that you heard the first cracker go off while you were actually talking to Mr. Witcombe in the passage?"

Carol agreed.

"And why," Rousdon demanded, "when we asked you yesterday evening to tell us what you were doing all that afternoon, did you not mention this little excursion?"

"Well, we were all very upset and I really didn't think of it at the time. I didn't know it was important."

"But you were asked where you were and you didn't mention going out into that passage. You must have realized that that was important; you knew, for one thing, that the gun-room is there and that the pistol came from the gun-room."

"I never thought about the gun-room," Carol replied. "I don't suppose I've ever been into it. Why should I remember a thing like going to fetch my handbag?"

"Your cigarette case, I thought it was?"

"Of course, the cigarette case was in the handbag; it was because of the cigarette case that I wanted the bag."

"If you had been waiting for Mr. Witcombe at that door you would know, of course, that he hadn't been out of it before?" Rousdon suddenly suggested.

Carol said she had been a bit taken aback; "he jumped at me so"; but she had replied that if Mr. Witcombe had gone out earlier she would have seen him while she was still in the hall. She had come out of the library and left him there, waiting about, she said; then she wanted a cigarette and went out of the door at the back of the hall to Jenny's room, where she had left her case. She hadn't seen Mr. Witcombe again after leaving him in the library, until she had been to Jenny's room and was returning to the hall, when he came out through the door into the passage. "I'll swear to that," Carol had said.

"I hope, Miss Wynford," said Rousdon nastily, "that you would be prepared to take your oath, if necessary, on everything you have just told me."

Carol agreed to this.

Then, "in that horrid, sudden way of his," Rousdon asked Witcombe, "How long did you talk to Miss Wynford in the passage?"

"Oh, really I don't know; a few minutes perhaps, not very long, because I had to go on to the servants' hall with the presents."

"And what did you talk about?" Rousdon snapped at Carol.

"Oh, nothing in particular; just how things were working out and whether it would all go off all right." Carol complained afterwards that "Inspector Rousdon seemed to think that suspicious, but it was quite natural really; everyone was a bit jumpy about the Santa Klaus plan and afraid it would lead to a scene of some sort with grandfather, and people must have said a hundred times during that afternoon, "Seems to be going all right?""

The upshot of all this was that Inspector Rousdon had insisted that Witcombe must go off with him in the police car to Wellbridge police station and make a statement about the gloves and the scrap of paper. I think Rousdon's idea was that this procedure would overawe Witcombe and he would confess to something.

"And that's that!" said Kenneth. "I hope Witcombe won't lose his head again; I advised him to say nothing but the truth and not too much of that, and if he is charged with the murder to say nothing at all except that he's not guilty and wants to see his solicitor."

"You advised him!" I gasped. "Are you helping the police or are you acting as detective-adviser to the accused?"

"Witcombe isn't accused of anything yet, so far as I know; if he has been charged with anything it's probably assault," Kenneth pointed out; "I advised him merely out of the kindness of my heart, as a fellow man. He can't tell you anything helpful, I'm sure of that. The poor chap is simply puzzled. If he's driven into a corner and tries to explain things, he'll simply make up a lot of stuff that'll confuse everybody."

I asked him if he had any plan of action in his mind.

"Wait!" he advised. "We shall get the eyewitness accounts to-morrow and those will give us something to work on. Also I think that something will happen; I feel sure it will."

I was afraid he had planned some devilment, but he assured me that he had done nothing all day but talk to people and hang about and think.

He pointed out that, if one believed Witcombe's story, it was clear that someone else in a Santa Klaus dress had gone into the hall with crackers as soon as Witcombe was clear of it and had almost certainly gone on through the library into the study and fired the shot. I had reached that conclusion myself. If Witcombe had returned to the hall so conspicuously, distributing crackers, as Miss Portisham and Mrs. Wynford said he did, why should he hope to be believed if he denied it? But Witcombe must know, I maintained, who the other man was, because he must have lent him the outfit and waited to get it back again from him. And how did Carol come into that, if she had been hanging about in the passage?

"I'm not sure of that," said Kenneth. "I don't believe Witcombe comes into this at all. That's to say, sometimes I don't believe it. But when I ask myself one question, I feel he must be connected with the plot in some way. Why was he at Flaxmere at all?"

I understood that he was invited and hadn't thought any special explanation of his presence was called for.

"But none of them like him," Kenneth insisted. "You don't normally accept an invitation to a house in which you're not generally welcome, unless you're desperately hard up for somewhere to go. Witcombe wasn't that; he's got a home and parents and plenty of friends. He can't have had a very pleasant time at Flaxmere, where they all tend to cold-shoulder him."

I reminded Kenneth that Sir Osmond liked Witcombe and that he was supposed to be paying court to Jenny.

"That's all my eye. Jenny doesn't care two hoots for him; in fact, she rather dislikes him since her father tried to force him on her. There was never the faintest chance that Jenny would marry Oliver Witcombe and he knew it. He may be obtuse but he's not so obtuse as all that. No, he didn't come to Flaxmere to ask Jenny again. And do you really suppose that he came for the sake of the company of Sir Osmond, a man forty years his senior, just at the time when that man would be much engaged with all his family? The family, of course, would be even less cordial towards Witcombe than usual if they noticed that their father was confiding in him and making a pet of him."

There might be something in this point of view, but I didn't really feel it had much value. I discussed the facts of the case with Kenneth for a bit because, even if his ideas are erratic, it's often helpful to get a perfectly fresh point of view. I hoped he might have been able to pick up some information about the telephone call which Sir Osmond had been expecting when he went to his study on Christmas afternoon. Since it had never been made, it was almost certainly the murderer's trick to ensure that Sir Osmond would be in his study alone at the appointed time. But on the question of how and when Sir Osmond had been told to expect the call I had so far drawn a blank. Kenneth could tell me nothing. He was not proving any more helpful than I had expected.

There were a number of other clues that I wanted to follow up and I told Kenneth that I should go over to Flax-mere in the morning to make inquiries. I asked him one more question; if he was sure of Witcombe's innocence, how did he explain the finding of one of his gloves in the library?

"That's not difficult; if the murderer had planned to implicate Witcombe he wouldn't find it difficult to nab a pair of his gloves beforehand. Much better, in any case, to use someone else's gloves in this sort of business. He deliberately dropped one and returned the other to its place. Witcombe may be obtuse, but he's not such a fool as to leave the glove lying there; if he could take one back to his room, he could take the other."

"Bingham thought it was only by chance he found it among the paper."

"Shows the ingenuity of the hider. He arranged it so that anyone picking up the paper would be bound to see it and would yet think that it had really been hidden."

It strengthens one's own ideas to have them confirmed by conclusions reached independently by someone else, and for that reason, if for no other, I was glad to have Kenneth's co-operation. If he spent another day with the Flaxmere family, as I gathered he intended to do, he might be able to throw some light on their private alarms, suspicions and motives. I thought I knew them pretty well but some of them were behaving unaccountably. I was reluctant to ask Kenneth if he could explain Dittie's state of nervous terror, but I hoped he might of his own accord throw some light on it before long.

Chapter Thirteen

Bad Dreams

by Col. Halstock

I had another talk over the telephone with Rousdon that evening. It occurred to me that newspapers would be published the next day and he would already be besieged by pressmen. I didn't want them to get the idea that Witcombe was under arrest, for the more I thought about it, the surer I felt that his guilt wouldn't explain half the problems of the case and would raise several new ones.

I told Rousdon about Sir Osmond's notes for his revised will and that the last name was not Witcombe's. As for the glove clue, if Rousdon accepted that at its face value, he must thereby admit that the police who had thoroughly searched for the gloves, particularly in the rooms near the library, had done their job very badly. Wasn't it far more likely that the thing had been planted later? The third point I urged was that facts suggested, on the whole, that the murder had been carefully planned beforehand. If Witcombe had thus planned it, was it credible that he would have arranged to draw so much attention to himself on the way to commit the crime as he had done by his second entry into the hall with crackers? He could easily have distributed these (if they were needed to drown the shot) before he went out and then have returned unseen to the study through the dining-room and library. His actual movements, assuming that all these were Witcombe's movements, of which I was doubtful, pointed rather to the idea that he had been made a dupe by someone else.

Rousdon apparently heard all this, but the telephone was still bewitched and I could hardly make out what he said about the finger-prints, which had now been sorted out. I asked him to meet me at Flaxmere the next morning with a couple of men who could be relied upon to carry out a thorough search of the house. Moreover, I didn't think that the residents ought to be left to their own devices as yet and two resourceful officers should be posted there for the night.

That evening I shuffled the pieces of the puzzle to and fro and tried to make a pattern of them. I believed that Sir David Evershot ought to be fitted in somewhere and was not satisfied with the idea that he came in as an accidental accessory who found the body by chance and didn't like to mention the matter. There ought by rights to be a more definite connection between the open window and the man who had gone outside for a breath of air at the time when the murder was committed. Dittie's state of alarm, too, would be natural if she had found something in the study which showed that her husband had been there.

I considered the concealed door between the dining-room and library, which was usually locked but had been open on Christmas Day so that the servants might go that way into the library to see the Christmas-tree. Only someone familiar beforehand with the Christmas plans could know that the door would be ready for their use. If it had not been known that this door would be available, then the study window would seem to provide the only chance of entering or leaving the library unseen from the hall. But we had already dismissed the possibility of anyone getting in at the window without Sir Osmond's knowledge or connivance, and from whatever angle I considered the picture I couldn't see Sir Osmond calmly inviting Sir David to come in out of the wet through his study window.

I threw aside that very awkwardly shaped piece of the puzzle represented by Sir David, and began to consider the piece called Carol. The fact that neither she nor Witcombe had mentioned their meeting in the passage until he was pressed to prove an alibi, and that she hesitated to admit it even then, until he pointed out to her that his situation was serious, looked queer. I couldn't help thinking that she had waited in the passage, near the gun room too—nasty thought!—intentionally to meet him. She would have benefited substantially under the proposed new will and that money would mean more to her than to any of Sir Osmond's own sons or daughters. It would mean an open way to the career she had set her heart on and the certainty of being able to build up her position in that career with the support of an independent income. I thought that money itself didn't mean much to Carol, but what money could buy for her at this moment meant a great deal.

The conclusion to which all this led revolted me, who had known Carol since her childhood. Witcombe may have had the notes of the will alterations from Sir Osmond and have jumped to the conclusion that they had been properly carried out; he may have confided in Carol; she met him by appointment as he left the hall and then, while he returned with crackers and created a diversion, she crept through the dining-room and library to the study and fired the shot. But how explain the gloves? Considering Carol critically and unsentimentally, I could see a streak of hardness in her, a determination to get her own way which might be relentless. She might be capable of the shooting, but could she be capable of a plan which, as she would be quick-witted enough to see, was bound to direct suspicion towards Witcombe, and could she be base enough to strengthen that suspicion by deliberately dropping one of his gloves in the track of the murderer?

There was a possible, though not very plausible, explanation of why Witcombe had denied any connection with the crackers, after entering the hall and distributing them so obviously. Was it conceivable that he didn't realize, when the plan was worked out, how guilty he would seem to be? Perhaps his exit from the hall, after the cracker-pulling, was planned to be through the door at the back; he may have gone into the library on a sudden impulse, to make sure whether Carol had carried out her role satisfactorily. I recalled that curious phrase of his, "having made sure that Sir Osmond was dead." He might well have been doubtful whether Carol really had the nerve and brutality to fire a shot straight into her grandfather's head. Supposing all this, he might suddenly have realized, when he was being questioned, that his second visit to the hall with the crackers and especially his mistaken exit by way of the library, made things look very black against him, and have decided to disclaim that second visit. How he expected to be believed I could hardly imagine. But, yes,— I could. He had talked it over with Carol before his interview with Rousdon this morning and had persuaded her to agree that, if necessary, she would admit meeting him in the passage and would declare that he couldn't have been dealing out crackers in the hall because she heard them going off while she talked with him.

I went over this theory again and again. No one had given evidence of seeing Carol in the hall during the important time. In fact, she had been unsatisfactorily vague about her movements during the afternoon. Witcombe's stupidity in going from the hall into the library was on a par with his stupidity in making such a pother about destroying Sir Osmond's note when he suddenly realized that he still had it and that it would be a nasty bit of evidence if he were arrested—of which, as he began to see, there was some danger.

I reluctantly admitted to myself that there was yet another point against Carol. Kenneth hadn't liked my question as to why he didn't include Carol in the writers of "homework." If he, mixing with the family as I couldn't do, had detected in her the signs of an uneasy conscience or had even picked up some scrap of evidence against her, he would think it useless to ask her to write an account, or he might shrink from trying to trip her up by such a method. If he had nothing definite against her, he would not say anything to me as yet, hoping probably that further evidence would point in a different direction.

The whole thing seemed horribly clear. An ingeniously contrived plan with just those patches of stupidity in the execution of it which generally occur to give the policeman his chance.

I spent a wretched night, dreaming of Carol; Carol with a smoking pistol in her hand, firing it again at me and then turning, running across the hall of Flaxmere, out of the front door, down the emerald slope of the lawn, standing for a moment poised at the end of the diving board which overhung the pool—she was now in a bright blue bathing dress, as I had seen her last summer—and plunging in with a frightful shriek, breaking up the smooth pewter surface with ripples which spread and spread, lapped over the edge of the pool, crept up the slope of the lawn, flowed strongly round my feet where I stood on the gravel drive.

Sir Osmond climbed out of his study window and came up to me, with a hole in his head, holding out a cracker.

"Pull this! Pull this!" he shouted like a maniac. "It will drown the shot! Drown the shot! Drown!"

Then again Carol appeared, walking in my own garden at Twaybrooks, wearing a pair of masculine hogskin gloves, and pointed to an immense edifice sprouting from my own tennis courts, rather like the tower of Bristol University but of bright pink brick.

"I designed that!" she announced proudly. Looking at her face I saw that it had become horrible; it was Carol's face and yet it was cruel, greedy, monstrous.

Chapter Fourteen

A Pair of Eyebrows

by Col. Halstock

I reached Flaxmere early on the morning of Friday after Christmas, feeling old, empty and harassed.

Parkins opened the door and he, too, looked older and seemed worried.

"If you'll excuse me, sir, there's something I'd like to say to you in private, that I should perhaps have said to you sooner, sir, but not thinking it was of any consequence and not wishing to give offence in any quarter, and of course a promise is a promise although in a case of this sort it's hard to know where duty lies."

It struck me that there was something pathetic about Parkins, evidently trying to be loyal to the family and yet, for some reason, coming to the conclusion that another duty superseded that loyalty. On re-reading last night my notes made on the evening of the crime, I had found that there was a question I must put to Parkins. I now thought he was about to volunteer the answer.

He followed me into the library and there began further explanations.

"Inspector Rousdon asked me about this yesterday, sir, and somehow I couldn't bring myself to tell him, but it came over me that I ought to tell you, sir, you being a friend of the family and so understanding, perhaps, though it doesn't seem of any consequence, except that any comings and goings on such a night, maybe, ought to be notified to the proper quarters."

"Well, what is it, Parkins?" I asked impatiently, feeling sorry for the old man, but unable to bear his meanderings any longer. "Are you going to tell me how you came to give a message to Miss Wynford on the evening of Christmas Day?"

Parkins looked astonished; his mouth fell slightly open, giving him a ludicrously frog-like appearance.

"Message, sir?—Why, yes, sir; that's correct; I had forgotten the message, though of course it comes back to me now, because the message was, in a manner of speaking, about the car. It was Ashmore's car, sir. You'll remember John Ashmore who drove the old Daimler for Sir Osmond? Well, sir, it was Ashmore who was here on Christmas Day, in that same car which he drives for hire in Bristol. He came up after lunch, sir, with a message for Miss Jennifer and Miss Carol, to thank them for some Christmas hamper they'd sent him, which was doubtless most welcome, him not being in too comfortable circumstances nowadays, and he thought it right to express his gratitude immediately, but they considered it best, sir, not to mention to Sir Osmond that he was here, and I acted accordingly, not wishing to make any trouble and Sir Osmond being, as you well know, sir, if you'll pardon the liberty, a gentleman who didn't like to be crossed."

So that was the car which Caundle had met at the gates as he drove up to Flaxmere. I could understand how, if Jennifer and Carol had extracted a promise of secrecy from Parkins, he would hesitate to say anything about Ashmore's visit. I asked him when Ashmore had arrived.

"Soon after lunch, sir; and I informed Miss Jennifer during the Christmas-tree ceremony, sir, and she ran out immediately afterwards to speak to Ashmore and asked him to stay and have tea. But later on, sir, when it got through to the servants' hall that something had happened, though us not knowing then that it was a fatal act, but only understanding that it was some accident, then Ashmore said he'd better be leaving and asked me most particular to give a message to Miss Jennifer and Miss Carol, that he thanked them for their kindness. So I went to deliver the message and not finding Miss Jennifer I looked in her own room—you'll know it, perhaps, sir; the one at the end of the passage, and there was Miss Carol, so I delivered the message and she seeming in ignorance that there was anything wrong I told her there had been an accident in the study."

I asked if he knew at what time he had found Carol.

"I couldn't say, sir, but there was no one about in the hall, sir; they had all gone into the study, I believe."

Carol, therefore, hadn't returned to the hall. She couldn't face the others and she skulked in Jennifer's room, waiting for the alarm to be given when she might join the party unnoticed in the general confusion, and any distress she showed might be considered natural.

I dismissed Parkins and sat down to consider the plan of action. Apart from my personal feelings, the case was difficult. There was little direct evidence against Carol, and it wasn't easy to see where we were likely to discover more.

Presently Rousdon arrived and I eagerly demanded his account of what he had done with Witcombe and what he had got out of the man.

Rousdon was dissatisfied and grumpy. He had found, before leaving Flaxmere on Thursday evening, that Mrs.

Wynford and Miss Portisham and others who had seen Santa
Klaus enter the hall with crackers, could not swear that this
was Mr. Witcombe; they were only sure that it was someone in an identical costume, with the hood pulled rather
low over the eyes. They hadn't looked at him particularly,
of course, assuming at the time that it must be Witcombe,
but evidently some of them had realized since that it might
have been someone else, and they had been very guarded in
what they said to Rousdon.

At the police station Witcombe had asked for time to
think things over and at first had said he would like to see
a solicitor. This was not easy to manage on Bank Holiday
evening, and before Rousdon had got hold of one Witcombe
had said that "if they were not accusing him of anything,
but merely asking him for information," he didn't want legal
advice. He was completely innocent, he maintained, and
quite ready to tell anything he knew, but he must have time
to think things out and remember the details.

First of all he said that the piece of paper bearing Sir
Osmond's notes had fallen out of the *Tatler* as he was reading it and, thinking it was rubbish, he chucked it into the
fire. Later he said he'd like to withdraw that and tell the
truth. He gradually made a long statement. Sir Osmond,
he said, had talked to him on Tuesday evening and told him
he was going to make a new will, in which he intended to
leave Jennifer a large sum provided she was still unmarried
at the time of his death. The old man said that he did this
because he had plainly told Jennifer that he wanted her to
remain at home and he meant to make it worth her while
if she chose to obey his wishes. He also—he hinted—was
hoping that Jennifer's future husband would realize that it
was worth his while to wait for her. Sir Osmond suspected,
however, that Jenny intended to throw herself into the arms
of young Cheriton, and if she did so they would both see,

when he was dead, what fools they had been. He was telling Witcombe all this so that Witcombe might drop a few hints to Jenny and also, perhaps, to Cheriton. There was some idea, too, in Sir Osmond's mind, Witcombe thought, that he might thus be enlisted as Sir Osmond's ally in looking out for and frustrating any plan for elopement which Jenny and Cheriton might make.

Witcombe declared that he hadn't said a word about all this to any member of the family. He didn't think he could influence Jennifer and in any case he had had no opportunity as yet to discuss the matter with her. But at the end of his conversation with Sir Osmond, which took place in the study, the old man left the room first. Witcombe, politely standing aside, looked round at the table where they had been sitting and saw that the sheet of paper with names and figures on it had been left lying there. Under the impulse of curiosity Witcombe pocketed it. Sir Osmond had said nothing about his other legacies and Witcombe couldn't help wondering how they were planned. He confessed to Rousdon that it was "not quite above-board" to pick up the paper but seemed to think that his declared intention to return it to the study later purged his behaviour of real dishonesty.

He had studied the paper in his own room and had evidently gloated over his possession of information which members of the family had fished for in vain. He had put it away in his pocket book so that he could be ready to take any chance of slipping into the empty study and putting the paper in Sir Osmond's blotting pad. After the Christmas Day happenings he had forgotten it until he was harassed by Rousdon's questions. Then, he said, he asked himself what they had against him, and he remembered Sir Osmond's notes and felt uneasy about them because he had no business to be in possession of them, so decided to destroy them.

"I see now," he said to Rousdon, "I was very unwise not to hand the paper to you, in case you might know it was missing and be looking for it. But, of course, it's of no real importance now, because Sir Osmond hadn't made this will."

Witcombe's story was just credible, Rousdon thought. In any case, it didn't seem likely that he had stolen those notes from the dead man's pocket. As for the gloves, Rousdon agreed that they were not a very good piece of evidence. Witcombe said he had worn them to church on Christmas Day and had put them away in a drawer in his room; in the front of the drawer, he thought. Anyone could easily take them from there. Witcombe had apologized for the attack on Constable Mere, excusing it by saying he had been thoroughly startled when the man rushed at him, and didn't see that he was a policeman.

By the time all this had been thrashed out and Witcombe had divulged all that he admitted he knew, it was after midnight. Rousdon offered to send him back to Flaxmere but he was not at all keen to return and so had remained at the police station as a voluntary guest. He was sleeping what Rousdon regarded with some doubt as the sleep of the just when Rousdon looked in this morning, but would be sent back later in a police car.

The most important point in all this was Witcombe's statement that Sir Osmond had not executed the new will. Giving Rousdon the facts about the will, I pointed out that since Witcombe knew the state of affairs he could have no motive, either alone or in collaboration with Carol or even Jennifer, for murdering Sir Osmond. In fact, if he hoped to share either Jennifer's inheritance or Carol's he had every motive for keeping the old man alive.

Rousdon studied my notes of the provisions of the will and the proposed revision.

"Strikes me that Lady Evershot would be the person most likely to want to prevent that new will being made," he suggested. "Any possibility that Witcombe told her what her father meant to do?"

I thought it most improbable, though I still wasn't satisfied that Dittie had neither knowledge nor suspicion about the identity of the murderer.

Rousdon now told me the report of the finger-print expert. Jennifer's finger-prints were on the pistol, all over it, on the muzzle as well as the butt, but not on the trigger. There were no other prints on it at all. That was what I expected, remembering George's remarks which I heard through the telephone and her own admission that she had touched it.

"But why did she want to smear it all over like that?" Rousdon persisted. "Who did she think she was protecting? Strikes me we ought to look into Mr. Cheriton's movements more carefully."

The shutters showed the prints of the maid, Betty Willett, and Dittie had left her mark there too.

"Lady Evershot closed those shutters, I've no doubt," Rousdon said. "What's more, she either opened the window or tried to shut it. She's had her fingers on the bottom of the sash, as if she'd tried to pull it down. There were no marks on the upper part, where you'd naturally put your hands in pushing it open, so I should say it was opened by the murderer with those gloves on."

I asked if there were any sign of Sir David.

"Not a trace. Got a good record from his hair brush, but we can't match it anywhere."

So my idea that Sir David had climbed in by the study window out of curiosity was washed out. He would hardly have put on his gloves when he went out casually to cool his head on the drive, and bare-handed he could not have climbed in over the window-sill without leaving some mark.

But Dittie had been trying to protect someone; someone who, she thought, had used that window.

As Rousdon and I sat staring at each other glumly over these problems, there was a tap at the door and in walked Miss Portisham and George's son, Kit. The child strutted in, very pleased with himself, and yet a little nervous. I couldn't think for a moment what made him look so absurd. Of course, it was the eyebrows! He had tufts of bushy white hair stuck on to his brows, rather crookedly, one of them taking a satirical list towards his temple.

"I thought it only right," began Miss Portisham timidly, "to show you this—"

"What the—we're attending to serious business!" snorted Rousdon, furious at being interrupted by what he took to be a childish game.

"I've got Santa Klaus' eye-brushes!" piped Kit.

"He won't say where he found them," Miss Portisham continued plaintively; "but they weren't in the nursery and he's been routing about the house. I hope I did right to show you?"

"Where's the rest of the outfit?" I asked Rousdon. "You must have dropped these when you carried it away."

Rousdon got very red and looked as if he might burst. He shot out of his chair and charged into the study, where he dialled a telephone call to the police station and I heard him demanding that the blank blank idiot who had carried the Santa Klaus outfit from Flaxmere, to be preserved as "exhibit A," should come to the 'phone. Then he growled out a series of infuriated questions.

"You've got them there? Go and fetch them and bring them here—no! not *here*; to the 'phone; and let the Super tell me if you've really got 'em. You know the difference between eye-brows and a beard? Describe them! Now read me the list of the items of the costume originally collected from the drawing-room at Flaxmere. Did you ever see any other eye-brows? No, not growing on anyone's face, you blankety blank; any others like those you've got there, loose ones, lying about here at Flaxmere. You're dead sure? Hm!" He slammed the ear-piece on to its hook and returned to the library.

Whilst listening to this half of the lively dialogue in the next room, I was questioning Kit about where he had found the eye-brows, but I could get nothing out of the child. He, too, was interested in the telephone conversation and instead of answering me he cocked his head and jigged about from one foot to the other, exclaiming, "D'you hear him? Who's that man talking to? OO! I wish I could hear the other man!"

Rousdon stumped in, glared at Kit and suggested to him:

"Now, you be a good boy and tell me where you found those things!"

The child's face crumpled; he stammered, "I w-w-won't! I w-w-w-won't!" and began to yell.

Miss Portisham took him on her lap and tried to soothe him. He kicked at her viciously and yelled louder. I advised her to take him back to the nursery and see if the nurse could get anything out of him.

"And you might detach those things from his face and bring them back to us," Rousdon commanded. They departed.

"That's the first vestige of the second Santa Klaus costume," I told Rousdon. "I want two men to search the house thoroughly for the rest of it. If a child can find it, a policeman should be able to."

"They'll find it all right, if it's here," Rousdon snorted.

I thought that it must be here and probably downstairs. The outfit would be too bulky to be carried about unnoticed, the front staircases could hardly have been reached unobserved by anyone on the evening of the crime and access to the back staircase, which began near the door of the servants' hall, would be almost as difficult. Rousdon went off to give instructions for the search.

Miss Portisham returned with the eye-brows. "Kit had got hold of some gum they had been using to stick pictures in a scrap-book and stuck them on with that," she explained. "They weren't very tight. But really, Kit is a very difficult child. I'm sure I tried my best to get it out of him, but he won't say a word. You see, I was going upstairs after breakfast and there he was at the back of the hall, prancing about as pleased as Punch. I can't *think* where he found them. Really, I did what I thought was best but there's a terrible commotion upstairs with Kit howling himself into hysterics."

The library door swung open and in swept Patricia, now Lady Melbury.

"Really, Colonel Halstock, really, when the *children* are to be put through the fourth dimension or whatever you call it, and terrified, poor little things, out of their lives, really, it is *too* much! And, Miss Portisham, I think you are taking *too* much responsibility upon yourself! If you had brought the child to me I could have used my judgment as to how he should be treated. But really, without a word to his mother, to bring the child before strangers who have not the least idea how children should be dealt with, and to give him a shock from which his nervous system may *never* recover—!"

Poor Miss Portisham shrank; her lips trembled; she looked appealingly at me.

I did my best to mediate, trying to make Patricia see that Kit's eye-brows might be a very important clue, which it was essential to tell us about at once. I couldn't explain to her, of course, that once she had got hold of the boy and the eye-brows we could never have been sure whether he had really found them or when or where he had done so. In fact, she might easily have detached them and flung them into the nearest fire and we should have had only Miss Portisham's word for their existence. I did, however, impress upon Patricia that we must somehow find out where the child discovered those clues. I disguised my opinion that he was a spoilt little brat, howling out of sheer naughtiness, and expressed tender concern for the state of his nerves. Miss Portisham managed to melt away during this difficult conversation.

Before I had got rid of Patricia, Gordon Stickland sailed in, his smooth, pinkish face looking, as usual, as if it had been well polished. He was smiling and pleased with himself.

"Understand, Colonel, that you want to know where Kit unearthed those eye-brushes, as he calls 'em? He found 'em in the cupboard under the stairs, the little beggar! No business to be there, of course, routin' about in the dust, so he was scared to tell; but I got it out of him."

"Oh, Gordon!" Patricia reproached him. "Kit has been so dreadfully frightened already; I *do* hope you haven't upset him again. He's so highly strung, you know and I always say that *nothing* can be so important as the necessity to protect a child's nervous system; nothing in the world!"

"Now, Patricia, don't get all het up about him; he's right as rain; come and see for yourself. I just showed him a new game of hiding and finding and in the middle of it he told me all about the eye-brushes without any trouble. Come along now! That all right, Colonel?"

I thanked him for what he had done and—silently— for removing Lady Melbury. When they had gone off to the nursery, I went in search of Rousdon and together we inspected the cupboard under the stairs. It was a large, dark place, running in under the main flight of stairs and open-ing into the passage behind the hall. All sorts of oddments were stored there, old motor rugs, golf clubs, baskets, brown paper, hockey sticks, a croquet set. Rousdon called up one of his men who searched the place systematically with an electric torch—the cupboard had no light—but we found no trace of the rest of a Santa Klaus costume. Kit had a little torch of his own, we found, and probably he had selected the big cupboard as a suitable place in which to use it.

Rousdon dismissed the constable to continue the search of the rest of the house and we returned to the library to discuss the problem. The cupboard was obviously an ideal place for anyone to use as a dressing-room if he had to get into a Santa Klaus costume and out of it again without being seen and as near to the hall as possible. The gun room was conveniently close at hand, too. I cursed myself for not having searched the cupboard at the beginning but we had not guessed that there was anything to search for.

"He's got the stuff away out of the house, that's certain," Rousdon grumbled. "That's to say, if there really was a second outfit. We'd better make quite sure that those eyebrows weren't in the house beforehand, part of some acting properties."

We questioned Jennifer and Miss Portisham, and even George, with the idea that he might know of a theatrical property box which had been in the house before he married. They were all sure there had been nothing of the sort, and certainly we found nothing else in the cupboard or elsewhere to justify this idea. George declared bluffly that that sort of thing wasn't in his line. Jennifer said they had never done much acting except some impromptu charades organized by Philip Cheriton—who was rather a good actor—during the previous Christmas visit of the family. They had no special properties. Miss Portisham confirmed this. She remembered the theatricals last year and was quite sure that no one bought any properties beforehand. "It was because I was quite convinced that those eyebrows did not belong to the house that I brought them to you immediately, Colonel Halstock," she assured me, rather reproachfully.

"Now how did he get the stuff away?" Rousdon considered. The house had been thoroughly searched by now, without result. "My men have been here all the time and they've watched everyone who went in or out. By Jove! That open window! I always thought it was a bit pointless to open that heavy, noisy window just to throw away a key which need not have been thrown away at all. But supposing he wanted to hand the costume out to an accomplice who was waiting there—Sir David, in fact—who would get rid of it? Where would he get rid of it?"

"And what about the eyebrows? How did they get back to the cupboard—where presumably he originally dressed up?"

"Maybe he hadn't time to put on the eyebrows, or had forgotten the gum. Or else—yes! Snatching off the things in a hurry he might forget the eyebrows till Sir David was well away. Then he tears them off and skips round to that cupboard and chucks 'em in before he goes back to the hall. Pity he didn't forget 'em altogether! Now, let's consider Sir David; he hadn't much time; he was back in the drawing-room, or at any rate in the house, before the alarm was given."

"The pool!" I cried. I suppose it was in my mind because of my dream. "It would be a matter of a few minutes to run down the lawn, tie the things up in a bundle and sink them. Or would they float? A stone—there's the rock garden at the end of the pool—done up in the bundle, would do the trick. That bundle must be near the edge; we can find it."

For once Rousdon liked my idea. We were neither of us very satisfied with the casting of Sir David for the part of assistant, but it would be odd if there had been someone else hanging about near the study windows, whom Sir David had not seen.

"Seems to me that only another lunatic would take him in as accomplice!" Rousdon commented as he went to give orders for rakes and hoes to be collected from the gardener's shed, for poles to be bound to their handles to lengthen them, and for his men to start dragging all round the edges of the pool.

Chapter Fifteen

Dittie Explains

by Col. Halstock

The inquest held that Friday morning was a short formal affair at which George gave evidence of identity. The other members of the family, having been assured that no further details would be inquired into, were not present. The proceedings were adjourned to the following week, and Rousdon was able to return to see how his dragging operations were getting on.

I sent a message to Lady Evershot, asking her to come and speak to me in the library. I had not seen her since I had shared that uneasy lunch with the family the day before, and then she had sat at the other end of the table, between her husband and Kenneth Stour, very quiet and preoccupied but still a bit jumpy, I thought.

When she joined me in the library I remembered my wife's remarks yesterday. Dittie, I thought to myself, cannot be more than thirty-two, but one might have taken her for forty and not a very well preserved forty at that. She had never been so lovely as Eleanor, who had perfect features and the knack of always posing in a becoming attitude. But before the girls were married I had always considered Dittie the more attractive, because she was more lively and intelligent. Now, as my wife said, she had a hard look. There was something impersonal in her expression, and a tightness of the lips, a recklessness of make-up resulting in crudity, which would have justified a description of her as middle-aged and embittered.

I asked her to tell me again, very carefully, exactly what she had done on the afternoon of Christmas Day when she heard the news of the murder. To make it easy for her I said I realized that everyone was very upset when I questioned them that evening and might now be able to give clearer accounts of the events.

She sat in the chair opposite to me, her face in the full light of the window. Her hands were clasped in her lap and before she began to speak she clenched them more tightly and drew a deep breath, as if bracing herself for an effort. She looked past me, out of the window.

"I was sitting in the drawing-room with several of the others. I was on the *qui vive*, I suppose, because we were expecting a summons to the hall for the final scene of the Santa Klaus masquerade, as my father had planned it. Oliver Witcombe came in, in the Santa Klaus dress, looked round and went straight to George, who was twiddling the wireless knobs. I could see there was something wrong—no; don't ask me how I could see; it wasn't *seeing*, really of course; it was one of those occasions when one feels something tingling in the atmosphere. Oliver spoke to George in a low voice and I got up and joined them. I was sitting fairly near them. The others didn't seem to have noticed anything unusual. I suppose that, living with David, I've become specially sensitive to people's feelings. You know, I expect, that David is—well, unbalanced; badly shell-shocked. One must always be ready for an upset."

She had been talking almost as if I wasn't there; as if she were recalling the scene for purposes of her own. Now she paused and turned to me.

"I'm telling you as a friend, Colonel Halstock. I expect that's irregular. I know you're questioning me as Chief Constable. But I can explain things more easily like this, if you don't mind. I was stupid before, because I was—well—frightened, and so I was on my guard. I don't think I told you anything untrue but I didn't explain as much as I might have done. I'll try to make up for that. After the finger-print business yesterday, I realized that I should have to explain and I meant to, even if you hadn't asked me."

"Go on, Dittie. Tell me in your own way," I urged her. "Probably you all think me a tactless brute, but I'm doing my best to help you all and I'm most profoundly sorry for you all."

"Yes," Dittie agreed dreamily. "It's horrible." Then, suddenly, she asked: "You haven't got a policeman concealed anywhere, taking shorthand notes?"

I assured her that this was a private conversation, though if she told me anything that was of importance to the case, I might have to ask her to make a statement afterwards. She nodded and looked out of the window again and went on.

"I got to the point where I went up to George and Oliver in the drawing-room, to find out what was wrong. I'm trying to explain to you how it was that I reached the study before anyone else, as you probably know. I quickly gathered that something was seriously the matter, in the study. I didn't wait to hear details. George was beginning to fuss about what was to be done. I slipped away from the drawing-room and through the hall and into the library."

"You didn't go to the door that leads from the hall straight into the study?" I asked her.

Dittie turned to me with a look of faint surprise.

"No; I didn't. I don't quite know why, except that we often used that way through the library into the study. I found the study door locked, but the key was in it, so I opened it and went in. I saw my father—you know how he looked. I went up to his table to see just what had happened. There was a pistol lying on the table and just behind him was an open window. Of course, I thought—someone—had come in through the window and shot him. I couldn't think what to do; I felt I must do something, but my mind wouldn't work. I could only think of the window and I pulled at it, but it was stiff and I thought I had only a few minutes, so I closed and latched the shutters and as I turned round again the door opened and Hilda came in, and some others. Of course I see now that it was hopelessly silly; that if things had been as I thought, I had done nothing to help; nothing. But I couldn't think clearly."

She paused, but I judged that it was only to find words for the rest of her explanation. Soon she began to speak again, in a faint, strained voice.

"Colonel Halstock, I suppose you know what I thought and why I was so desperate. I had seen Kenneth on Monday at the Tollards. He didn't tell you because he guessed I hadn't mentioned it and he didn't want to make you think I was being secretive. No one else here knows that I was there, except David. We said we were going to lunch with the FitzPaines at Manton and David went there, but he dropped me at the Tollards. I simply had to see Kenneth. He had been in the States for a year and is only just back. I didn't want to tell the family and have a lot of gossip and all of them telling me what they think my duty is. I'd rather they didn't have to know."

I couldn't see that her visit to the Tollards affected the case, but I reminded her that any fact which was relevant couldn't be concealed.

"Yes, I know," Dittie said listlessly. "I've made up my mind to all that and I'll go through with it. You're wondering why David collaborated in this. It isn't easy to explain because David's character is so contradictory, but he is fond of me and he wants to keep me and yet he realizes that he's a pretty tough sort of husband. Yet we get on together on the whole and understand each other pretty well. He knows I'm fond of Kenneth and should manage to see Kenneth in any case, so he has the sense not to make a fuss about it. I can't bear hiding things and pretending and I'm always at my worst if I have to do it.

"Well, I talked to Kenneth on Monday and he asked me, not for the first time, to go away with him and leave David. I said I couldn't—not for any virtuous reason but because I am a coward. I am so desperately afraid of being poor—what I should call being poor, which is not being able to have every sort of convenience and to pay people to see to everything that's troublesome and to travel and run away from oneself. I know it's despicable, but those are the things that make life bearable. I suppose you can't believe that I'm really fond of Kenneth. He's rich now, I know, but the stage is so uncertain and actors, even successful ones, so often end in miserable poverty.

"It seemed to me that there were two possibilities. Either we stayed in London and I should be continually meeting David's friends, and Eleanor and her friends, and they would all think me a cad, and although I despise their opinions, I can't stand up against them. Or else we should go abroad—which Kenneth suggested—and then his career might go to bits and we should be poor. And, you see, I should be cut out of Father's will if I went off with Kenneth. That was certain, and I couldn't face losing what I felt I really had a right to and that meant so much to me. Comfort and security—they mean a terrible lot. I can't take risks. When I told Kenneth that, he said rather bitterly that after Father's death, when we might both be too old to care, he supposed I would go to him.

"When I saw the open window, I thought of that. Of course now I see that the idea was absurd, but I couldn't think. I was sure that Kenneth had shot my father; that made me his murderer, too, because I had given Kenneth the idea that it was the only way of getting me. I closed the shutters—when I couldn't shut the window—so that you wouldn't know anyone had come in from outside. When I saw Kenneth the next day, I thought he had rushed over to see if I had changed my mind about him. And I hadn't; that seemed, in a way, the most awful part of all. I had been awake all the night, thinking over the situation. Father was dead; I should probably be pretty well off. It would be *safe* to go away with Kenneth. Yes, I'm a coward; I wouldn't risk anything; I had to be safe. And yet I knew I still wouldn't go. It wasn't just people's opinions; it's horrible to feel that everyone is despising you, but I could get away from them. It's—it's just David." Her voice broke. Her eyes were shining and a tear trickled down one cheek. "He's so dependent on me. If he was more of a brute I could leave him. The story of inherited lunacy, by the way, is all bunk. He's just neurotic, through shell-shock. But it's not his fault. It would be so horribly mean to leave him, when I'm the one person who can be of help to him. Oh, do you understand?"

She dropped her head, propping her forehead in one hand, to hide her face, while she dabbed at her tears.

I thought I did understand. While she had been rather morbidly proclaiming her cowardice and worldliness as the reason for her refusal to run away with Stour, it was really a very honourable determination to stand by her husband and give him what help she could.

I tried to comfort her and told her that she had explained a good deal, but I wanted to ask her a few questions. To begin with, what had convinced her that Kenneth was not the murderer? Had she lighted upon some clue?

"No," she told me. "We're all utterly in the dark. I wish you could get to the bottom of it—well; I suppose I do; but of course we're all frightened of what the solution may be. Not that we have any definite suspicion, but just that it's all such a wretched mess. Kenneth explained that he couldn't have done it; I could see he was speaking the truth and there must be a dozen people who can witness that he was at the Tollards' party all that afternoon. You must know that, of course."

I asked her if she had never suspected Sir David. She turned to me in amazement.

"David! But why should he? Surely *you* don't think David did it? He couldn't have any motive at all! Besides, if he did anything so frightful, he couldn't keep it to himself. I should know something was wrong."

I asked her what she could remember about her husband's movements that afternoon.

"David was certainly in the library at first and he went out and came back after about ten minutes. He told me afterwards that he went out of the front door to get some air. I've known him do that before, and he probably wanted to get away from the noise of the crackers; he can't stand bangs. I had asked Father not to have crackers, because of that, and he had promised that there shouldn't be any, so I was surprised when I heard them. But I thought he had just decided, as usual, that my fussiness ought not to be taken into account."

"Do you remember just who was in the library when Witcombe came in?" I asked.

"Oh yes, because I looked round before I left. I think I was trying to guess how they would all behave and what sort of a fuss there would be. I think I told you on Christmas Day that I couldn't remember. It was true—then; I couldn't bring my mind to bear on anything except what I thought Kenneth had done and how I could protect him. But I'm sure, now, that Gordon was there, with Shakespeare and the *Times* crossword."

"Shakespeare?" I inquired, taking him for a hitherto unmentioned guest.

"Yes, Shakespeare's works," Dittie explained, with a hint of a smile. "There was a special crossword, with all the clues taken from the plays. George was there, as you know. David was there, too; he had come back. And when he came back he was quite calm and undisturbed. That would show that he couldn't have done anything frightful when he went out, or even have known about it. I don't think there was anyone else. Patricia and Eleanor had gone into the hall when the crackers began and Aunt Mildred had gone to fetch her knitting."

"Miss Melbury hadn't come back?" I asked.

"No, I'm sure she didn't come back."

"And Philip Cheriton?" I asked.

"No, he wasn't there at all, nor Jennifer."

I asked if she could remember who was in the hall, but she shook her head. "I went straight through; there were the children and several others, but I didn't really notice. I don't think I can tell you anything else."

I asked her one more question. Had there been any talk about a new will which Sir Osmond may have made or may have intended to make? Did she think her father had confided in anyone his intended method of dividing his property?

"I'm sure he hadn't told any of us. We all had suspicions that Miss Portisham knew all about it, but of course we could hardly ask her. There was a great deal of talk; the others were always worrying about what Father would leave them. Oh, yes! I was too; I was just as bad as the others; worse, perhaps. But we none of us knew a thing, and we don't know yet."

I thought she was speaking the truth. Just before she went out she turned and said:

"I'm glad to have got this off my chest. You and your wife were always nice to me. I'm glad you know all this. I've had a pretty awful time, but somehow it's a relief to know how I stand. I always thought that Father's death might make a difference, and now I see that it doesn't, and I know I've just got to stay as I am and stick it out. I've made up my mind to it now."

Poor Dittie! It was a pretty grim prospect, I thought, tied to that morose unbalanced husband. But perhaps, if she could make a job of it, it would be a finer thing than a runaway match with Kenneth Stour.

I was trying to convey this idea to Dittie when we heard a timid knock at the door. I called "Come in!" and Miss Portisham appeared and immediately withdrew in a fluster of apology. Dittie hurried out after her and sent her in. She was carrying a wad of typewritten sheets clipped together.

"I hope I did right to bring this to you, Colonel Halstock?" she inquired. I had forgotten for the moment about what Kenneth called the homework, and I looked surprised.

"My account of the events of—of that terrible day," she explained. "I do hope it is what you require. I tried my best, as you said, to write just as if nothing had happened. I am afraid you may find that much of what I have put down is trivial, but of course, it is so hard to judge. I did my best to put down just what I saw and noticed."

Having those neatly typed sheets in my hand, I could not refrain from sitting down to glance through them and see if any significant facts were embedded there. I skipped over a good deal of wordy explanation at the beginning and through what seemed the unimportant events of the morning of Christmas Day, until the sentence, *Sir Osmond then told me he was going to the study*, caught my eye. I read on, and so came to the astounding evidence of the anonymous letter. I think I let out some sudden exclamation of amazement, for I heard a little startled squeak from Miss Portisham and realized that she was still standing there, evidently uncertain whether she had been dismissed or not.

"It's this typewritten letter with no signature which Sir Osmond received on—when was it—Christmas morning," I explained. "It may be important. Why haven't we heard of it before?"

"Really, I didn't know that it was important. Everything is so—so—unusual. I find it very difficult, Colonel Halstock, to judge what it is right to do. In the ordinary way, of course, I should never have mentioned that letter to anyone, it being evidently Sir Osmond's private business. I was not asked about it, of course, and really it did not come into my mind until I came to write this account, when it struck me that it might have some bearing on the case, though of course, that is only my idea. I hope I did right to mention it now? I should not like to feel I have been guilty of any breach of confidence."

I wondered what more the girl might have locked away in her confidential safe deposit of a mind, but apparently there was nothing else that she could think of, that she had not mentioned in the account. The facts about the typewritten note seemed to be that Miss Portisham had found it on the hall table, where letters and papers were usually put, and had brought it to Sir Osmond. She assumed that it had come by hand because it had no stamp or postmark, but she did not know who had brought it. It was in an envelope of ordinary kind; in fact, similar to some which were kept in the study and generally used by her for Sir Osmond's business letters.

After Sir Osmond had read the letter, he had looked at the envelope rather carefully and had then torn it across and thrown it into the waste-paper basket. The letter he had folded and put in his breast-pocket. Miss Portisham had observed that it was typed on a small sheet of white paper, which also was similar to some kept in the stationery rack on her typewriting table in the study, though she could not be sure that it was exactly the same. He had made no comment on reading the letter, "except a sort of *Hm!*"

"Do you think it had been written on your typewriter?" I asked her.

"Oh, Colonel Halstock, I never thought of such a thing! I naturally thought the letter was brought to the house by someone, who wrote it to make an appointment of some sort; an arrangement to telephone to Sir Osmond at a stated time, I supposed."

"He didn't say anything about a telephone call?"

"Oh, no. I just thought it must be a telephone call; that seemed most likely. And of course no visitor did come."

"Nor did any telephone call come through, as far as we know," I pointed out.

Miss Portisham had last used her typewriter on the morning of the day before Christmas (Tuesday). She had not looked at it after that, she was sure, until she took it away from the study on Boxing Day. The study had been empty on Tuesday afternoon, when Sir Osmond had taken Kit and Enid for a walk and Miss Portisham herself had been busy about the house with arrangements for Christmas Day. She didn't know if any members of the family could type, excepting Jennifer, who had once asked Miss Portisham to show her and had practised occasionally. "Of course, she had not attained any speed," Miss Portisham explained condescendingly; "but she understood how to work the machine and how to open it and put the cover back. She would never have left it as we found it, with the cover not properly fastened." Mr. Cheriton could type and had once, on a previous visit, borrowed the machine for some work of his own. He also knew how to put the cover on, Miss Portisham was sure. She did not know whether any of the others had ever used a typewriter.

It struck me that amongst the uninitiated, rather than amongst the practised typists, we should seek the writer of the anonymous letter who had failed to replace the cover properly. Anyone could open the machine and pick out a few words on the keys. I dismissed Miss Portisham and went to tell Rousdon of the latest clue. I warned her not to touch the typewriter again, but feared it was now too late to identify any finger-prints left by the unknown typist.

Remembering that George had spoken very definitely of that expected telephone call, I interrupted him in a gloomy examination of some of his father's papers, and asked him just what he really knew about it. Blandly he admitted that he knew nothing at all. He had heard someone, Miss Portisham probably, say that Sir Osmond was expecting a telephone call and had assumed that it must be so and had, with a great effort of his generally limited imagination, further supposed that his father had arranged for the call himself. I couldn't make him realize that he was definitely misleading us in giving "information" of this sort. He maintained that he had it from a reliable source and so he "knew" it perfectly well—until it turned out that what he knew was wrong.

"We all make mistakes," said George, "but Miss Portisham, the lady who is always right, seems to have made this one. No use blaming me. Might as well blame me for putting my money on a dead cert. that ties his legs in a knot. It's not my fault."

I had to leave it at that.

Chapter Sixteen

The "Homework"

by Col. Halstock

It was now past midday, with a gleam of sunshine brightening the wintry garden; most of the Flaxmere party had strolled out to see what was going on down by the pool. There was no sign of Jennifer or Miss Melbury, but Eleanor, wrapped in furs, was seated becomingly on a bench and Sir David hung over the back of it, inspecting the procedure morosely and conjecturing, as I passed by, that they were "hoping to hook the missing murderer, I suppose!" Patricia, also in furs, fussed about amongst the children on the edge of the pool, whilst Gordon Stickland made a fool of himself, prancing on the end of the diving board, to amuse the children, who skipped about delightedly. Carol came racing down a path, her golden hair tossing, with Kit in chase. Kit informed me in a shrill squeak that they were fishing for Santa Klaus' beard. Carol greeted me cheerfully. She is one of those girls who always give the impression of being well turned out, though one knows she has very little money to do it on. She favours a tailor-made style, which my wife tells me is the most difficult to do cheaply, but she has one of those slick, lithe figures which clothes seem to mould themselves on to.

I detached Rousdon from supervision of the dragging operations and strolled with him round to the far side of the pool. He told me that although they had been dragging for an hour and had brought up a miscellaneous catch, including a thermos flask and a roll of camera film, they had found nothing that seemed to have even a remote connection with Santa Klaus.

I asked him to send one of his men to secure Miss Portisham's typewriter and test it thoroughly for finger-prints, though there seemed little hope now of finding any other than her own. I told him that I had elicited information from her about the typewritten letter, but I did not let him know about her written account, which I meant to keep to myself, because it was somewhat unorthodox. It seemed that the finger-print expert who had gone over the study had ignored the typewriter, concentrating chiefly on Sir Osmond's table and the window and the things in that corner of the room.

"There's something I don't like about this," said Rousdon. "She gets hold of the typewriter on some pretence of having work to do, dabs her fingers all over the cover on the excuse of showing you how the thing should be fitted on, and when all is made safe, then she remembers to tell you about the typewritten note."

"But since the thing hasn't turned up, she could easily have avoided telling me at all," I pointed out. "That, by the way, is what the murderer was searching for in Sir Osmond's pockets presumably, and it's not likely that we shall ever see it now."

Rousdon said he would himself make inquiries about the possibility of the letter having been delivered at the house, but we didn't hope for much from that direction.

"Look here!" he exclaimed. "Someone might write and say he had important information to give, which he wanted to give secretly, and ask Sir Osmond to be in his study and open the window, to provide an unseen entrance!"

I thought that too theatrical. Why shouldn't the unknown ask Sir Osmond to meet him outside the house, instead of risking himself in the house. Moreover, if the murderer was already in the house—which the pistol from the gun-room suggested—why should he take the suspicious and dangerous course of going outside and entering again by a window. True, Sir David did seem to have left the house unseen, but he couldn't have been sure of doing so. And could anyone be sure that Sir Osmond would agree to such a hare-brained plan and leave the window open?

I left Rousdon and strolled away from the pool, along the paved path under the study windows to the yard at the back, which was surrounded by the garages and various outbuildings. I wanted to make a survey of other possible hiding-places, as we seemed to be drawing blank at the pool.

Bingham was cleaning the Sunbeam in the yard. He looked up from his work on the radiator and inquired, "Found anything yet, sir?"

The discovery of the eyebrows was common knowledge and those who had quickly guessed that we were now hunting for a second Santa Klaus costume had not been slow to tell everyone else.

"It's my belief, sir—a-course, speakin' as a amatewer-like—that the stuff 'as bin got away from 'ere," Bingham proclaimed. "You won't find it, sir; though a-course I 'opes as you may."

I wondered if the man knew anything and to sound him I suggested that there hadn't been much chance for anyone to take anything away from Flaxmere.

"There's tradesmen's vans, sir—" he hazarded.

178 Mavis Doriel Hay

"I hardly think a tradesman would keep silent if he discovered a Santa Klaus outfit, complete except for a pair of eyebrows, in his van," I pointed out.

"Well, mebbe no!" Bingham agreed sadly. He scratched his head and considered. "A-course there was Ashmore with 'is car on Christmas Day. 'E's a good sort orlright, sir, is 'ole Ashmore; do anythink for the fambly, 'e would, an' I'm sorry for a man like 'im wot's down on 'is luck, on'y through bein' a bit outer date, as it were. I don' bear 'im any ill will, though I've got 'is job. But if someone was to arst 'im to take away a little bundle an' nothin' said; well, sir, would 'e refuse—'im not knowin' there was anythink wrong? Drop it in the river mebbe, 'e would, orf that suspension bridge. I don't want to barge in, sir," he added hastily; "mebbe I've said too much; it just come to me, like. I don' suppose there's anythink in it, but a-course we're all thinkin' where that stuff coulder got to and the idear jus' come to me."

"No harm in telling me, though I don't honestly think there's much in the idea. And you'd better not repeat it to anyone else. It might be a case of slander, you know." I didn't want the man to go prowling about sowing unfounded suspicions about poor old Ashmore. "You didn't see anything suspicious, I suppose? Didn't see him talking to anyone outside the house that afternoon?"

"Not me, sir! Ashmore was there in the servants' hall along of us all, and we got the news that there was something up and Ashmore, 'e said 'e'd better be orf an' orf 'e went. An' mind you, sir, I wouldn't say anythink aginst 'im, not for anythink. If 'e 'ad any 'and in this, it was unknowin'-like, you may be sure."

When I returned to the house, Parkins was beating the gong for lunch and as soon as this important ceremony was over, he came up to me and announced:

"Miss Melbury's compliments, sir, and this, sir, is what you were wishing for, and if you would like to speak to her, she is alone in the drawing-room. I was to tell you as soon as you came in, sir. And, excuse me, sir"—he surveyed me anxiously with his watery eyes—"I suppose there's no news from the pool? That is to say, sir, nothing that you would be able to tell us?"

I told him there was nothing to report at present and then on a sudden inspiration I asked him a question. I was almost surprised to hear myself ask it, but I had been thinking a good deal about Carol and what she had really been doing on Christmas afternoon and had realized that I filled in from my own imagination one part of the picture for which evidence was available.

"Who did you tell me, Parkins, was with Miss Carol in Miss Jennifer's room on Christmas afternoon, when you delivered the message from Ashmore?"

Parkins looked a little surprised. "Why, Mr. Cheriton, I believe, sir; but I may be wrong there, sir, because he was in the arm-chair with his back to me, and I saw little more than the top of his head and had no cause to notice particularly, sir. If I am wrong about that, sir, I wouldn't wish it to cause any inconvenience, because it's hard to identify a gentleman, sir, to swear to him, as the saying is, from the top of his head."

"Quite so, Parkins; don't worry about it."

He departed sadly.

The object which he had delivered to me with Miss Melbury's compliments was a flat brown paper parcel. I sought out Miss Melbury in the drawing-room, glad that the summons of the gong might help to curtail our interview.

"I see you have not yet had time to examine my little offering," she began. "I hope that it may be the means of directing your inquiries along more fruitful avenues. Of course, I am not a *trained* observer, but I flatter myself that I do not remain in ignorance of what goes on around me, and I have endeavoured to set down in those pages the result of my quiet observations, so that you may draw your own conclusions. Of course, what I have written is *confidential*; I have been frank, as you will see; nothing, I may say, would have persuaded me to be so frank but the conviction that my statements may be of some little help to you. Of course I have refrained from drawing any inferences; that is not for me to do. But we cannot help having our own thoughts; they may be mistaken; I always realize that I *may* be mistaken, though I do not think I often am when the motives or intentions of those I know well are in question. Of course, when the *denouement* of this terrible affair is reached, I do not ask for any credit; I prefer to remain in the background; the limelight is not for an old woman like me. The private knowledge that I have done my poor best to assist will be sufficient reward."

I hardly knew how to reply to this harangue. The old woman, sitting up very primly in a straight-backed arm-chair, looked so self-satisfied and so disagreeable. She was rather a big, stout woman with an insignificant nose, a long upper lip and a discontented mouth. It was just as well that I had not even unpacked her manuscript before I saw her, because when I had read its venomous insinuations and its accusations so vague as to be easily disclaimed if they proved wrong, I was in no mood to be polite to the author. As it was I managed to mumble thanks and gratitude and withdrew.

By my own request I had a luncheon tray in the library to-day, with Rousdon, who was already wolfing small jam tarts in great crumby mouthfuls when I arrived. He reported that the pool was a wash-out. They had been all round the banks and he felt sure that no one could hurl an awkward bundle of that kind very far out, especially in the dark, when you couldn't risk getting too near the slippery edge. We decided to search the outbuildings thoroughly. They could be quickly reached from the study window by the paved path, and although Bingham had told me that the garage doors were always locked when the car was put away, to prevent people from borrowing his tools, there was a shed where firewood was stored, the door of which, I had noticed, was only fastened with a catch.

After explaining this, I mentioned Bingham's suggestion.

"No flies on that young man!" Rousdon remarked. "That car of Ashmore's was standing in the garage yard, even handier than the shed for anyone wanting to get rid of a bundle. I've worried all along about that car. It might be a coincidence, him being here, but it looks nasty to me. And the way he took himself off as soon as he heard something was up!"

"I don't believe the old man would lend himself to help in the murder of his old master, even if he did feel a bit sore about the way he had been treated," I pointed out. I knew vaguely that Sir Osmond had not been generous to his former chauffeur.

"Ah!" said Rousdon. "But he didn't have to know it was murder. He might even think it was some sort of practical joke. Someone ought to see the man. Bristol, isn't it? I'll ring up and get them to make inquiries."

I urged him to tell the Bristol police not to frighten Ashmore. If he was concerned and had been ignorant of what he was really doing, he was probably in a blue funk by now. If any member of the family was involved, his loyalty to them might well keep him from reporting to the police. If he were bullied he would probably insist that he knew nothing. So we asked that a plain-clothes man should be sent to interview Ashmore tactfully and to make sure that, in case it turned out that he had no part in the plot, his reputation was not injured by general knowledge that "the police had an eye on him."

Having done this, Rousdon began to doubt the possibility of Ashmore having had anything to do with the plan.

"Seems a risky game!" he meditated. "Could they rely on him to keep quiet when he realized what he was mixed up in? He may have been heavily bribed. Anyway, we'll begin to search the garden and outbuildings while we're waiting to hear from Bristol."

He flicked the crumbs of pastry from his mouth and left me to finish my lunch. I settled down to study Miss Portisham's and Miss Melbury's "homework." The latter was a discouraging collection of sheets of Flaxmere embossed notepaper, covered on both sides with spiky script which was thick with effacements and alterations. I was surprised to find a good deal about Eleanor and, groping through this to discover its significance, if any, I came across one of the few definite statements of fact in the whole effusion, the record of a conversation overheard between Gordon and Eleanor in Sir Osmond's study on Tuesday afternoon. The actual words seemed to me unimportant, though Miss Melbury evidently intended me to find some sinister significance in them, but the fact that Gordon was in that room, where the typewriter was kept, might be important.

Gordon and Eleanor seemed the most unlikely people to have any hand in the murder. They would be losers, to a comparatively small extent, under the revised will, and Gordon Stickland, the astute business man, was just the one to know accurately, if anyone did, the fact that the revisions were merely proposals, which might yet be prevented from becoming fact. But Dittie had now declared that Gordon was occupied with Shakespeare in the drawing-room during the important time on Christmas afternoon. Eleanor had gone out into the hall. But Eleanor? Gentle, rather characterless, rather brainless, Eleanor? No, it wouldn't do.

However, to clear the matter up I went in search of Gordon Stickland and found him in the drawing-room trying to spur a bored audience to interest in another of the diversions which the *Times* of Boxing Day had benevolently provided to fill in the two blank days before its readers could again be regaled with real news. Only Miss Melbury was getting worked up about the correct order of precedence for an unlikely collection of distinguished personages.

George was grumbling, "None of us is ever going to entertain that lot at once, so why bother?"

When I had detached Gordon and was taking him off, Eleanor remarked sweetly, "I'm so grateful to you for removing my husband, Colonel Halstock. He's really too frightful when he comes over all highbrow, like this."

"I have information," I told Gordon, when we were alone in the library, "that you were in the study on Tuesday afternoon. Did you happen to go there to type a letter?"

He laughed genially. "No, no, Colonel! I *can* pick out a tune on the machine, mind you, with one finger, but I don't do it for fun. If I wanted something typed I should ask the admirable amanuensis."

I asked him if he had noticed the typewriter at all, but could get nothing out of him on this point. No one else had been in the study, except for Eleanor, who had followed him in. He had expected to find Sir Osmond, had gone in to see him, but the room was empty.

"You want to know what I was trying to get hold of Sir Osmond alone for? In fact someone, who overheard a bit of what we said before the door was shut, has reported some incriminating conversation? I don't know what they have told you, and I can't remember exactly what words we used, but we certainly didn't refer to the typewriter, neither to the machine nor to its seductive operator! It's a bit awkward. I'm not keen for the others to know this, as you'll understand. The late Lady Melbury had some fine jewels, in particular some emeralds. I'm a bit of a connoisseur and Sir Osmond once showed me those stones. I believe she left them all for him to dispose of at his discretion, and although he gave some to the girls, he still had a good many. I was particularly anxious for Eleanor to have those emeralds. Both she and I would appreciate them and you'll not find anyone who could wear them to better advantage. You'll admit that, I think?"

I agreed that Eleanor would look lovely in emeralds and emeralds lovely on Eleanor, and wondered if I was going to be told that Sir Osmond had them in his breast-pocket on Christmas Day.

"I had told Eleanor," Gordon continued, "that I meant to ask Sir Osmond, on this visit, if he would now give those emeralds to her. Fact of the matter is, I was a bit afraid he might do something foolish about them; might get an idea, you know, that emeralds would look well with auburn hair. Sheer waste! That girl would be better pleased with something from the synthetic diamond store.

"Eleanor didn't want me to speak to her father. She was afraid we'd lose the treasure for good if we seemed too eager for it. Eleanor and I aren't often at loggerheads, but she couldn't see eye to eye with me over this. I felt sure that if I caught the old man in the right mood, he'd be delighted to hand them over to his favourite daughter. That's what I was seeking him out in the study for on Christmas Eve. I thought I'd given Eleanor the slip, but she had chosen to make a great cause of this affair and was keeping an eye on me and followed me. So that's how it all came about."

There wasn't much more. The emeralds were kept in the safe, he believed. He hadn't seen them on his visit and he never got another opportunity to speak to Sir Osmond about them. He only hoped that when the will was read it would turn out that the testator had done the right thing about them.

We did later on check the valuables in the safe and the emeralds were snug in their case.

When I was alone in the library again, I turned my attention to Miss Portisham's neat typescript. The girl had obviously made a great effort to remember every detail correctly and it seemed to me that she had remembered far too many.

The first point I noted as important was that apparently two Santa Klaus costumes had been ordered, of which the first never turned up. Miss Portisham's description of the family's behaviour when the alarm was given, I found interesting, but I noted no special facts until I got to the end of her story. The order in which people arrived in the study or library might tell us something, I thought. It was: Dittie, Hilda, Witcombe, Miss Portisham, George, Jennifer—who all entered the study. Then into the library came Eleanor and Gordon, Witcombe (again; he having gone out into the hall, apparently, to tell the others) and Miss Melbury, and Patricia. Then there was a pause and, last of all, Carol "sort of burst in," followed by Philip Cheriton.

So Parkins had not delivered Ashmore's message to Carol until everyone else had heard the news and flocked into the library. That bore out what the butler himself had said. Also he was clearly not mistaken in thinking he had seen Philip Cheriton in Jenny's room with Carol. In any case, there was little possibility of a mistake, for Cheriton has thick, black, unruly hair, unlike that of anyone else in the house. Witcombe's hair is fair and neatly waved, Sir David's is thin and dusty-looking, Gordon has a bald patch and George has a very closely-clipped head.

While I was wondering what sort of a plot could possibly have been hatched between Carol, Philip and Witcombe, Witcombe himself put an inquiring head round the door. I knew he had returned to Flaxmere early that morning, but he seemed to have lain very low since then and I had not seen him. He grinned his silly grin at me.

"May I come in, Colonel? I've thought of something I'd like to tell you. It's a bit hard, you know, to think out the reasons for things when they're sprung upon you, the way your Inspector fellow sprung that one on me yesterday about the hairs on Sir Osmond's coat. Of course, I'd never thought of it before; didn't know there *were* any hairs on his coat; so how could I explain them? But lying on my little prison bed last night, I thought the whole thing over. Great place for thinking, a solitary cell! Of course, when they took the coat off the poor fellow's body, they folded it up! I left a little nest of bunny hairs on one side, and they spread all over the place. They stick to anything they touch! So that's all right, isn't it?"

I said guardedly that it might be.

"And there's another thing! Of course we all know what you're looking for and I saw it!"

This staggered me, but I asked him to explain exactly what he saw.

"Why, a whole Santa Klaus outfit, the exact image of the one I wore!"

I nearly went off the deep end at that. The house seemed to be full of lunatics who never gave away anything they knew until it was just too late. But I did manage to tell the fool to explain himself.

"I saw it in the mirror," he told me. "I didn't grasp the idea at the time; thought I was seeing myself, though it did seem a bit odd. Thought it must be some scientific trick to do with refracted light and it occurred to me that we might make a good game of it later on. Angles and rays and that sort of business."

With great difficulty I brought him back to the point and drew out of him that as he left the hall to take the presents to the servants and crossed the passage he approached a big mirror which is fastened to the wall opposite to the door of the cupboard under the stairs. In this mirror he saw for a moment the reflection of a Santa Klaus, who immediately slipped away "out of the side of the mirror, y'know!"

"I thought it was a bit rum and I walked backwards and tried again, but I couldn't catch the reflection a second time," he explained. "But I've been experimenting since I came back, and if someone stands just in the dining-room doorway, and you come out of the hall and cross the passage to the opposite door, you catch a glimpse of him when you're almost up to the mirror."

I took Witcombe to the passage and he showed me what he meant. The passage is lighted by windows high up in the wall which separates it from the hall, and if its own electric light is not switched on, it is gloomy. A man lurking silently in the doorway of the dining-room, at the end of the passage, would probably be unseen by anyone crossing the passage to go to the servants' quarters. If the murderer, rigged up as a duplicate Santa Klaus, had waited there to make sure that Witcombe had left the hall before he entered it, he forgot the tell-tale mirror which revealed him just for an instant, before he slipped away.

"You didn't go to the dining-room, I suppose," I asked Witcombe, "to see if there really was anyone else about?"

"It never entered my head that there could be another one! I was sure that I'd seen myself, only I didn't quite make out how it happened. You see, Carol came out of the other corner while I was experimenting, and then I forgot all about it."

"What do you mean by *out of the other corner?*"

"From somewhere behind me, to my left. From Jenny's room, I suppose. She called out to me and I turned to talk to her and forgot all about my ghost."

I remarked that he seemed to have forgotten a great deal.

"You're right there, Colonel," he agreed amiably. "I had

such a shock when I found the corpse in the study that my mind went blank. It's all coming back now."

Nothing else of any importance seemed to have "come back," however, so I returned alone to the library.

Again the clues were leading unpleasantly to Carol. At the moment when Witcombe might have discovered the second Santa Klaus, Carol—after perhaps having helped that second one to dress up—distracts Witcombe's attention and saves the situation. Having kept him talking for a few minutes, she sees him safely on his way to the servants' hall and then waits in Jenny's room—for the return of the murderer? And who did join her in that room? Philip Cheriton who, whatever he knew or did not know of the will, had strong motives for murdering Sir Osmond. Perhaps, after all, Witcombe had begun to drop a few hints about Sir Osmond's proposed new will; not quite the hints Sir Osmond intended, but a suggestion to Carol that she was going to gain substantially. If she misunderstood him and thought that her grandfather had already executed a will leaving £25,000 to her and £50,000 to Jenny, providing she were still single, she might plan to draw in Philip as accomplice. By one shot he could win Jenny and a fortune and, incidentally, help Carol to another one. They would not bring Jenny into the plot. Even if she could be capable of such villainy, her naïve, emotional character was not the stuff of which murderers are made. But she might well suspect that something was wrong and if she had guessed enough to jump to the conclusion that Philip had fired the pistol, that would account for her handling of it to blot out his finger-prints.

Jennifer's room seemed to offer a possible means of getting the Santa Klaus outfit away from the house. Opening, as it did, into the passage, it was freer from observation than other parts of the house. If Philip had put on the costume in the cupboard where it had been kept ready, he may have forgotten the eyebrows and left them there; he could have returned to Jennifer's room to change. Or possibly he changed again in the cupboard, picked up the things and took them to Jennifer's room and never noticed that he had left the eyebrows in a dark corner. We must survey the garden outside Jennifer's windows for a possible hiding-place.

I had reached this point in my speculations when Kenneth Stour appeared, with an untidy mass of manuscript, which he dumped on the table in three heaps labelled on top sheets in his own handwriting: *Cheriton, Mrs. Wynford,* and *Jennifer Melbury.*

"I sat with Jennifer in her room most of the time while she wrote hers," he informed me, "to make sure there was no collaboration between her and young Cheriton. But they are in no mood to collaborate. I suppose you've noticed the coldness between them? They are hardly on speaking terms. I'm sorry for little Jenny. Philip sat up most of the night over his little effort, I gather, and delivered it as soon as I arrived this morning. It doesn't tell us very much, I'm afraid, except how unfair the family always is and always has been to Dittie. Dittie's so confoundedly honest and that's not a quality which most Melburys can understand."

"I have noticed that they have little use for the truth," I agreed.

"I'm almost sorry I asked them to write the beastly things," Kenneth continued. "But here they are. I haven't had time to read Jennifer's and Mrs. Wynford's thoroughly, but I have extracted one bit of information. The Santa Klaus affair was planned in the week before Christmas and an outfit was sent for, which was expected by post on Saturday but didn't arrive. That is to say, no one admits to knowing it arrived. It may have come, though not necessarily on Saturday. I don't know whether any members of the household, besides Jennifer, knew of the plan, but evidently most of the visitors didn't know of it until Monday morning, when Jennifer told them."

Casually I asked him if he had worked out exactly who was at Flaxmere then.

"Yes; I've got a note of the order in which they came; Aunt Mildred on Friday; Hilda and Carol by train on Saturday morning, met at the station by Ashmore; George and family by car on Saturday evening; Dittie and David by car on Sunday; Eleanor and family on Monday morning by train, also met by Ashmore; Cheriton on Monday afternoon and Witcombe on Tuesday morning."

I flicked over the leaves of Jennifer's story as he talked, and Carol's name jumped up at me from the third or fourth page. Jennifer "knew Carol had some shopping of her own to do in Bristol" on Monday morning. I felt an intense distaste for all Kenneth's ridiculous homework idea and I picked up the whole mass, including Miss Melbury's and Miss Portisham's compositions, and handed it to him, telling him to take the lot and go away and work through it.

"It's about time I left Flaxmere," he agreed cheerfully. "Old George is beginning to wonder what on earth I am and if they forget their own troubles sufficiently to get really inquisitive, they'll give Dittie hell. I'll go home to the Tollards and work though this stuff systematically. I'm getting the germ of an idea but there are blank spots in my knowledge and I may want a good deal from you."

I reflected that I might cope with him better when he had been chastened by reading Miss Melbury's sketch of his character, so I told him to drive to Twaybrooks and invite himself to dinner and I would talk to him afterwards. He went to borrow from Jenny a dispatch case in which to cart the manuscript about and then he took himself off.

Chapter Seventeen

Jennifer

by Col. Halstock

I thought I would take a look at Jennifer's room and see what hiding-place was suggested by the garden outside the windows. Jenny's own voice invited me in when I knocked. A litter of paper on a table and a waste-paper basket beside it, full of sheets of paper crushed into tight balls, indicated that she had only just finished her "homework" and presumably Kenneth had brought it to me straight from her room. Jennifer herself was sitting in a low basket-chair by the fire and as I came in, her attitude and expression of expectancy relaxed into indifference and she threw herself back listlessly. She looked pale and tired and almost plain. Her prettiness depended so much on her youth and health and her usual vivacity and, perhaps, I thought to myself, on her charming, frivolous, frocks. She was wearing something very severe and of dark colour, which made her look older.

I told her I wanted to know exactly why she had picked up the pistol which had been used to shoot her father and had handled it so lavishly.

She sighed and stared at the fire. I looked at the fire myself. That's another thing that would make this room useful to the murderer, I thought. A fire in which to destroy an incriminating note! I strolled across to the french-window at the end of the room, which opened on to a terrace, below which was the rose garden. Jennifer began to speak, in an artificially cheerful voice.

"It was silly of me but, you see, I thought for a moment that Philip must have shot Father. I had absolutely no *reason* for thinking it." She turned round in her chair and looked at me anxiously. "He hadn't said anything to me suggesting such a thing, and I hadn't seen anything to make me think he could have done it. But of course—well, you know I want to marry Philip and Father was against it, and it was all so complicated. When I saw Father dead, like that, I couldn't help thinking all at once that I was free. I wish you'd come here and sit in the chair opposite, so that I can see if you believe this!"

I did as she wished, with a glance out of the side windows, at the border beyond them with its dead-looking stumps of plants, and the red-brick wall beyond that, which enclosed the kitchen garden.

She ran a hand over her smooth fair hair and then propped it under her chin and gazed at me steadily from her childish blue eyes.

"*Can* you understand how I could be horrified at seeing Father dead like that and, at the same time, could think that there was nothing now to stop me marrying Philip?"

I agreed that it was possible, if she and Philip had thought of it in that way beforehand.

That seemed to worry her a bit, but she admitted, "We had, in a way. Father himself put it like that. He said he wanted me to stay at Flaxmere as long as he was alive. So the question before us really was, were we to wait, perhaps years and years, or were we to risk it and marry at once? We had actually decided, Colonel Halstock, to get married this spring. Hilda and Carol can tell you that; we discussed it with them both."

"So you had decided that there wasn't anything to stop you, in any case; or that there wouldn't be anything to stop you, by the spring?"

"That's not a fair way of putting it!" Jenny protested. "There was something to stop us, in the way I meant: Father's ban and the fact that I shouldn't get any money from him. But we decided that we wouldn't let that stop us. But what I felt when I saw Father dead was that—Oh! I'm all muddled; you've tied me up with your beastly questions, but you know what I really mean." Jenny opened her eyes wide and looked at me appealingly.

I hardened my heart and told myself that I had to get to the bottom of all this and that if—out of kindness to little Jenny—I didn't insist on hard facts, I might be unfair to someone else. So I suggested that what she really felt when she saw Sir Osmond's body was that his opposition to her marriage, and any fear of financial hardship resulting from it, were both removed.

"I suppose that was it, in a way; though I didn't think it in words like that," Jenny admitted.

"You knew you would inherit a good deal under his latest will?" I asked.

She raised her brows a little in surprise. "I didn't know anything for certain; none of us do. We don't know when he made a will. But it was always understood that he would divide everything, more or less, among us."

"To return to that pistol. You thought Philip had shot your Father, because you saw that his death made things so much easier for you and Philip, so Philip obviously had a strong motive. Isn't that a bit thin, Jennifer?"

"What do you mean?" she asked indignantly. "It's perfectly true—except that you put everything in such a beastly way."

"I mean this; that it was rather rushing to conclusions to assume immediately that because Philip would gain by your Father's death, therefore Philip must have shot him. Hadn't you any other reason for thinking so?"

"I was afraid you wouldn't believe me," Jenny confessed sadly. "But it's perfectly true. I wish I could have made up something that would seem more likely to you. But I always thought the police considered motive very important. You find a murder done and there's nothing at the moment to show who has done it, so you at once try to find out who had a motive for the murder. Isn't that the way you do it?"

"It may be. But even the police take character and other points into account; above all, they consider facts."

"Oh! I know you're thinking me a beast to suppose that Philip could be a murderer! But—" she stopped short, suppressing something she had been going to say. "But someone obviously was, and apparently someone in the house. And I was horrified; so horrified that I suppose I was a bit off my head. Can't you imagine how frightful it was? I thought that somehow Phil—it had happened. My one idea was to protect Philip somehow. He'd left the pistol there, out of carelessness, I thought, and his finger-prints would be on it and you would find them, so I picked it up and handled it, hoping to rub them out!" Jenny shut her mouth tightly and glared at me defiantly.

"Didn't it occur to you that that was very dangerous? That you might be accused of the murder?"

"I hadn't done it, so I didn't really think anything could happen to me, especially as I didn't know anything at all about it. Besides, I had been in the hall all the time. People must have seen me there."

"Whereas people hadn't seen where Philip was, and that might tell against him. In fact, you yourself didn't know where Philip had been, and perhaps that made you suspect him?"

"No; it wasn't that!" Jenny cried vehemently. "I know where he was; I'm perfectly sure! He's got an alibi; Carol can tell you. You *must* believe Carol! After that first awful moment I *knew* he couldn't have done it. Oh, you must see that he couldn't possibly!" Her repeated assertions were those of one who tries to convince herself as well as someone else.

"You've nothing against Philip, nothing whatever!" she went on. "Except that one thing, that we haven't tried to deny, because it's perfectly obvious, that he would benefit by Father's death. But so would all of us! We all expect to get some of Father's money! You *can't* think Philip did it! You can't! Oh, what can I say?" Tears blurred her eyes and she fumbled for a handkerchief.

Her distress seemed genuine, though one always suspects a woman's tears on an occasion of this sort because they give her a convenient breathing space and may put her opponent off his guard. I tried to preserve an attitude of moderate sympathy which only took the edge off a stern desire to get on with the business. After a good deal of sobbing and sniffing and mopping, she responded to my exhortation that she should pull herself together and explain how she had become convinced of Philip's innocence.

"When you asked us all those questions on the evening of Christmas Day," Jenny continued, "I didn't know what to say because I hadn't had a chance of talking to Philip. But after you'd gone, he explained it all; how he had seen a chance of getting hold of Carol to have a talk alone with her and arrange how she should help us. Carol had rather a way with Father, if she took the trouble and he was in a good mood, and she always manages to get a thing done when she sets out to do it. I was sure that if she helped us with all the plans for Philip and me getting married and Hilda coming to live at Flaxmere instead of me, they would be sure to work out all right. That's what Philip was doing all the afternoon. It's perfectly simple."

I reminded her that in her first interview with me she had left out another item, apparently unconnected with Philip—her visit to the servants' hall to speak to Ashmore.

She cheered up at that, relieved, I think, at getting away from the subject of Philip. "I'd forgotten that. Yes, it happened while Oliver was talking to Father in the study. I ran out immediately the Christmas-tree business was over and I only stayed a minute or two talking to Ashmore because I imagined that as soon as Father had told Oliver exactly what he had to do, Father would appear on the scene again and probably want me to organize games or something for the children and would be fed-up if I wasn't at hand."

I asked her when she got back to the hall.

"Just before Oliver came out of the library—at least, I suppose it was Oliver? I'm so muddled now about who was who. But anyway, a Santa Klaus came out of the library just after I got back to the hall."

"And what about Ashmore? Why had he come and why was there a conspiracy to deny that he was ever here?"

"It wasn't a conspiracy! You do make everything sound so much worse than it is! I'm sorry about it, but when you began questioning us all I thought how awful it would be if you went and questioned Ashmore, just because he had happened to be here. He didn't know a thing and he's terrified of the police 'getting their hands on him,' as he says. They got their hands on him once when he was a boy, for something frightfully trivial, like robbing an orchard, and he nearly lost his job here because of it and he always thinks that if they should get their hands on him again, even for parking his car in the wrong place, and that old business should come out, he'd be finished. So I thought it better not to say anything about him and I passed the word to Carol not to and we asked Parkins not to. We'd already kept it rather secret, because we particularly didn't want Father to know he was here. Father might have been furious, because he had some idea that Ashmore wasn't properly grateful and hadn't behaved well. Father always took any kindness we showed to Ashmore as a criticism of his own behaviour—which I suppose it was in a way."

I asked again why Ashmore had come to Flaxmere, which Jenny had omitted from her flood of explanation.

"Carol was most frightfully sorry for him when he drove her and Hilda up from the station," Jenny explained. "He looked ill and seemed so worried. So we decided to send him a big Christmas hamper and Carol went into Bristol with Patricia on Monday and ordered the things. He was awfully pleased and came all the way out here to thank us. Parkins told me he was here, so I just rushed out and said *Happy Christmas* to him and all that and told him to stay to tea. I suppose that if you can't believe a thing I say and you must ask him, then you must. But do—please—do it kindly. He really is a poor old thing."

I promised we would be tactful with Ashmore and told her—what was worrying me a bit—that he could not be found. Bristol police had telephoned to say that they had called twice at his house but his wife would only say he had gone out that morning without saying where he was going or when he would return. His car was in its garage. His wife seemed worried, they thought.

"I suppose he's gone off on affairs of his own," Jenny conjectured. "His wife is a whining sort of woman and I don't wonder if he wants to get away from her sometimes. He's sure to be back to-night. I'll swear he has absolutely nothing to do with this affair and I don't suppose he even knew my father was dead until he read the papers this morning. Why don't you ask Carol about him? She doesn't muddle things up like I do and perhaps you'll believe her!"

I had decided that I wanted to talk to both Carol and Philip before Jenny had a chance to tell them of her interview with me, and perhaps it might be a good plan to question Carol in front of Jenny.

Jenny watched my hesitation and suggested, "Shall I go and find Carol? I think she's doing something to her new black frock. Oh! I suppose you think I might give her some private instructions on the way! You needn't worry about that. We're quite ready to tell you the truth about Ashmore."

Jenny rang the bell and gave instructions to the maid who answered it. To ease the situation I walked over to the side windows and looked at the bare garden and brick wall and made some aimless remarks about spring flowers. Jenny carried out some hasty repairs to her face. I was thinking that Jenny still suspected Philip. She didn't quite trust his explanations and she was jealous of Carol. But she would stand by Philip to the last, protesting her belief in him in the face of the blackest evidence.

When Carol appeared I was struck again by the fact that this girl seemed much less affected by the general anxiety and distress than anyone else in the house. There was a resilience in her, the resilience of self-confidence and youth. Or was it of callousness and grim determination? The latter seemed absurd when you looked at Carol's fine—one might have said sensitive—features and candid eyes.

As soon as she sailed into the room Jennifer exclaimed:

"Carol! Ashmore's gone away—disappeared! What can have happened?"

Jenny was evidently more disturbed by the man's disappearance than she had admitted to me. Carol looked startled and very grave. She turned to me accusingly.

"What have you done to make him go? How do you come to know that he's gone? It's wicked if he is dragged into this beastly mess!"

"Just consider!" I urged them. "If the man is, as you say, completely innocent of any complicity and, in fact, ignorant of what actually happened, then you yourselves are to blame for making a great fuss about nothing. First your conspiracy of silence, then a car seen leaving Flaxmere when everyone in the house says that no car has been here. If Parkins had not very properly confessed to me, Ashmore might have had to undergo a very close questioning as to what he was doing here secretly that afternoon."

"Yes, I see now that we are to blame and that it was idiotic of us not to tell you he was here," Carol agreed, after considering this. "But we were none of us quite normal that evening. A horrible thing had happened and more than our judgment was upset. But don't let's argue about who's to blame. If he has really disappeared, he must think you are after him and he might do something desperate. He must be found at once. One of us must go and tell him that it's all right. But you haven't explained. Why should he have gone?"

I told her what I knew.

"Well, of course," she burst out indignantly. "If you sent police to his house, he'd be awfully upset—"

I pointed out that they were plain-clothes men.

"I'm sure he'd know what they were; they'd look like policemen, even in their best mufti, and they'd talk like policemen."

I managed to get in a word to the effect that Ashmore had apparently taken himself off some time before the first plain-clothes man called.

"Are you *sure*?" Carol asked. "I can't believe that. He has absolutely no reason at all to be worried. Unless there was something horrible in the papers. There might be. Some journalist might have routed out the fact that Ashmore was here."

I didn't think that likely, but we sent for all the papers which could be collected in the house and when they were brought we studied the pages announcing what most of them called the Christmas Crime, or the Santa Klaus Murder. There were plenty of lurid headlines, but very little real information, the lack of it being made up for by wordy and inaccurate descriptions of the house and family. There was no reference to Ashmore, nor could we find the least hint that he, or anyone in his position, was connected with the crime or under suspicion.

"There may be some other awful screaming rag that Ashmore reads," Jenny suggested.

"Or perhaps, as Jennifer suggested to begin with," I mildly ventured, "he has gone out on his own affairs and will be back this evening."

The two young women looked at me suspiciously and coldly.

"You don't really think that," Carol accused me. "Your police have said something that makes you sure there's some important reason for his disappearance."

The Bristol police had actually reported that, from all they could discover, it was unheard of for Ashmore to go out, even for an hour, without telling his wife where he would be and when he would return. This was important for his business, to which he attended diligently. Some inquiries in the local public houses had not been very helpful. One publican knew Ashmore who, he declared, was "almost a teetotaller" and hadn't been in the bar for days.

"Look here!" said Carol suddenly. "If Jenny or I could go and see Mrs. Ashmore, I believe we might get something out of her. Naturally she's suspicious of your plain-clothes police!"

I suppose my face showed my doubt of the wisdom of this plan. Anyhow, Carol looked at me and laughed.

"Oh, blast! Of course we're all under suspicion and observation and the rest of it and you daren't let us out! Well, come yourself, if you like; only keep in the background! Or send another guard with us. Let Jenny go, with a nice fatherly policeman!"

I was sorry that Kenneth was not at hand. There might be something in Carol's idea that she or Jenny could get more out of Mrs. Ashmore, and I began to think that Ashmore did know something and it was important to find him. I felt that Jenny certainly, and Carol possibly, really believed in Ashmore's innocence. Perhaps he had picked up some clue quite by accident. Yet I was reluctant to turn either of those girls loose in Bristol, though I had no definite idea of what mischief they could do. I took a few steps up and down Jenny's little room, whilst they watched me anxiously. Reaching a decision, I sent for Rousdon and held a colloquy with him in the passage outside the door.

We decided to let Bingham drive Jennifer to Ashmore's house, and they should be followed by a plain-clothes man on a motor bicycle who was to keep himself in the background unless he noticed anything unusual or unless they overstepped their instructions, which were to go to the house, make the inquiries and come straight back to Flaxmere. Bingham—who had been helping the searchers of the outhouses, drawing their attention to lofts, producing ladders, unlocking doors—was supervised whilst he placed a rug in the Sunbeam and drove it round to the front door. The car itself had already been searched.

Jenny had put on a black hat and coat which she had selected from amongst the goods which deputations from two or three of the chief shops in Bristol had brought to Flaxmere that morning. Looking small and frail and anxious in the back of the big limousine, she drove off alone with Bingham.

Chapter Eighteen

Mr. Ashmore's Story

by Jennifer Melbury

It was a relief to get away from Flaxmere, where we had all been cooped up so unpleasantly for what seemed weeks, though it was really only from the evening of Christmas Day—Wednesday—until this Friday afternoon. Colonel Halstock had been pretty unpleasant, but now that I began to think it over calmly, he had really been no worse than we all were. Everyone seemed perfectly beastly during those awful days. Oliver must have had the hell of a time, because although we all agreed that it seemed utterly idiotic that he should shoot Father, yet it did look like that to begin with. I don't wonder that he was quite pleased to spend a night in prison and that he kept away from us when he returned to Flaxmere.

Then when we all grasped that there must have been what we called a "second Santa," the suspicions grew worse, because none of us could see who it could possibly have been. Some people, Aunt Mildred and Patricia especially, who are quite impervious to reason, obviously wanted it to be poor Grace Portisham, though we all knew that Hilda had been talking to her in the hall all the time when the murder must have been committed. They evolved an idea that she might have done it immediately Oliver left the study, and it was true that she hadn't joined Hilda till a bit later and no one could exactly remember when she came into the hall from the library, where she had stayed behind to clear up the litter when most of us drifted out. However, that wouldn't account for the second Santa, and anyhow I was sure that poor Grace simply worshipped Father and wouldn't dream of shooting him, even if she was going to get a lot of money by his death, which everyone was afraid of.

Bingham had said he knew the way to Ashmore's house, but as we began to get into Bristol he stopped the car and slid back the glass partition behind him. I thought he was going to ask about the address, but instead of that he said, "Excuse me making a suggestion, Miss, but if I might be so bold, wouldn't it be better for me to draw up just at the corner of the street, as it were, and for you to go up to the door by yourself? Make less stir in the street, like, if you understand my meaning."

It seemed a good idea, because there would be sure to be a lot of excitement and talk if the big Flaxmere car were seen outside Ashmore's door, and what Carol and I were specially anxious about was to avoid publicity for Ashmore. He had such a horror of it and it was all through trying to keep him out of it that we had apparently made such a mess of things, and brought him under suspicion.

Bingham stopped the car in a busy street, just before the corner of the little road, with small houses in two grim rows, in which Ashmore lives. We were very inconspicuous, stopping there, as I might have been going to a shop.

I knocked at Ashmore's door and it was opened a crack, and a voice behind it said surlily, "What is it?"

I said who I was and the door opened wider to show Mrs. Ashmore. She was always rather a draggled woman but now she looked more down-at-heel than usual, furtive and red-eyed. She took me into the parlour and then it suddenly came over me that I didn't know quite what I was to say to her. I didn't want to make her think I had anything to do with the police by asking straight out where her husband was. However, she got me out of the difficulty by pouring out a flood of sympathy and indignation about Father's death.

"We was anxious, you'll understand, all the Boxing Day, Ashmore having come back on Christmas Day with news of some accident to Sir Osmond, by reason of which he left hurriedly without knowing rightly what was the matter. We thought it might be that he had another stroke like he had in the summer. Ashmore would have rung up if it hadn't been that he thought Sir Osmond would answer the telephone himself, as like as not, if he was in good health, we having no suspicion, of course that the poor man was lying dead, and thinking he might consider the inquiry uncalled for."

She ran on like this, explaining just how anxious they were and what they said to each other and so forth, and I told her I was very sorry I hadn't thought of letting them know and asked if Ashmore was at home.

"No, he's not; and that's the trouble!" she said.

I inquired whether anything was wrong and she burst out: "I don't know what should be wrong or why there should be anything wrong, but Ashmore's bin that upset since yesterday evening and this mornin' off he goes with nothin' to speak of inside 'im except just a cup of tea, and I'm not to say anything to anyone, though there's little I could say if I wanted to, but the way he said goodbye to our Ada—she's the weakly one, you'll remember, Miss, an' always at home an' her father that devoted to her, would make your blood run cold. Jus' as if he never thought to see the girl again an' I says to Ashmore, I says, thinkin' he was jus' takin' a short run, as he often does mornin's, 'I s'pose,' I says, 'you'll be back within the half hour.' At that he gives me a queer look an' says, 'There's no knowin',' says he, 'but anyway, you know nothing, old girl, and you'll say nothing to any as may come making inquiries.' An' with that off he went and hasn't bin seen since, and how he thinks we're to get on without him, with nothing comin' in but what he gets by the car and little enough of that, and me not knowin' what to say to people when they ring up, I'm that worried I don' know what to think!"

I tried my best to get out of her whether there could be any other reason for Ashmore's disappearance; anything not connected with Father's death. Mrs. Ashmore seemed to have an idea that he had gone away because of that, though exactly why she could not or would not say. She declared that he had no reason for leaving, nothing to do with his home or business. She maintained for a long time that she hadn't the faintest idea where he had gone, but at last she told me that there was some place he had talked about last night, after he began "to get in a state," a place he had often talked about before. He had been there on a day trip in his youth and he always said it was the most beautiful place in the world but she could never get him to take her there. Sometimes she was doubtful whether it ever existed, except that other people had talked of going there. She couldn't make out what he saw in it, for he admitted that it wasn't the seaside and there was no promenade, but just some ruins. Last night he had said he'd like to see that place again, for the last time, he had always promised himself that he's see that place again. Could she remember the name of it? She didn't think so; she wasn't good at remembering names, but

Ada might know. She went to consult her invalid daughter and returned with the information that it was "Tinnun."

Considering the ruins and Mrs. Ashmore's slurred Bristol accent, I suggested Tintern and she thought that might be it.

"Though, mind you," she insisted, "I don't say he's gone there. There's no sense in it, to me, an' it'd cost a fair sight, though they run trips in the summer."

Then she seemed suddenly anxious as to whether she had done wrong in giving away this clue. What was I going to do? Was I sure no harm could come to him through what she had told me?

I told her I was dead sure that Ashmore had no reason for bolting, but I thought he was run-down and in a very nervy state and must have imagined something which was preying on his mind. Mrs. Ashmore agreed that he hadn't been at all himself for some time and was "suffering with his nerves" through worry over bad business and her own illness, about which she began a detailed history. I managed to head her off and told her that if Ashmore came back, or she got news of him, she was to telephone to Flaxmere at once and ask to speak to me. We would do all we could to find him, I assured her. "You won't put those police on to him, will you, Miss?" she implored, and I promised that I wouldn't, with some doubt about whether I could fully keep the promise.

The visit of the policemen in plain clothes hadn't been mentioned, except for a vague reference by Mrs. Ashmore to "people who come nosing round for no good purpose."

I began to say good-bye and she wanted to know how I was getting home, so I told her the car was round the corner and she came along the street with me. When we got to the corner we saw the car a few yards away, with Bingham sitting at the wheel. Mrs. Ashmore looked hard at him and then plunged forward in a sort of half run. Bingham saw me and got out to open the door, so Mrs. Ashmore caught him on the pavement.

"So it's you, Mr. Bingham! And so I thought!" she raged at him shrilly. "An' I'd like to know what you have to say for yourself, you who took away my husband's job and now you've taken away his senses, you with your cock-and-bull tales, whatever they may be, that have sent him, as good a husband and as good a father as ever there was, off to goodness knows where."

People passing by on the pavement were beginning to stare and pause to see what was going on. I got quickly into the car. Bingham behaved very well, saying he was sorry if anything had happened to Ashmore but he knew nothing about it, and so on. He didn't lose his temper but answered her quietly and then got into his driving seat. I opened a window and asked what was the matter.

"Just you ask him!" she cried. "Ask Mr. Bingham! Ask him what he told my poor husband on Boxing Day! That's what I'd like to know!"

I dreaded being involved in a scene in the street and I thought the woman had lost her senses and was putting the blame on Bingham because probably she had always felt bitter about him since he got her husband's job at Flaxmere. I assured her that Bingham had nothing to do with the affair and implored her not to get so upset about it or to jump to conclusions too quickly. Then I told Bingham to drive on and we left Mrs. Ashmore standing on the pavement, shaking her head of straggling hair.

When we were clear of Bristol again, Bingham drew up and said he would like to explain what Mrs. Ashmore had meant, before we got back to Flaxmere. So I went and sat in the front and we drove on.

He told me that yesterday—Boxing Day—he had to drive Mr. Crewkerne, the solicitor, from Twaybrooks back to Bristol and after dropping him Bingham decided to call at Ashmore's house and break the news to him. Bingham explained that it was hardly at all out of his way and although Colonel Halstock had instructed him to return to Flaxmere at once he thought there was no harm in stopping for a moment. The Ashmores, he realized, wouldn't have heard what had happened at Flaxmere and he thought he could save them the shock of reading it in the papers next day. Bingham said he was rather "come for" at the way Ashmore received the news. "All broke up, he was, seemed to take it to 'eart somethink orful. I wouldn't be surprised if the man 'as done isself a mischief."

"But why?" I asked. "Even if he were upset at hearing of Father's death, I don't see why he should behave like that."

Bingham said mysteriously, "There's no knowin' what a person'll do," and I could get no more out of him. He was worried about his own position. He had disobeyed Colonel Halstock's orders because he thought it would be a kind-ness to old Ashmore to break the news gently to him and he had never dreamt that his visit would cause such a to-do. He understood that the police now wanted to get hold of Ashmore and if they found out that Bingham had seen him just before he went away, Bingham would be for it, he was afraid. He would take it as a great favour if I could forget to mention to Colonel Halstock that Bingham had ever been there. He reasoned very ingeniously that it was simply the news of Father's death which had sent old Ashmore off the deep end, and if Bingham hadn't happened to deliver that news the day before, Ashmore would have got it from the papers this morning, so his visit was really of no importance.

I wasn't going to make any promises to Bingham, but I decided that I wouldn't bring him in to the story at all if I could avoid it. I did tell him, however, that the police didn't really want to get hold of Ashmore, not in the way he implied. They had wanted an explanation of why he was at Flaxmere, but they understood now that he had a perfectly good reason for coming and it was Carol and I who were anxious to find him because we were worried about him, though we were perfectly certain that he had nothing to do with what had happened or any knowledge about it.

Bingham replied that he would venture to suggest that we left any search for Ashmore to the police, who knew how to manage things. It mightn't be a very nice business for young ladies to mix themselves up in.

I don't quite know what he was implying and thought it was rather cheek of him, though I suppose Ashmore's behaviour did look so queer that no one could be blamed for suspecting him of at least some guilty knowledge.

Chapter Nineteen

Carol and Oliver

by Col. Halstock

While Jennifer was driving to Bristol I talked to Philip Cheriton. He is a shortish, rather stocky young fellow, generally a bit untidy in his dress, although he had shown enough respect to the mourning atmosphere of the house to appear in a grey suit in place of his usual sloppy flannel trousers and sports coats. He wears his hair too long and has an irritating habit of twirling a lock between his fingers and then leaving it on end.

He blurted out as soon as he came into the room, without waiting for me to say anything, "I know I'm in a deuced awkward position, Colonel! What I mean to say is, it's quite obvious to anyone that this clears the ground a lot for Jenny and me. I'm sorry I didn't spill the whole story to you right away on Wednesday evening, but as I wasn't in the business at all I thought it didn't matter a row of beans to anyone just where I was that afternoon. I thought you'd have the fellow by the heels in no time."

I told him, pretty severely, that we had small chance of clearing up the affair until people in the house told us the truth.

"Oh, of course; I see that now. I'm ready to come clean. I was sitting in Jenny's room, talking to Carol, trying to persuade her to be an accomplice—in our plans for eloping, you know!"

I questioned him, but his story was simple. He left the library with the others and gave Clare, George's youngest child, a pick-a-back round the hall. That led to some words with Patricia, who thought he was exciting the child too much, and he talked to her for a bit, or rather listened to her exposition of the right way to treat children, to put her in a good humour again. He saw Santa Klaus go out of the door at the back and he saw Carol run after him and then Santa Klaus returned with crackers and he pulled some of these with the children. When all the cracker-pulling was over and he had helped Kit to get his train running, he looked round for Carol, thinking this might be the opportunity to have a quiet word with her. He didn't see her and it occurred to him that she hadn't come back to the hall, so he went off to see what she was up to. The natural place to look was in Jenny's room, since the door was so near the door of the hall through which he had seen her go.

There she was, looking a bit flustered, he thought.

At that point he pulled himself up. "Good Lord! What have I said? I don't know what made me say that! Carol was all right and she sat down quite calmly and listened to my plans and we discussed how she could help, by getting her mother installed here, and there we were when Parkins came in, very solemn, with the message from Ashmore and some rather confused remark about an accident in the study, which sent us both off to see what had happened."

"And when you found out what had happened you realized that the need for an elopement, with its probably unpleasant financial consequences, was gone?" I suggested.

"Naturally it occurred to me before long that Jenny and I were now on velvet, but a lot of other things occurred to me first. Really frightful for the family, it would be. Something so sordid about murder! It's one of the things that you think can never happen in your own family. Nasty shock for Jenny, too. I noticed the minute I got in to the library that she looked pretty well knocked out."

I told him I didn't think he had really explained why he did not tell me the truth about his whereabouts during the afternoon, when I had particularly asked each one of them to describe their movements accurately.

"To tell the truth, by the time you began asking your questions I had begun to wonder—I suppose all of us had—just how the affair had happened and who had done it. I'd been rather out of it, away there in Jenny's room and there was only Carol to say that I had really been there. You were obviously suspecting all of us and I thought you might well suspect me if I admitted I hadn't been with the rest of the party, but with the kids racing about in the hall and crackers popping and people going to and fro between hall and drawing-room, I thought no one would notice I hadn't been there. It does sound a bit thin, I know," he finished apologetically. "But there is it."

"The thinnest part," I pointed out, "is that Miss Wynford might have given you away, unintentionally. How could you be sure that she wouldn't tell the truth?"

"You do put your finger on the spot, every time," Cheriton remarked, in a sort of mocking complaint. "I have to admit, I suppose, that I passed the word to Carol not to say we left the hall and she seemed to think that was all right.

Poor girl, she couldn't do much but agree, for she hadn't any opportunity to argue and she was smart enough to see that at all costs our stories must tally."

He didn't seem to realize that they had been perjuring themselves and obstructing the police and all—according to his story—because they thought it might sound better to say they were in the hall rather than in Jenny's room. It wasn't a good story and yet there was nothing tangible against the man except this untruthfulness.

〉〉〉

Meanwhile Rousdon had pursued his search into the walled kitchen garden, which adjoined the servants' quarters of the house and came close up to the windows in the side of Jenny's room. It was entered by a gate in its wall on that side and also by a door from the house near the kitchen. There was a potting-shed and other outbuildings in this garden but, being used by the gardeners, they were unlikely hiding places and they had yielded nothing.

He had explored all the gardens round the house and found that from Jennifer's windows there was no direct way to the garage yard; you had to go round the front of the house and along the path on the other side, unless you went through the kitchen garden and the back part of the house. So if the Santa Klaus costume had to be conveyed to Ashmore's car in the garage yard, the study window was a more practical outlet than the windows of Jennifer's room.

Rousdon was confident that his men had thoroughly examined all possible hiding places in the grounds which were within easy reach of the house and he was coming round again to the idea that Ashmore had taken the Santa Klaus outfit away in his car. That seemed to implicate Jennifer or Carol, for we could not discover that anyone else, excepting the domestic staff, knew of Ashmore's presence. Philip

Cheriton, I thought, might have heard of it from Jennifer, but it was unlikely that she would tell anyone else.

Rousdon had also made sure that there was no typewriter about the place except Miss Portisham's and that had, as we feared, yielded no clue to the person who may have used it on Tuesday afternoon, or perhaps even earlier.

He had also, at my suggestion, set inquiries on foot about the delivery of parcels at Flaxmere before Christmas. They came in the mail van and the back drive was used because that happened to be the more convenient route. The post office people would make inquiries but they did not hold out much hope of being able to tell us whether a box from Dawson's, containing the Santa Klaus outfit first ordered, had really been delivered at Flaxmere, and if so on which day, and who had taken it from the postman. So many parcels had been sent up and there were so many temporary postmen, who did not know the houses nor the residents, that it was unlikely they could give us any definite facts, unless something unusual had happened to that parcel before it left their hands.

Jennifer returned from Bristol while we were reviewing the situation and I sent for Carol to hear what she had to tell us.

She reported that Mrs. Ashmore was confused in her statements but had made it pretty clear that Ashmore went off early this morning, long before the first plain clothes man called. She maintained that Mrs. Ashmore was very worried and, although the woman apparently knew of no reason why Ashmore should want to disappear, yet obviously thought that he had gone for good.

As soon as Jennifer finished her story, Carol burst out furiously: "You must find him! It's horrible! We're all responsible! He must be found, I say!"

Whilst Jennifer gave her account of the interview, I had watched Carol closely. She sat listening eagerly, her eyes fixed on Jennifer's face, biting her lip.

"I agree that we must find him," I told her seriously. "We must know the reason why he has run away."

"The only reason," Carol cried emphatically, "is that he doesn't know what he's doing. Mother and I saw that he was on the edge of a nervous breakdown when he drove us on Saturday. And then on Christmas Day Jenny knows what he was like."

We all looked at Jenny. "Yes," she said; "it's difficult to explain but he was so frightfully grateful just for an ordinary Christmas hamper. It was—well, rather ghastly— that anyone could be so—so abjectly grateful for that and for being asked to stay and have tea. It made me feel ashamed. He—he was almost in tears. I told Carol afterwards."

"Look here!" Carol announced. "I'll tell you everything, the whole beastly story, if only you'll let us look for Ashmore. I think he means to do away with himself and if we follow him at once we may be in time to save him."

"Can you tell us where to follow him to?" I asked.

"I can!" Jennifer volunteered, and told us rather a fantastic story of Mrs. Ashmore's belief that the man had gone to Tintern. It sounded very unlikely.

"There! That shows you he's half crazy!" Carol declared. "And if you put your police on his tracks, plain clothes or not, that'll be the last straw. Now listen; I'll tell you every blessed thing I know and perhaps then you'll believe me!"

We settled down to hear this extraordinary confession. Jennifer looked uneasy and I caught a questioning look from her, but signed to her to stay.

"To begin with," said Carol; "I never went to Jenny's room to fetch my handbag. I followed Oliver Witcombe when he left the hall because it occurred to me that he would see

Ashmore in the servants' hall and might ask who he was when he found there was no present for him, and would then tell grandfather. He's rather officious, you know, and it would be just like him to go butting in. So I ran out after him and found him in the passage admiring himself in the mirror, though there wasn't much light. I told him about Ashmore and how grandfather mightn't like the man being here, when he hadn't invited him, and asked Oliver to keep quiet about him. Oliver looked very prim and made some idiotic remark about it being unwise to run counter to grandfather's wishes. I was fed-up and told him that if he wasn't a cad he just wouldn't see Ashmore in the servants' hall. Oliver very solemnly took me by the arm and led me into Jenny's room. Then he unhooked his beard and threw off his red hood, but evidently forgot all about his rouged cheeks and the white eyebrows, which made him look a perfect ass. He gave me a solemn lecture about the importance of keeping in with grandfather. Said that grandfather thought a lot of me, and hinted that I should probably come in for a lot of money under his will if only I behaved like a good girl. I told him I thought it was immoral to play for anyone's money after their death by being nice to them in their lifetime. Then he came over all sentimental and said he was very fond of me himself and he couldn't bear to see me throwing away my chances. He said: if I was honest with myself I'd admit that it would mean a lot to me to have enough money to follow my career; made out that I was being proud about it because I didn't believe him. He said he knew what he was talking about, though he hadn't breathed a word of it to anyone else and only told me because he was fond of me. It was nauseating!

"There was a good deal more of it and I only got rid of him by laughing at him. Of course I don't know if he really knew anything. If he did, if what he said is true, I'm sure he was just making up to me because of the money.

"When later on I heard of grandfather's death, it was horrible, after what had happened. But it didn't strike me that Oliver could have had anything to do with it, because I had seen him go to the servants' hall. Of course, Oliver might have shot grandfather in the study immediately after the Christmas-tree, but everyone seemed to think it had been done later—because of that cracker business.

"When you began making inquiries, Oliver got hold of me and pointed out that he would be in an awkward position if I told you about our conversation. It would lead to all sorts of nasty questions, he said, and it was just bad luck that he happened to say all that to me just at such a time. Jenny and I didn't want Ashmore brought into it, so I asked Oliver to say nothing about him and promised that if he kept quiet about that I would keep quiet about his remarks to me. Naturally I didn't want to be cross-questioned about them and I didn't think the incident could matter to you in the least.

"That's all, I think, except that just after Oliver had gone off to the servants' hall, Philip came in. I saw Oliver go through the door at the back of the passage, but then I went back to Jenny's room because I was all het up and wanted to cool down. Philip came to look for me there and he wanted to talk to me alone so he took the opportunity to tell me about his and Jenny's plans and how I might help them. I expect you know all that?

"There's one other thing. I did tell you a lie when I said I knew Oliver was talking to me when the crackers went off, because I heard them. You see, I do know that he had come straight out from the study because I had watched him from the hall and followed him, but we didn't hear the crackers at all in Jenny's room. I was in a bit of a hole because I didn't want to confess that we were in that room; it would look so much like a private conversation. So I had to invent hearing a cracker. I'm sorry. But now I really have told you the whole truth and I suppose Oliver will have to endorse it. If it gets him into a mess, I can't help it. I did what I could for him; a lot more than he deserves. It's much more important now to do something for poor old Ashmore and I'm furious to think that it was partly to save Oliver's beastly feelings that I began telling you lies and made you think there was something fishy about Ashmore."

Rousdon had left us in the middle of this story to answer the telephone in the study. I had been watching Jennifer. It was evident, from the way she followed Carol's words, anxiously and with some disgust, that the story was new to her. I was shocked at the way these young people lied or prevaricated on the slightest excuse and then came out with another tale and confidently expected to be believed.

Carol stood up and looked round at us.

"Now, will you let me go and look for Ashmore? If there is anything to be found out from him, I'm sure I can get more out of him than any of your policemen, and I believe I could find him, too. I feel it in my bones. Really, it's desperately serious. And it's no good sending anyone who doesn't know him by sight. Descriptions are so hopeless. You know yourself that you could never recognize anyone from one of those descriptions issued by the police; medium height, fresh complexion, and the rest of it. If you get a photograph of him it's bound to be ten years old at least, and the man looks awful now, an absolute wreck, not a bit like he did a few years ago."

I never knew anyone like Carol for overwhelming one with good reasons for any course of action she wants to pursue. I dismissed her and Jennifer so that I could discuss the situation with Rousdon.

"I'll be ready to go at any minute!" she declared before she went. "I can drive the Sunbeam, or George's car, if you don't want to send Bingham."

"No one can go to-night, in any case," I decreed. "It's ridiculous to set out in the dark to hunt for a possible case of lost memory in the Wye Valley. I'll do whatever seems best, but I must ask you not to stage any melodramatic attempt at escape, against which I shall take every precaution."

Rousdon came to tell me of the rather queer report which had just been telephoned to him by the man who had followed Jennifer and Bingham in the Sunbeam. During Carol's story quite a new picture of the murder had been taking a shape in my mind and it was the first solution into which it seemed possible to fit all the known facts. I now laid it before Rousdon and, leaving him to confirm a few details, I returned to Twaybrooks. I hoped that the "homework" might provide me with some of the missing links in this new chain of evidence and if Kenneth had really spent the afternoon in intensive study of the untidy mass of manuscript, he should be able to find the answers to my questions.

He had done his job well, so well that it seemed unfair to keep him in the dark and I told him everything that would help him to put the story together for himself.

The result of our deliberations was that I rang up Flax-mere that night and after some conversation with Rousdon I told Carol to be ready at eight o'clock next morning, when Kenneth would call for her in his own car. I also arranged that a detective officer in plain clothes should have a seat in the back of that car, but I did not tell Carol this.

"Oh, thank you! Thank you!" she said in a low voice. "I do hope we shall be in time."

Chapter Twenty

Excursion to Tintern

by Kenneth Stour

The Tollards' household in which I was a guest rose (that is exactly the right word) in splendid style to the effort of tearing me from my bed, putting nourishment into me and packing me into my car by half-past seven on Saturday morning. A grim morning it was at that stage, only half lighted, dank and raw. At the entrance of the Flaxmere drive I picked up the plain-clothes man, who settled himself gloomily into a corner of the back seat.

"Didn't understand that it was an open car, sir!" he muttered sadly, pulling the rug about him.

Carol was standing on the steps of the house when I crested the steep drive. I was glad to see her fur coat. She looked at the unhappy passenger and asked me in a low voice, "Is he coming?"

Learning that he was, she dashed back into the house and soon returned with a capacious old leather coat, which she threw at him unceremoniously, saying, "You'll need it!"

As we swept down the drive she whispered, "Who is he?"

"A detective," I told her. "And since you had to ask, it's evident that he's fulfilling his intention of appearing to be just an ordinary man."

"I knew. I only asked to make sure. I was surprised that the Colonel allowed me to go with you, but now I understand. However, I don't grudge him the coat. It's an old one of George's that I've often borrowed. I've got Jenny's to-day. Now, there's something I think I ought to tell you, though I don't know that it's any good, since we've started."

She then related what Jennifer had not told Colonel Halstock on her return from Bristol, but had divulged to Carol later; Mrs. Ashmore's accusation of Bingham and Bingham's own explanation to Jennifer. The fact that Mrs. Ashmore had screeched out some reproaches and that Bingham on the way home had stopped the car and spoken to Jenny, who had then moved into the front seat, had all been reported to Rousdon by the man deputed to follow the Flaxmere car, but I thought the additional information might be helpful, so stopped at the next telephone box and rang up the Colonel. Carol was rather indignant at the delay.

"I almost wish I hadn't told you," she said. "But I did promise to tell the Colonel everything I knew and after I'd done that he let me come, so I felt it was a bargain and it wouldn't be fair to keep this back, though of course Jenny ought to have told him really."

"Your conversion to a belief in telling all the truth is rather sudden, isn't it?"

"I've come to the conclusion that it's best," she replied haughtily. "We really did get ourselves into a bit of a mess by trying to select—though we had perfectly good reasons."

"By the way, I'm not sure that Colonel Halstock would appreciate the idea of a bargain. You'd better not suggest it to him, I think."

"Oh, of course I shouldn't. But you seem to know a lot about everything! You're not the police yourself, are you? I don't see how you can be, unless you're not Kenneth Stour at all, but some one impersonating him."

I assured her that I really was myself and had not joined the police, but had been doing what I described as clerical work for the Colonel out of kindness, having known him for years.

We were on the main road to Gloucester, speeding along as well as Mr. Belisha would allow us. I had decided that this would be quicker than trusting to the Beachley ferry, about which I had some uncertain information, but the "30" signs had a depressing effect on Carol.

"I suppose you *have* to take notice of them? We shall never get there. When you're on business for the police and it may be a matter of life or death, aren't you allowed to let her rip?"

"Being held up and having to give name and address and all the rest of it, might delay us even more than these thirty touches," I pointed out.

We drove in silence for some time. I was thinking of the solution I had tentatively worked out in the Colonel's study at Flaxmere during the previous afternoon, with the help of the pile of homework. The Colonel and the police were wandering in a maze of clues; they followed one here and one there, but they could not see which led towards the goal and which were blind. I, not having to concern myself with these misleading details, was able to go back in my mind to the beginning and to draw up a series of questions as to who had at various stages of the case the necessary knowledge and the necessary opportunity. This led on to other questions, on who had, at later stages, taken action to lay a false scent. If one name would answer all the first two sets of questions and some of the last set, I thought we had solved the case.

When Colonel Halstock had arrived home on Friday evening I had a pretty little scheme ready for him, into which the facts of which I was ignorant and which he was able to give me fitted to a T. The Colonel believed that he had reached my conclusion by himself and was very cock-a-hoop about it. That was just as well, because there was a good deal more to do and he would work out the last details with far more enthusiasm if he really believed in the idea as his own. I thought we had a pretty water-tight case, but it depended on whether one or two experiments turned out successfully this morning, and I couldn't help being anxious.

Gloucester's market-day livestock and shoppers and traffic were beginning to cumber the streets as we drove in, but we were through the town and out on the good Chepstow road before nine o'clock.

Carol suddenly asked: "Would you mind awfully if I drove your car? I haven't driven this before but I'm quite a good driver of wide experience."

"I don't really mind letting you try; if you do it badly I shall take over again. But won't it slow us down a bit? I thought you were all for getting on?"

"Yes, I am," she agreed; "but after five minutes I don't think I shall be any slower than you, and I can hardly bear to sit still. I'm so worried. It would be an enormous relief to me to be able to drive!"

The astonishing part of it was that she appeared quite composed. No one would have guessed that she was in an agony of anxiety, except perhaps from a strained note in her voice. That did convince me that she was sincere and not merely covetous of the opportunity of sitting at the wheel of a powerful car. I let her change over and noticed a pained query in the chilled expression of the passenger, but soothed him with a nod of reassurance. She handled the car beautifully. It is a joy to drive and Carol appreciated all its points and got the best out of it with amazing skill. I settled down in the passenger's seat with relief.

For some time she concentrated on her work and then she asked suddenly: "Can you tell me exactly why the Colonel did let me come? I know it wasn't really a bargain."

"Can you tell me in return just why you are so anxious about Ashmore and feel it so necessary to go in search of him? I don't want to imply that you haven't really told the whole truth, but perhaps I haven't heard all of it."

"There isn't any definite reason," Carol said slowly. "There are no *facts* that I haven't told that would help you to understand. It's just that it came over me, when I heard that he had gone away, that something frightful was happening. I've been worried about him ever since Mother and I saw him last Saturday. He looked so awful, quite out of control. You see, until he left Flaxmere he had a good safe job and he's not used to the hand-to-mouth existence he has led since. When things went wrong, he couldn't stand the strain. You read in the papers often enough of bodies fished out of rivers and verdicts of *suicide while temporarily insane*, and you can find just this sort of a story behind those verdicts. A man desperately worried by bad times and the insecurity of his position and finally tipped right off his balance by something just as absurd as the suggestion that because he left Flaxmere just after grandfather was murdered, he must have had something to do with it."

Her summary of the situation seemed plausible. I was only surprised that anyone as young as Carol could have so much insight into the sordid facts.

"We sent him a Christmas hamper and gave him a good feed and a temporary feeling of comfort but that didn't really help him much. We had done nothing at all to relieve his main troubles. That worried me and I don't want to fail him still worse. But I don't think the Colonel believes in my point of view."

"I think I do," I told her. "The real reason why you are here is because we believe that Ashmore may be able to tell us something important and you are useful to identify him, to reassure him and to persuade him to tell us what he can."

"You don't think it's anything discreditable to him?" she asked quickly.

"I'm pretty sure it's not. I think the thing that finally tipped him off his balance, as you put it, was a devilish act by someone I am anxious to identify quite definitely."

At Chepstow we began to make inquiries. Rousdon had sent out information and instructions the night before and the local police had picked up traces of a man who might be Ashmore who had got out of a train on Friday afternoon and asked the way to Tintern. A kindly porter had been sorry for the man's feeble condition and had persuaded him to get a cup of tea and a sandwich, intending to treat him. But the old man produced some money and insisted on paying, saying that he would have no more use for it. The porter "didn't like the look of him," but he seemed sensible, though a bit dazed, so he directed him on his way. There was no other news.

"You haven't—there hasn't been—anything found in the river?" Carol asked the sergeant who gave us this information.

"You'd be thinking of a body, Miss? Oh, no! Though of course they don't always come up at once. Not that I've much experience myself; this isn't the sort of river they go dropping into much, not this isn't."

We drove slowly up the Wye Valley. Bare dripping trees clung to the slopes above the river, which swept down to meet us, thick and soupy. Then at last we swung round the corner which showed us the dark, broken relics of the abbey on their green terrace by the river's brink. I believe we were all unreasonably expecting some discovery as soon as the abbey came into sight, but the valley here was just as mournfully empty as it had been all the way up. So we crept on. I had taken the wheel again, so that Carol could more easily jump out to question the occasional wayfarers, which never produced any useful results.

As we rounded the bend Carol, staring across at the swampy meadows gasped, "Slow, slow! Oh, I think it must be! Down there, yes. Oh, stop! But don't shout or do anything sudden. Just stay here and keep *him* here"—a backward jerk of her head indicated our passenger; "and I'll go and talk to him."

We watched her swing over a gate and pick her way across the boggy grass to an unmoving figure, almost like the hulk of a dead tree, on the river bank.

Nibley, our detective, was anxious and he followed her across the road and stood by the gate, hidden from her behind the hedge. We watched her walk gently up to the figure, which came alive with a jerk and plunged clumsily towards the water. In one instant Carol had seized him by the arm and was dragging at him with all her strength and weight, while Nibley was over the gate, squelching across the meadow. I followed and lost sight of them all until I was over the gate. There were still three of them, Nibley in the middle of the boggy tract and the other two swaying on the very brink of the sweeping current. Before I could reach them, Nibley had them safe and Ashmore stood limp and passive. He trembled violently and was wild eyed.

"Let me go!" he appealed, quite gently. "You don't understand. You ought not to hold me. I should've done it yesterday, but I couldn' do it."

Carol was panting from her struggle and looked pale and scared, but now she stood in front of Ashmore and said to him, slowly and distinctly:

"Ashmore, don't you know me? I'm Carol Wynford; Miss Carol. Yes, of course you remember. Now listen; there's been a dreadful mistake. You needn't be worried; there's nothing wrong; there was no need for you to come away; no one is going to bother you."

"Ah, Miss; you don't know. It wasn't my fault, but there's no getting away from the police. You don' know."

"But I *do* know," Carol insisted. "And I want to say I'm sorry for what happened and for you being so upset, but it's quite all right now and we can take you home."

"They'ah be waitin' for me there!" the old man insisted.

"No, they won't. You've got absolutely nothing to worry about."

He looked doubtful, but his eyes stared at us with more intelligence and with some surprise.

"My feet are damp, standing in this wet place; let's get to the road," Carol suggested in a matter-of-fact voice, and Ashmore, gently guided by Nibley, moved with us towards the field gate. Remembering a thermos flask of coffee laced with something more inspiriting, which the Tollards' cook had sent out to me, I hurried on ahead and poured some of this into a mug.

We got the shivering old man into the front seat of the car and persuaded him to drink the potion.

Nibley suggested; "As quick as you can back to Chepstow, I would advise, and to the best hotel there, where we could get a private room and a fire and some food."

Carol got in beside him. He had been so unobtrusive and yet so useful at the right moment, that she was regarding him with less disfavour and there seemed to be some confidential conversation passing between them as we sped back down the valley.

It was Carol who went into the hotel and arranged for our reception. Ashmore looked at the building doubtfully.

"This is a good pub," I told him. "We all need something to warm us."

"I hardly touch it," he said weakly. "But I don' know but that a drop mightn' do me good now.'

Charmed or bullied by Carol—I don't know which—the manageress of the hotel led us quietly to a room with a blazing fire, promised that no one should disturb us and sent, in surprisingly short time, soup for Ashmore and biscuits and drinks. He swallowed the food with difficulty, but gulped down some brandy. Nibley and I moved away a little and left Carol to tackle him.

"Can you tell me now, Ashmore," she asked; "just what was said to you to make you come away? I do want to clear up the mistake and I can't do that until I know just how it began."

"It's a bit awkward, Missie, because I wasn't to teh, an' it was meant in kindness, I've no doubt—"

"I'm quite sure you ought to tell me now. We ought to know."

"Weh, Missie, I s'pose it's aw right. I fee' a bit mazed an' not rightly abeh to judge, but if you say it's aw right—. Bingham, you see, Missie—who's a right smart young fellah, there's no denyin'—Bingham come along to my place in the evenin'—when was it? Where are we to-day?"

"Saturday morning," Carol told him. "And I think you came to Tintern yesterday afternoon—Friday."

"That's it; Tinnun. I wanted to see that place again; but it's not quite the same as it was. An' I misremembered how the river went, it's not so easy to do as you might think. I went up to the Suspension Bridge before I came here, but I couldn' do it. A terribeh long drop that is, Missie."

"So you came here on Friday afternoon," Carol reminded him. "Now when was it that Bingham came to your house?"

"Thursday evenin' it'd be. That's it. He said not to teh anyone, he was goin' beyond orders to come, but he thought I might be wishfu' to know what had happened at Flaxmere. Sir Osmond had been shot in the head, he said; murdered. Now do you mean to teh me, Missie, that it was aw a mistake?"

"No; I'm afraid that's true, but there *is* a mistake somewhere. Tell me the rest."

"I'm right sorry to hear it, Missie. Not a good end for a man like that. Bingham to' me that he'd bin shot by someone dressed up like, so's they wouldn't know who he was. I diddun unnerstan' rightly, but these togs he wore, whoever he may be, was put in my car, Bingham says, when it stood in the yard back of Flaxmere, for me to bring away, so's they'd not be found, but the police, he to' me, knew of it and would be comin' to see me, and would they believe me when I to' them I knew nothing about it? 'You bet your life, no!' Bingham says—if you' excuse me, Missie, for repeatin' such an expression. Weh, I was struck aw of a heap, but I says to Bingham, 'There's nothin' in the car,' I says, 'for I took it out this mornin', an' I saw nothin', an' if them things was ever there, which is a fair wonder, how is anyone to know?' '*They* know!' Bingham says. 'They know everything, the police. There's finger-prints and what not. I shouldn' be surprised if they was watchin' when the man, whoever it was, came late on Christmas night to your garage and took the things away. Teh me,' he says, 'did you search the car when you came back that night?' Weh, of course, Missie, I diddun so much as look in the back."

"But do you really think the things were there?" Carol asked, as Ashmore paused.

I interrupted quickly: "I'm pretty sure they never were there. In fact, they have now been found in quite a different place." I thought this bold assumption of what I hoped to be a fact was justified. Carol shot a startled look at me, but said nothing.

"Weh; Bingham seemed to know," Ashmore said uncertainly. "He was sure, and it was aw up wi' me, he says, unless I got away at once, for good. If you help a murderer, he says, it's as good as doin' the murder, in the eyes of the police, an' who's to believe that you drove them things away from Flaxmere an' knew nothin' about it? Weh, I was pretty weh shook up, but I waited that night an' the police diddun come, but Bingham had said, mebbe they won' come at once, but they watch an' wait, though you never catch a sight of 'em, an' they come in time. I couldn' stan' it any longer an' so I come away, no' tellin' the wife anything, hopin' it'd be aw right for her that way."

"She's worried about you being away," said Carol; "but she's all right, and Ada too. We must get you back to them as soon as possible. It's absolutely certain that the things never were in your car, and nobody thinks they were and you've nothing at all to be frightened of."

Whilst Carol borrowed a couple of thick rugs from the kindly manageress of the hotel, who seemed to think that we had discovered a long-lost ancestor, and I put up the hood of my car and wished I had taken George's staid old saloon instead, Nibley went off to the telephone and put a trunk call through to Inspector Rousdon. It was then about half-past eleven. We muffled the old man up in the front seat like a papoose and raced back to Flaxmere.

Chapter Twenty-One

End of the Search

by Colonel Halstock

The funeral took place early on Saturday morning. The procession went by the private gate from the park into the little churchyard at its edge and so the family did not have to go beyond their own domain. The church was pretty full of villagers and the household and estate servants. A few enterprising pressmen, who had not been able to discover the time of the funeral but had guessed the date and place, arrived early enough to see the ceremony and there was a bit of a scuffle between a photographer who climbed on to the churchyard wall to get some pictures of the family, and one of Sir Osmond's gamekeepers, who pulled him down. Except for this incident, everything went off quietly.

As soon as the procession had moved off down the drive, a squad of police under the direction of Rousdon began a second intensive search of the outbuildings round the garage yard. This time they lacked the assistance of Bingham, who was attending the funeral, but they found what we had hunted for so long. Rolled up in some sacking, the costume was neatly packed in the middle of a pile of wood blocks.

"Well, I'm jiggered!" said Constable Mere. "We looked in that pile! I'd've said there couldn't be a dead rat left in it, let alone Father Christmas' Sunday suit!"

It turned out that Bingham had been very helpful in that part of the search. He had said that from his own knowledge that pile had been there, exactly like that, for at least a month, but they had better look through it, all the same. He had lifted the blocks himself and in the middle of the work, Mere remembered, there had been a diversion. Bingham had thought they ought to look behind some heavy boxes of potatoes in another corner, and Mere had gone to help shift these. Bingham had gone on moving blocks alone, though he hadn't got to the bottom by the time Mere returned, and they finished the job together. Bingham said they need not put the blocks back again, so they left them as Bingham had piled them in the course of the search.

Rousdon carried off his prize to the "dark room" at the back of the house—the disused dairy which the doctors had used as a mortuary. When he examined it there he found that the outfit was complete except for a pair of eyebrows. It was more than complete, for tucked away in a sleeve there was a folded sheet of paper on which was typewritten:

```
If you wish to hear some confidensial
information re certain members of your
family be in your Study from 3.30 to 4.30
on Christmas Day Afternoon and you will
hear from
                              Well Wisher.
```

"Well Wisher! Seem to have heard of him before!" Rousdon remarked when he showed this to me. "Evidently the man recovered his decoy note from Sir Osmond's pocket and then got into a panic lest it should be found on him before he could destroy it, so he shoved it in here!"

I received this news when I returned from the funeral and whilst the family was gathered in the library to hear the will read by Crewkerne. None of them knew yet of the discovery of the Santa Klaus costume. I could imagine them all sitting on the edges of their chairs and Crewkerne nuzzling short-sightedly in the document and then lifting his head above it to peer at them down his long nose.

After their anxiety had been allayed, and whilst most of them were congratulating themselves that it might have been worse, George, who was one of the executors, and Crewkerne had a short interview with Miss Portisham in the study. She was delighted to hear that she would receive one thousand pounds.

"Really, I never expected it! It is—was—very kind of Sir Osmond to think of me in that way. I certainly never expected it, though Harry Bingham did say I should be sure to get something. Perhaps I ought not to mention that and of course I never heeded him, but this will come in very handy, for you see, Harry Bingham and I are engaged. I suppose you will not be needing my services any more, Sir George? Of course you will understand that nothing can make up to me for the death of Sir Osmond and I never hope to work for a more appreciative employer, but it is nice to know that he remembered me. Anything further I can do to help in going through Sir Osmond's business papers will be a pleasure—that is to say, it will be a labour of love—" Miss Portisham blushed in confusion and continued hastily—"but he left everything in such perfect order that there should be no difficulty at all. He was always so particular that nothing should be put aside until the matter was completely settled. So methodical! I'm dreadfully sorry, Sir George!" Miss Portisham fluttered away.

"I've said some hard things about that girl," George remarked; "but, Good Lord! I'm sorry for her—if you're right, Colonel!"

George and Crewkerne rejoined the others in the library and as George paused with the communicating door half open to ask me something about my plans, I heard Miss Melbury's acid voice declaring that Osmond was mean, he always had been mean, but that he should class her with his valet and his chauffeur, and a little below his secretary, it was too much! She wouldn't touch a penny of his money!

I, too, was sorry for Miss Portisham. I had never liked her better than when, all of a twitter with gratitude and excitement over her legacy, she had blurted out those ridiculous remarks to George and had hurried off to tell her fiancé. I hated the plan which we had adopted because Rousdon was sure it would bring some further evidence which we lacked. Had I known that we were to discover this in another form, I would never have consented to his scheme.

I went into the hall and stood looking at a newspaper until Miss Portisham came in about a quarter of an hour later, by the door at the back. Out of the tail of my eye I saw her hesitate and look round and then come slowly towards me. She looked troubled.

"May I speak to you for a moment, Colonel Halstock? I—I don't quite know what to do. It is very upsetting. I— I was so happy; that is to say, of course, we are still under a dreadful cloud, but getting such a windfall I couldn't but feel pleased. It's like this, Colonel Halstock; Harry Bingham says there must be some mistake. He's in such a way about it; really I feel afraid. But he said I must speak to Mr. Crewkerne before he leaves. I don't quite like to go and look for him, seeing that he is still with Sir George, I believe, and the others. But Harry says I must speak to him before he goes because Harry thinks they haven't got hold of the right will.

He's sure Sir Osmond made another one and left me—well, a lot more than Mr. Crewkerne said. I want to make it clear that I am more than satisfied and I thought Harry would be so pleased, but he is taking on so dreadfully about it. I thought, Colonel Halstock, you might advise me?"

I asked her if Bingham had given reasons for his belief in another will.

"Well, not exactly, but he does seem so sure. I think it likely, Colonel Halstock, that Sir Osmond spoke to him on the matter. It was not unusual for Sir Osmond to talk to him about business he was engaged on, of course in a general way. Naturally he would regard anything Sir Osmond may have said as confidential and would not mention it to anyone. He told me just now I was not to say a word about this to anyone except Mr. Crewkerne himself, because it is so confidential, but I thought it only right to consult you, Colonel Halstock? I do hope I have acted for the best? It seems so ungrateful, but I assure you it is not meant in that way."

I told the girl that I thought Bingham was mistaken, and even let her know that Sir Osmond had intended to revise his will but had never carried out that intention. I promised to speak to Crewkerne and advised her to go to her own room until I sent her a message.

Then I heard the telephone bell ring. Miss Portisham instinctively started for the study and checked herself. I told her not to bother as I thought it was my call, and she went off upstairs. I joined Rousdon in the study, where he was listening on the telephone to a report from Nibley.

After that we went in search of Bingham and found him in his own flat above the garage. We entered very quietly, Rousdon first, and saw the man sitting in a chair, biting his nails and making the most horrible grimaces. We had a momentary glimpse of him like that; then he sprang to his feet and faced us. Two constables stepped forward and clipped on the handcuffs, while Rousdon charged him with the murder of Sir Osmond Melbury and gave the usual warning.

"It's a dirty lie!" Bingham spat at us. "A dirty lie, and I can prove it! I've an alibi! You can't cook the evidence of the whole servants' hall! I know why you're doing this; oh, yes, I know! You want to cheat that poor girl out of what's due to her! But I'll show you up! You can't silence me like this. Warn me, do you? Evidence—I'll give you some evidence!"

They took him away and at once began to search his rooms. For a long time we thought that these would yield nothing, but Constable Mere, nettled by the way in which he had been cheated over the pile of wood blocks, was determined to repair his reputation as a zealous officer and he would leave nothing unexamined. His diligence was rewarded by the discovery of a crumpled and soiled piece of paper in a finger of one of Bingham's driving gloves. It proved to be another note in Sir Osmond's writing of his proposed alterations to the will. It was evidently an earlier draft than the one Witcombe had purloined, and the various eighths, sixths and quarters had been juggled about and crossed through, but "*Grace Portisham*—£10,000; say 1/16" was clearly written and underlined. We conjectured that Sir Osmond had written it in the car, crumpled it and left it on the floor, where Bingham had found it. It was amazing that the man had put such faith in it as definite evidence of a clause in the will to this effect, but it is probable that Sir Osmond had mentioned a will to Bingham and had perhaps even added that he meant to leave Miss Portisham something considerable.

Evidently Bingham couldn't bear to destroy this tangible evidence—as it seemed to him—of his opportunity of marrying an heiress, and he doubtless gloated over the feel of it against his finger whenever he drove the car.

›››

Having seen Bingham and his escort off the premises, I went to tell the family that our investigations were complete. It was evident from their various expressions of consternation, anger and uneasiness, that they had now inspected Sir Osmond's tentative embellishments to his will. Only Jennifer looked quite uninterested. She was lounging in a big arm-chair near the door, with her head flung listlessly back, staring miserably at the ceiling.

I gave them the news and watched her sit up, lean forward and grip the chair as I began to speak. She literally gaped in amazement and then relaxed in relief. Looking round, I saw that as great an astonishment gave way gradually to varying degrees of relief in all the other faces.

"Good Lord! Bingham!" George gasped.

"I always distrusted that man!" Miss Melbury announced. "But of course Osmond was a very poor judge of character." She looked across the room at me, superciliously. "I am sure we must be grateful to you, Colonel Halstock, for *at last* relieving us from the terrible anxiety we felt so long as the criminal was still at large; we must all feel thankful that we, at least, are still alive. To *think* of that assassin having the run of the house, and a family of defenceless women and children in his power!"

"I say, Aunt Mildred, draw it mild!" George protested. "I mean to say, *I* was here, and Cheriton and the rest of us—"

Jenny had risen and was quietly moving towards the door. I opened it for her and as I did so I saw young Cheriton moving restlessly about on the other side of the hall. Once Jenny reached the door she was so quick that I couldn't help see her rush at him and throw herself incontinently into his arms.

Postscript

by Colonel Halstock

I have been asked to set down the questions which Kenneth Stour had drawn up, with the help of the homework, on Friday afternoon, and the answers which identified the murderer of Sir Osmond Melbury. I give Kenneth credit for his work in setting out this evidence in orderly form and so confirming the conclusions I had arrived at. It will be noticed that several other names would provide answers to some of the questions, but only one name would answer them all.

KNOWLEDGE

1. Who knew, at the time, of Sir Osmond's visit to Crewkerne to discuss a new will?	Bingham, who drove him.
2. Who knew of the Santa Klaus plan at least by the Saturday before Christmas?	Bingham, who mentioned it then to Miss Portisham and on learning of it abandoned his earlier plan for a day off with her.

OPPORTUNITY

1. Who was on the spot to intercept the first Santa Klaus costume if it came on Saturday morning, as expected, or on a later day?

Bingham. He might well be able to intercept a parcel at the back door.

2. Who could keep unobtrusively *au fait* with the Santa Klaus plans and would know at once that a second costume was obtained?

Bingham, through Miss Portisham.

3. Who had opportunity to use the typewriter on Tuesday afternoon?

Bingham, who was fixing Christmas-tree lights in the library, next door to study.

4. Who had opportunity to get hold of a glove from Witcombe's and plant it in library?

Bingham, when he helped carry the body upstairs on room Thursday at lunch time. He was the one person who had no need to plant the glove in the library; merely to say he had found it there.

5. Who had opportunity to remove the Santa Klaus costume from the house after the murder?

Bingham, under the rug which he carried out on Thursday afternoon, before driving Col. Halstock to Bristol.

ATTEMPTS TO LAY FALSE SCENT

1. Who attempted to divert the search for the costume away from Flaxmere by suggesting that Ashmore had taken it away?

Bingham.

| 2. Who prevented the finding of the costume on the first search of outbuildings? | Bingham, who so obligingly helped the police. |
| 3. Who tried to implicate Ashmore by frightening the man into flight and perhaps into suicide? | Bingham. |

We were not sure until Saturday that the two last questions and answers were true statements, but even before the costume had been found and Ashmore had told his story, we had circumstantial evidence for them. As for Bingham's knowledge of the contents of Sir Osmond's will, there was a possibility that he had confided in his secretary, as all his family thought he might. In that case it might have been difficult to regard Miss Portisham as completely innocent of any complicity. Her written story of the events of Christmas Day, in which she accidentally gave Bingham away, implied her innocence and I am glad to say that eventually this was fully established.

Bingham had been ruled out as a suspect because he had an alibi. There was ample evidence that he reached the servants' hall before Witcombe and assuming that Witcombe went straight there, Bingham couldn't have committed the murder. But later we found that Witcombe had dallied on the way and had even gone into Jennifer's room, thus happening to leave the murderer a clear route along the passage to the cupboard under the stairs and thence to the servants' hall. Philip's, Witcombe's and Carol's prevarications had falsified all the evidence about time and had presented Bingham with a convenient alibi. The mist of suspicion created by rash actions and untruths obscured for a time the fact that Bingham's alibi crumbled when truth emerged.

Bingham had hustled Miss Portisham out of the library when everyone else had left after the Christmas-tree ceremony, and no one knew how long he remained there. Doubtless if Witcombe had gone straight to the servants' hall and Bingham's late arrival there had been questioned, he would have tried to establish an alibi by explaining that he had been kept busy with his electrical job.

I believe that he trusted to the false clue of the open window to cause a hue and cry after some supposed intruder from outside and a general confusion, in the course of which he may have hoped to get the costume out of the house and perhaps to dump it in some place where the fugitive might be supposed to have shed it.

Bingham was a conceited little man. He was confident that Miss Portisham was ready to fall into his arms at any moment and he cunningly refrained, before the murder, from getting her promise to marry him, but hastened to do so immediately afterwards, before he could be supposed to know that she was an heiress, as he thought. He evidently felt sure that she would not throw him over when she knew her good fortune.

He over-reached himself when, desperately anxious to prevent the discovery of the Santa Klaus costume, he threw suspicion upon Ashmore and further, to make sure that such suspicion should never be cleared away, tried to drive the old man to suicide. When I saw that hideous trick, any pity which I might have felt for Bingham was extinguished.

When it became clear that all the members of the Melbury family and Philip Cheriton and even Witcombe had disgorged the truth at last and were not implicated in any way, I felt as if I had myself been cleared from complicity in some horrible crime. Even Gordon Stickland's strange story about emeralds was true, as far as I ever discovered, and Eleanor did get those stones in the end and looked very lovely wearing them.

Kenneth's conviction that Witcombe would never have joined that Christmas party at Flaxmere without some sinister motive proved to be quite wrong. Kenneth told me that for a long time he had suspected that Witcombe must have some blackmailing hold over Sir Osmond, but nothing of the kind was traced and I believe the truth was simply that the man was so complacent that he never realized how unpopular he was. I have wondered whether he may have guessed some time before that Sir Osmond was considering Carol with great favour and have decided to abandon his courtship of Jennifer and lay siege to Carol instead. But I have never been able to decide this certainly.

Hilda is probably the only one of Sir Osmond's children who really misses him and mourns him, but she and Carol are soberly enjoying their new affluence and Carol is to begin her architectural training in the autumn.

As for Dittie, I think she will stand by her husband to the end of his life and I admire her courage and humanity. I think that she has made peace with herself and will now be happier because she is no longer waiting for something to free her from the bonds, which, she now realizes, she herself keeps fast and could cut if she wished to. She remarked to me about Sir Osmond's notes for the new will:

"He was right; that was all I deserved; perhaps not that. Carol deserves it far more and would do more good with it. But she thinks that she and Hilda have plenty and she won't take anything. She insists that Father only made those notes in a fit of spite and never really meant them. I'm not deceived by that. Carol is generous, for she might easily have made me feel uncomfortable about the money and I won't pretend to deny that I'm glad to have it. I'm going to make an effort to use it really wisely, because I think that's only fair to Carol."

George is now established at Flaxmere, with Miss Melbury in the Dower House at the gates. She loves to preside over gossip parties at which she explains how she always foresaw that trouble would come of those Christmas gatherings and always warned Osmond that he ought not to talk so much about his affairs; of course she saw *at once*, when "that terrible business" occurred, that "none of us" could have had *anything* to do with it; in fact, she was a good enough judge of character to discern pretty quickly where the guilt lay, and if it hadn't been for some timely hints which she dropped, the criminal might never have been brought to book.

There is a tacit understanding among the Melburys that there shall be no more family gatherings at Christmas time at Flaxmere.

To receive a free catalog of Poisoned Pen Press titles, please provide your name and address in one of the following ways:

Phone: 1-800-421-3976
Facsimile: 1-480-949-1707
Email: info@poisonedpenpress.com
Website: www.poisonedpenpress.com

Poisoned Pen Press
6962 E. First Ave. Ste 103
Scottsdale, AZ 85251

CPSIA information can be obtained at www.ICGtesting.com
Printed in the USA
LVOW11s1226061215

465611LV00006B/737/P